DOMINGO

— PARIAHS OF WAR —
• VOLUME 1 •

BOZWICK ABEL

Domingo (Pariahs of War Series Book One)
Copyright © 2020 by Bozwick Abel, Monticello Publishing

www.facebook.com/bozwick.abel

All characters and events in this book, other than those clearly in the public domain, are fictitious and any resemblance to real persons, living or dead, is purely coincidental.

All rights reserved. No part of this publication may be reproduced, distributed, or transmitted in any form or by any means, including photocopying, recording, or other electronic or mechanical methods, without the prior written permission of the publisher, except in the case of brief quotations embodied in critical reviews and certain other noncommercial uses permitted by copyright law.

For permission requests, write to:
bozwickabel@hotmail.com

Ordering Information:
Quantity sales. Special discounts are available on quantity purchases by corporations, associations, and others. Orders by U.S. trade bookstores and wholesalers. For details, contact the publisher at the address above.

Editing by The Pro Book Editor
Interior and Cover Design by IAPS.rocks

ISBN: 978-0-578-66526-9
    1. Main category—Historical Fiction
    2. Other category—Action & Adventure, Drama
First Edition

TABLE OF CONTENTS

PROLOGUE
Santa Fe, New Mexico *1*

CHAPTER 1
Peculiar Tree *3*

CHAPTER 2
Fish On *17*

CHAPTER 3
Unexpected Visit *28*

CHAPTER 4
Turquoise Pendant *46*

CHAPTER 5
Raven *51*

CHAPTER 6
Blood at the Gila *65*

CHAPTER 7
Heading South ... 72

CHAPTER 8
A Stir from the Brush ... 82

CHAPTER 9
Man's Best Friend ... 98

CHAPTER 10
Winchester Rifle ... 127

CHAPTER 11
White Man's Woman ... 143

CHAPTER 12
Blood from the Sky ... 154

CHAPTER 13
Retreat ... 163

CHAPTER 14
A Little Wooden Cross ... 165

CHAPTER 15
Fool's Gold ... 174

CHAPTER 16
No Mora ... 182

CHAPTER 17
Cozy Cave ... 188

CHAPTER 18
The Name's Domingo ... 191

CHAPTER 19
Bushwhackin' Bastard ... 205

CHAPTER 20

    Thunder from the South 211

CHAPTER 21
    Perseverance 225

CHAPTER 22
    Welcome to Santa Fe 243

CHAPTER 23
    A Familiar Face 259

CHAPTER 24
    Everything is in Front of Us 268

CHAPTER 25
    Old Friends & New Friends 275

ABOUT THE AUTHOR 287

ACKNOWLEDGEMENTS 289

This book is dedicated to the Wolves of North America. These restless spirits of the wild fully embody the beauty and freedom of our natural world. Hunted to almost extinction, to later be reintroduced and threatened once again, Wolves are the epitome of those who have suffered, those who still suffer, and those yet to suffer, but also those strong in spirit who refuse to surrender their way of life.

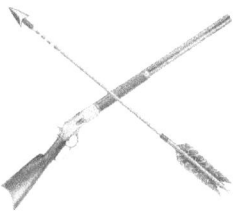

PROLOGUE

SANTA FE, NEW MEXICO

APRIL 1847

As the soldiers' horses dragged the Mexican outlaw by the irons clamped around his wrists, the man struggled to stay on his feet. He often fell to the dirt and was dragged until he could regain his stance. His wrists dripped blood on the ground in front of him, and his arms were bleeding so badly it looked like he was wearing a red-sleeved shirt. His clothes were ragged, and his face was covered in dirt. The outlaw cussed at the men dragging him while keeping a smile on his face to get under their skin.

The townsfolk stared at them as they made their way through town, and the soldiers just smiled and tipped their hats.

When they reached the jailhouse, the horses stopped. The outlaw collapsed to the ground, then he unsuccessfully tried to get back up. A young boy across the street rushed to his aid.

"Get back! That man is dangerous! A murderer!" shouted one of the soldiers.

Ignoring the soldier, the young boy pulled a hankie from his pocket and handed it to the outlaw.

The Mexican squinted as he lifted his head to see who was helping him, but he couldn't make out anything more than a silhouette. "*Gracias*," said the outlaw as the boy ran off.

The soldiers called the Mexican an outlaw, but that was only partially true. His name was Domingo, and he was a strong, well-built Mexican born in Guadalajara in 1808. His name came from his father, Devi Domingus Montoya, a Spaniard who had claimed his father, Fernando Montoya, was a Spanish military governor killed by Indians in 1771. Domingo wasn't sure if that was true or not. It was just something his older brother, Vicente, had told him. Vicente, being the oldest, had seen much more of their father than Domingo had. He could only remember seeing the man a few times as a boy, luckily, since his father had been abusive and a heavy drinker. The few times he had seen his father, he had been more excited when the man left again. Devi had been most abusive toward their mother, and Domingo despised him for that; however, being so young, there had been nothing he could do. After many years passed and no word from Devi, Domingo could only guess he'd been killed, or the drinking had finally caught up to him. Either way, he figured the world was better off without Devi Montoya.

Now Domingo was fighting for his life with little strength left in him. He lay on the ground, exhausted, dirty, and bleeding.

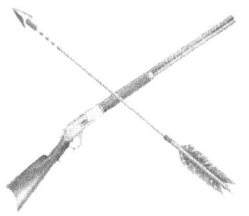

CHAPTER 1
PECULIAR TREE

Domingo met Arabella in 1831, when he was twenty-three and she was seventeen. A young man by the name of Pedro Lampas was her boyfriend and planned to someday marry her. Arabella's father had owned a blacksmith shop in the nearby town of San Juan Lagos. Pedro and Domingo's brother, Vicente, worked for Antonio and were good friends. When Arabella's family moved from San Juan Lagos to Guadalajara, Vicente had brought Domingo along to help. Domingo had been overtaken by Arabella's beauty the moment she walked into the shop. He was trying to set up a workbench and put tools away, but he could not stop turning around and staring at her.

"Bring me that shoebox, Domingo," Antonio said, pointing to the boy's left.

Domingo's love-struck gaze followed Arabella as she placed a basket of food she'd brought for them on a nearby table. She then went to a nearby bench with a pile of tools on it and started putting them away. Domingo picked up the shoebox and started heading toward Antonio while still staring at Arabella. He clumsily tripped on a stall jack, almost dropping the shoebox before quickly regaining his stance.

"Arabella, my darling, go help your mother in the house," said Antonio.

"Of course, Papá," she replied, making her way to the door in a very slow, sensual walk. Before exiting, she turned back and looked Domingo in the eyes with a sly smile, as if making sure he was still looking at her.

The widest grin spread over Domingo's face as he stuttered a nervous goodbye to Arabella.

"Get to work!" yelled Antonio.

Startled back to the task at hand, Domingo quickly looked away and continued working.

Antonio gave Arabella a stern look and pointed to the door.

Arabella frowned at her father but quickly made her way out.

Though refocused on the job at hand, Domingo could not stop thinking about her amazing smile. As he worked, he stumbled across some throwing knives in one of the boxes. He showed great interest in the knives, so Arabella's father said he could have them. Domingo had always enjoyed throwing knives to stick them in trees, but the knives would often break. The knives Antonio had given him were high quality, and Domingo was excited to try them out when the workday was finished.

Later that night at home, Domingo sat at the table, cleaning the knives. Vicente got a glass of water, then he made his way to the table and sat next to Domingo. Domingo looked over at Vicente a few times like he wanted to say something but didn't.

Vicente noticed his odd behavior. "What is it?"

Domingo kept polishing his knives and smiled. "What do you think about Arabella?"

Vicente sat his water down. "What do you mean?" he said in a stern tone.

Domingo replied, "She's quite beautiful. And she was giving me the eye at the shop earlier."

Vicente began shaking his head in disapproval. "Domingo, she is very pretty, I know, but there are so many women. Please don't put me in a position. Pedro is my friend. She was probably staring at you because you kept staring at her."

"No, I don't think so. I'm telling you she gave me the eye." Domingo sat a knife down on the table and looked directly at Vicente. "I am sorry, brother. I have to see her again. I absolutely must see her," he said with great urgency.

Vicente shook his head again. "Do you think she will not tell him of you?"

Domingo gave Vicente an angry glare. "Do you think I care if she does? Am I to be afraid of Pedro?"

Vicente picked his sombrero up from the table, put it on his head, and walked toward the door. Grasping the door handle, he turned back around and looked at Domingo. "I know no man you are afraid of, and I know no man whose advice you would follow." Then he closed the door behind him.

The very next day, Domingo went to Arabella's house and knocked on the front door.

Her mother opened the door and told him, "Antonio is at the shop."

"Actually, I came here to see Arabella. Is she available?"

asked Domingo while looking downward and shuffling his right foot across the ground.

Arabella's mother looked over the nervous young man standing at the door. "I am sorry, but she is busy helping me inside."

The door opened a little farther, and Arabella appeared beside her mother. "It's okay, Mama. He's a friend," said Arabella.

Arabella's mother made a not-so-friendly face at Domingo, turned, and disappeared inside the house.

"What are…" Arabella slipped outside, closing the door behind her. "What are you doing here?"

"I…umm…" Domingo could feel his heart pound in his chest as his hands trembled. He'd thought she would be more excited to see him. *"What are you doing here?"* he thought. *Yeah, what the hell* am *I doing here?*

This time, with her hand on her hip, Arabella asked again, "What are you doing here?"

Wanting to run away, Domingo could do nothing but laugh and then try to apologize for bothering her. She started to laugh as well. Then he was laughing so hard, his stomach started hurting. He finally caught his breath and regained his composure.

Arabella looked at him like he was crazy. "Domingo, I need to get back inside," she said as her mother called for her.

"Arabella, please, I need to tell you something." Domingo reached for her hand, stared straight into her eyes, and said, "Ever since I saw you, I cannot stop thinking about you."

Arabella stared right back for a moment, then she dropped her gaze to the ground. "Domingo, I'm with Pedro," she said softly.

Domingo shook his head as he accepted that fact. "I came

Domingo

here today, hoping for the chance to tell you how I feel. I am thankful I had the chance to do that. I would really like to see you again, but I promise I will not bother you." He smiled and turned to walk away.

"How about tomorrow?" replied Arabella.

Heart pounding, he turned back to face her and grinned with excitement. "Really?" he asked.

"Yes. Be here around six, and you can have dinner with me and my family," replied Arabella.

Domingo rushed to her and kissed her hand. "I will be here!"

Arabella's mother called out again, this time with more urgency.

"I'm sorry, but I have to go! Good day, Domingo," said Arabella as she spun around and rushed inside.

The more than an hour walk to her house felt like only fifteen minutes on the way back. He replayed the few minutes of seeing her—and the promise of seeing her again—over and over in his mind. He was so glad he'd gone and wondered if Antonio would welcome him when he returned for dinner. It was apparent that Arabella's mother had her reservations, but Antonio and Domingo got along pretty well at work, so he was hopeful.

The next evening, when Domingo arrived at Arabella's home, Antonio answered the door with a grin and simply invited him in. Domingo followed Antonio into the living room and sat in one of the chairs after waiting for his host to take the chair of his choice. Domingo nervously looked around while sitting up straight and keeping his hands together, hoping Arabella would soon walk into the room.

"So, Domingo, it seems you and Arabella became friends

awfully quick?" said Antonio as he crossed his legs and leaned back in his rocker chair.

"Well, I have only seen her a couple times, but yes, I would agree we did become friends rather quick," responded Domingo with a nod, looking over his shoulder for Arabella. He quickly looked back at her father. "I'd like to thank you again for the knives. I polished them, and they look great." Domingo then looked over his shoulder again.

This time, her father took notice. "She will be along shortly. She is in the kitchen, helping her mother prepare the food." Antonio pointed to the fireplace. "Can you toss a couple more logs in there?"

Domingo stood and walked over to the fireplace, picked up a log, and tossed it in the fire. Then he reached for the poker leaning against the wall nearby. "Where did you get those knives, if you don't mind me asking?"

Antonio leaned back in his chair and put his hands behind his head. "Oh, I got those during the war. Won them in a card game with some of my comrades."

Domingo turned toward him while picking up a second log. "You were in the war?" he asked with enthusiasm and curiosity in his voice.

"Sure was, for six years."

Domingo made his way back to his chair, feeling more comfortable than he had when he arrived. He spent the next twenty minutes talking to Arabella's father about the war of Mexican independence as they waited for dinner. The conversation was cut short when Arabella walked into the room, carrying some dirty rags from the kitchen.

Domingo quickly rose from his chair. "Hello, Arabella," he said, walking over to her.

Domingo

"Hello, Domingo," she replied with a smile.

Domingo moved awkwardly to give her a hug.

Arabella blushed, saying, "These rags are dirty. I'm taking them to the laundry. Dinner is ready, Papá."

Antonio leaned forward in his chair and got to his feet, then he headed for the kitchen.

"Follow me," she said to Domingo.

They made their way through the hallway to a storage room, where a basket and many unpacked boxes were stacked inside.

Arabella put the linens in the basket, then she gave Domingo a hug. "I'm so glad you are here. Sorry I left you alone so long, but my father wanted to greet you first." She straightened up Domingo's collar. "Now, let's head to the dining room before they come looking for us."

The pair made their way back through the house and into the kitchen, where Arabella's mother and father were already sitting at the dining table.

Domingo felt much relief when Arabella's mother stood from the table and greeted him with a much-unexpected hug, welcoming him to their home.

Arabella pulled a chair out for Domingo and instructed him to sit there, then she walked to the other side of the table and sat directly across from him. After a small prayer led by her father, the dishes were passed around. Domingo began thanking them for having him over and commented on how great the food looked. Silence filled the room once they all began eating.

A few minutes later, Arabella's mother put down her fork and reached for her water, then she looked over at Domingo.

"Your brother Vicente is quite the young man. He has been quite helpful at the shop and during the move."

Antonio simply nodded in agreeance since his mouth was full of food.

Domingo nodded as well. "When our father left, I was still a young boy, and Vicente was the man of the house, not only helping our mother with the children but working and making money to support us. He had to grow up very quickly."

"When was the last time you saw your father?" asked Antonio.

"Close to ten years ago, I suppose."

"What was he like?" asked Maria.

Domingo began to smile. "An asshole, I guess, best describes him."

Arabella kicked Domingo's leg under the table.

"Ouch," said Domingo, then he quickly apologized for his language.

Antonio chuckled as Arabella's mother tilted her head and sat her glass down on the table slowly. "Well, I guess I got my answer," she said.

"How are you liking your new home?" Domingo asked, shifting the conversation away from his father—and most certainly away from Vicente—fearing Pedro would eventually be brought up.

"It's been a lot of work, but we are starting to settle in. Luckily, we had you, Vicente, and Pedro to help," replied Antonio.

Domingo quickly nodded and looked back at his plate. He could see Arabella, through the corner of his eye, looking at her mother to acknowledge the discomfort of her father mentioning Pedro. "It's really been no problem. I appreciate the work, and the money is extremely useful. It's been tough finding any work around here lately."

"You ever thought about working as a blacksmith like Vicente?" asked Arabella's mother.

"Yes, I have, but I really enjoy working over at the Cortez ranch when they need me. Their ranch is just a few miles north of town. I'd like to have a ranch of my own someday." Domingo looked over at Arabella, who was smiling at him. He was beginning to feel comfortable with her family. He talked a little more about his ambitions and—very delicately—his fondness for Arabella.

After dinner, Domingo and Arabella helped clear the table and then decided to go for a walk around the property. As the two were walking, he explained about his abusive, alcoholic father he'd, luckily, rarely seen as a boy. He was beginning to tell her about his childhood dog that had been kicked by a horse when Arabella abruptly interrupted.

"Those are great stories. Can you tell them again?" asked Arabella.

Domingo laughed, and Arabella's eyes widened as she turned away with an unsettled look. She quickly turned back toward Domingo with a big grin.

Domingo laughed even harder and struggled to catch his breath.

"C'mon, I want to show you something," said Arabella, and she led him down a path to a strangely shaped tree. It almost had the shape of a cactus but was a pine tree. "Look what I found the day we arrived here," she said.

Domingo looked at the odd tree and smiled. "Well, that's unfortunate. Would you like me to cut it down?"

Arabella punched him in the arm. "Don't you touch it!"

"Are we still talking about the tree?"

Arabella answered him with another lick to the arm.

"You wanna know why that tree is shaped like that?" asked Domingo.

Arabella quickly looked up at him, tilting her head and putting her hands on her hips in curiosity and skepticism.

"Well, see there," said Domingo, pointing to one of the limbs. "That's pointing west, and that one there is pointing south."

Arabella shook her head and rolled her eyes.

"Seriously, this tree didn't just grow that way. It was shaped like this by Indians, so they knew which direction to go," explained Domingo.

"Are you being serious? When did you become such an expert on Indian tree bending?" said Arabella as she laughed and waved her hand, dismissing Domingo's claims.

"I'm not sure, but you wanna know the sad part?"

Arabella looked at Domingo, trying not to smile.

"These trees take decades to mature, and the Indians died of old age before they got to see their finished work."

Arabella tilted her head straight back, almost losing her balance. "You are so ridiculous!" She grabbed his hand. "C'mon and be quiet! You seem smarter when you don't talk," she said jokingly.

The two continued their walk, Domingo overflowing with anticipation of kissing her. As Arabella's home came into view, he stopped and gently pulled her toward him. Not wanting to be too forward, he leaned in and gave her a small, quick kiss. Leaning back, he looked down into her chestnut-colored eyes for a moment. He knew he could easily get lost looking into her eyes. They were quite lovely and pierced through his soul when he looked into them for any length of time. He then kissed her again, this time much longer and more passionately. They kissed for what seemed like several minutes, pressed close and lost in their mutual desire. Domingo had kissed other women before, but nothing compared to Arabella's kiss. This furthered his belief that they most certainly belonged together.

Neither Domingo nor Arabella wanted to break their passionate kiss, but they quickly pulled apart at the sound of the door opening. They regained their composure as Antonio came out to have a cigar on the porch, then they continued toward the house, both blushing and stealing glances at the other. After quickly thanking them for dinner, Domingo said goodnight to Antonio and Arabella.

Over the next couple weeks, Domingo went to see Arabella almost every day. She'd thought she loved Pedro, but she was learning what true love was and could not bring herself to tell him about her feelings for Domingo. It was Vicente who ended up telling Pedro, and when Pedro confronted Arabella, she did not try to talk her way out of it. She simply said she was sorry, but she was in love with Domingo. Very angry, Pedro waited outside Arabella's house for Domingo to arrive later that night despite her pleas for him to leave.

Seeing Domingo coming down the road, Pedro sprinted out to him. "You stay away from her, Domingo!"

Domingo kept walking toward Arabella's home.

"You hear me? Stop, you bastard!" shouted Pedro.

Arabella ran into the house to get her father.

Pedro got into Domingo's face, then pushed him two steps back.

Domingo recovered and walked around the jilted young man. He did not want to fight Pedro, mainly because he knew

Pedro was already hurting from losing Arabella, but he was also Vicente's friend and worked for Antonio. However, he was not going to be stopped from seeing the love of his life. When Pedro tried to punch Domingo in the face, Domingo turned out of the way and grabbed Pedro's wrist. Twisting his arm, he then delivered several blows to Pedro's face. Pedro fell to the ground as blood ran from his nose. Still holding his arm, Domingo drew back to strike again.

"Domingo!" shouted Antonio, coming up behind him.

Domingo froze and looked down at a bloody Pedro staring up at him.

"Not on my land, boy," said Antonio.

Domingo let Pedro's arm go and stepped back.

"I've known that boy for a long time, and I'm not going to sit back and watch you hurt him," said Antonio.

Domingo looked at Arabella, who was now crying, then over to Antonio. "I apologize, sir, but he did swing first."

Walking over to Pedro to see if he was all right, Antonio said, "He has a right to be upset, Domingo. Now come over here and help me get him to the house."

Domingo walked to Pedro and reached down to help him up, but Pedro pushed his hand away while making a disgusted and angry face.

"Have it your way," said Domingo, stepping back.

"Come inside, all three of you," said Antonio, helping Pedro along toward the porch.

After Pedro calmed down a bit and was cleaned up, the three men sat down at the table for a discussion. It went on for some time, and even though Domingo apologized several times, Pedro would never forgive him. After a short while, Pedro made his way out the door, and Domingo stayed behind to

Domingo

console Arabella. Pedro's friendship with Vicente did continue, but Vicente made every effort to make sure Domingo and Pedro were never around each other. Domingo and Arabella spent every day together they possibly could before eventually getting their own place. It was the happiest time of Domingo's life, and as each day passed, their love continued to grow as they became closer and closer. It was a love so powerful, they truly believed it could not have existed before and will never exist again. Within two years, they were wed, and there was a great celebration as many family, neighbors, and friends attended. Vicente and his girlfriend, Maria, were not present for the wedding, as they had moved to Tucson a year earlier in hopes of starting their own business. Pedro was also not present for obvious reasons.

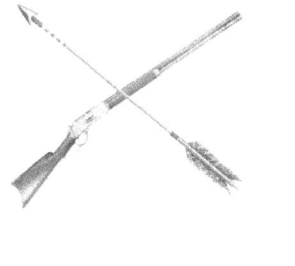

CHAPTER 2

FISH ON

While living in Guadalajara, Domingo worked as a line rider at a local ranch, and Arabella worked part-time at a local tailor shop. Within one year of being married, they welcomed their son, Marcello, followed four years later by their daughter, Camille. Times were tight, but Domingo managed to put some money away for his dream of starting his own ranch someday.

After repeatedly applying over several years, Domingo was finally awarded three thousand and four hundred acres just south of the Gila River in the Nuevo Mexico province, through a grant program with the Mexican government. The grant program was designed to populate the region with people loyal to the Republic. Domingo's new land sat near Camino Real Road, which extended from Mexico City to San Juan, making for easy travel to nearby towns. There were also ranches and trade fairs along Camino Real Road that many rancheros counted on to sell and buy livestock, among other things. There was already a partially built home on the property when he arrived. The roof was collapsed but could be rebuilt. The property was wide open and beautiful. Sunrise and sunset were both breathtaking. As the sun set, the rocky terrain spilled out vivid colors, and the cactus left long shadows that seemed to stretch for miles off the cliffs. Overall, he was quite pleased with his newly-allotted land.

Domingo and his son, Marcello, sometimes took long walks, climbing steep, rocky terrain until they reached the highest point where they would sit and watch for birds and other wildlife. Once while sitting there, a golden eagle flew right over them, so close you could hear the wind rushing from its powerful wings. Domingo stood and watched the bird glide over the valley, thinking how great it would be to fly like that great bird. He watched until the eagle finally disappeared from sight, then looked over to Marcello to share the moment, but the ten-year-old boy was busy flipping rocks and looking for lizards. The boy loved chasing lizards and snakes. The ones he caught, he kept for a while, until Domingo would eventually let them go or cook them. Domingo would cook up anything he could catch just to try it out. Times were good and food was plentiful.

Much of Domingo's time was spent repairing the home and building a bunkhouse for his ranch hands, Luis and Jose, two brothers he'd befriended on his way to the property shortly after receiving his land grant. He'd had big dreams of being a wealthy ranchero and making woolies his primary livestock, but the cost of building fences, a sheer shack, repairing his home, and purchasing sheep took an early toll on Domingo's finances. After several months, their supplies diminished, and there was no time left for sightseeing or rock climbing. Domingo realized he had greatly misjudged the cost of getting the ranch finished and had to come up with a plan.

Everyone, including his two children, had to carry their share of work, their survival and financial stability depending on them getting it done. He managed to get a milk cow, sixty-eight sheep, an ox, and many chickens. He was mostly on his own when it came to building and repairing structures, as Luis and Jose spent their time tending to the sheep and protecting them from predators and thieves. Although Marcello was a great help at ten years old, Camille was very little help at six. To make matters worse, his wife, Arabella, was pregnant and struggled to keep up with the constant chores. There was shearing, cleaning, teasing, spinning, and weaving to be done too. Domingo, Jose, and Luis always did the shearing because even though Marcello was learning fast, he was not yet strong enough to handle the sheep.

To help feed the family and ranch hands, Domingo decided to take Marcello to the Gila River to do some fishing. After being very successful on their first trip, they returned to the river frequently over the next month. After feeling the area was safe, Domingo began leaving the boy at the river by himself while he returned home to work on the ranch. He worried about leaving Marcello for several hours on his own but figured he didn't have much of a choice with so much work needing to be done.

At first, he took his son to the river once or twice a week, but soon it became every other day. He'd pack Marcello a little pouch of bread and beans, and they'd leave just before sunrise. Each trip to the river, Domingo and his son removed big rocks and debris from the trail and cut back branches to widen it, making traveling much easier and quicker. These trips to the river also made Marcello much more comfortable riding a horse. The boy learned quickly, and he soon led the way to the river.

They followed a little creek that hardly carried much water over a couple inches. Marcello liked that little creek and always jumped down from his horse to catch frogs and salamanders. Domingo would just keep going, and Marcello would soon climb on his horse and catch up. Lucky for the family, Marcello was quite the fisherman for his age, and many times, his bounty alone could feed the whole family. When he returned from the river, there were always more chores waiting for him.

Arabella gathered wild plants for her family almost every day, taking Marcello with her when he wasn't fishing or helping Domingo. She taught her son which plants could be used and which could not. Of all the tiresome chores, the boy seemed to enjoy these times with his mother the most. During peak harvesting, they took the oxcart and filled it within a couple of hours. Although, when they finished cleaning and stripping the plants, so little was left that could be used. Growing in abundance on the land and with so many uses, Agave made up the majority of what they gathered. Domingo especially enjoyed the tequila they made from the spiny-tipped plants. The crowns of the Agave plant were quite heavy, so Arabella liked having Marcello's help carrying and loading them into the cart. They also gathered berries, seeds, cota, lip ferns for tea, and bark for sweetener. Arabella spent countless hours making clothing and blankets for the family.

So far, everyone on the ranch had avoided any serious illness or injury, but with Arabella pregnant, she was slowly tiring of the situation. Domingo knew he had to get supplies to help ease the burden of continuous food gathering and clothes making. He had been stocking up the blankets and serapes Arabella made to sell and considered selling the nice throwing knives given to him by Arabella's father. He hated the idea of parting with them, but he knew they would be good to trade. He also planned to visit his brother in Tucson, about a two and a half days' ride west, to persuade Vicente and his wife, Maria, to come live on the ranch. Not only would it be nice to have his brother closer, but Vicente was also a blacksmith, and his skills would be extremely useful. However, Domingo struggled with leaving Arabella and the children for so many days.

Luis and Jose had left for Janos a couple weeks earlier after hearing their mother was extremely ill, and they would not return for another month. With no trade fair on the horizon, Domingo briefly thought about seeking out the Apache who lived to the northeast. This could be a dangerous endeavor since Mexicans and the Apache had been at war for many years, and from what he'd heard, the Apache were a bunch of thieves. If you traded with them, they were likely to steal it back the next day.

One evening while Domingo and Marcello were returning from the Gila River, Domingo spotted a mule deer. He got down from his horse and whispered to his son, "Marcello, wait here with the horses."

Domingo hunched down, walking slowly and quietly closer to get a clear shot. He strategically placed each foot to avoid making a single stick crack until he was close enough to take a knee, then he raised his rifle and adjusted the sight. Just as he was about to pull the trigger, he saw something else move in the distance. He remained still, looking and listening, until he could make out three men riding horses. The men were several hundred yards away, making their way down a rocky ridge in the valley that Domingo and his son usually walked the horses through. The good news was that they were heading away from Domingo and his boy. He wanted to tell his son to stay quiet and low but figured he was already doing that, and trying to make it to the boy might just get him spotted. He watched the mule deer he was after trot away, disappointed about missing out on a kill that would have been a much welcome break for his family.

"Fuck, what timing," he said under his breath. Domingo looked back at the riders, still heading away from him and Marcello.

Then the horses stopped and turned, heading straight for him.

"Oh shit," he muttered.

It wasn't that Domingo was scared. Whether it was Indians or outlaws, he felt confident in fighting them off. He was worried about his son. Unsure if they'd seen him or just spotted a trail he and Marcello had made, Domingo didn't know what to do. The riders were in between him and his home, and it was too late to high-tail it out of there. He tried to look through the brush and trees as they got closer to get a good look, but he still could not make out who they were. They soon passed through a clearing, and he could see it was Indians—either Apache or Navajo. Either way, it was not going to be good. He watched closely until he locked eyes with the front rider when they were no more than a hundred feet away, and sure enough, the rider was looking straight back at him.

Damn! Domingo thought. *How did they spot me?*

Glaring at Domingo without blinking, the front Indian looked like a chief because he was decorated in paint, feathers, and beads. The other two men wore animal hides and headbands. They looked almost angry, as the chief led the group straight toward Domingo and Marcello. The chief was quite muscular, with a strong chin and nose, and he had a wide face with a prominent jaw. Domingo thought he might be the meanest looking guy he'd ever seen. The chief towered above his horse, having to duck under tree limbs while making his way through the valley. He guessed the man was about thirty-five years old, but it was hard to tell with his face painted.

A noise behind him drew Domingo's attention. He looked back to see his son heading toward him. "Marcello!" he shouted.

The noise stopped.

"Wait right there, son. If you hear any gunshots, ride home as fast as you can! Don't look back. Just go!" shouted Domingo.

"Yes, Father," replied a frightened Marcello, sitting frozen in his saddle.

Turning back, Domingo focused again on the chief, now within thirty feet and not stopping. Still down on one knee with his gun pointed directly at the lead rider, he watched as the horses came to a stop no more than ten feet from him. The chief stared down at Domingo for a minute, then dismounted. Realizing then just how tall the chief was—probably more than six and a half feet—Domingo felt helpless on his knee in front of the giant man. He began planning an escape. He could shoot the chief and throw his rifle at the Indian still mounted on his horse, then beat the hell out of him. The problem was the third one, who was farther back with his rifle lying across his lap. He surely would get a shot off before Domingo could reach him.

As these thoughts ran through Domingo's mind, the chief waved his hand, signaling for him to point his rifle elsewhere.

Domingo took that to mean they weren't looking for a fight and just wanted to talk. He dropped the barrel down toward the dirt and stood up. Holding the rifle in his right hand, he slowly raised his left in a friendly gesture.

The chief took little notice of Domingo's gesture and looked around him at Marcello.

"That's my boy…my son," said Domingo.

The chief walked toward Domingo's horse, looking it over, then spoke to the other Indians riding with him.

Domingo could not speak Apache, but he figured they were checking to see if the horse was stolen since stealing horses and livestock was so common between Mexicans and Indians.

The chief pointed to the stringer of fish hanging from Domingo's saddle, then walked back toward Domingo and started talking to him.

Domingo had no idea what the chief was saying. He figured the chief was telling him he was trespassing on Apache land or some bullshit like that. Then the chief pointed at the trail and spoke more words Domingo couldn't understand, though he was sure the man was saying he had been trespassing for some time.

"I did not know the river and land was yours," Domingo replied in Spanish.

The chief looked at Domingo, seeming to understand him, then talked to his warriors again without taking his eyes off Domingo.

Domingo slowly unhooked the stringer of fish and held it out for the chief to take. He really needed the food for his family but figured he would go hungry to get out of this mess. "Here, take these fish and let us go in peace," he said.

The chief took the fish and tossed them to the closest warrior.

For a second, Domingo was hopeful that they would leave. Then the chief started talking and pointing to the trail again. They wanted something more.

"Well…fuck you," said Domingo quietly.

The chief stopped talking, seeming to know Domingo had said something offensive.

There was a long pause as the situation grew tenser.

Domingo began to smile, something he did when he was getting irritated. He thought about how if the chief was alone, he would knock his damn head off. He envisioned pushing his thumbs through the chief's ever-staring Apache eyes. However, he was outnumbered and had his boy to think about.

The more the chief carried on, the more Domingo started figuring out what he was saying. Domingo had taken a lot of fish, and the four on the stringer wasn't going to cut it. The chief began talking loudly, trying to make Domingo understand.

Domingo raised his hand to stop his shouting, leaned the rifle against a tree, and turned to get his horse. He slowly unhooked his saddle and set it down on the ground, then he rubbed the horse's neck and looked into its eyes for a minute. Having said goodbye to a reliable horse he was fond of, he then turned to the chief and handed him the reins.

The chief walked the horse over to his warriors and climbed up on his own horse. Still seeming angry, he yelled more words Domingo didn't understand as he and his men backed away.

Domingo just figured he always talked that way, and unsure of what the Indian was saying, replied, "Yes, señor! Sounds good!" then nodded and raised his hand to show agreement.

The chief and his warriors slowly rode off.

Domingo looked back at his son, relieved the Indians had left. "You okay, Marcello?"

"Yes, Papá," replied a teary-eyed Marcello, walking toward his father.

Domingo grabbed up the saddle and said with a smile, "What do you think? Think he liked me?"

Clearly shaken up by the ordeal, Marcello replied, "Father, I do not want to fish here again. I'm scared!"

Domingo walked over to his son and said, "I don't think there's any fish left in that river. You caught them all!"

Marcello smiled, seeming to relax a bit.

Domingo threw the saddle over his shoulder, and the two walked back to Marcello's horse.

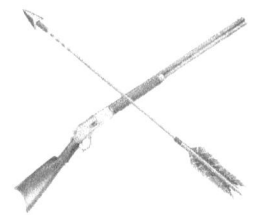

CHAPTER 3
UNEXPECTED VISIT

As Domingo and Marcello approached home, they noticed several horses and men gathered around the ranch. Domingo quickly picked up his pace while trying to see who it was. As they got closer, he realized it was more than several men. It was about twenty Mexican soldiers. Arabella was standing on the porch with Camille clinging to her leg, talking to men in Mexican officer uniforms.

All heads turned toward Domingo as one of the officers put his hand on his pistol and glanced back at the man who must have been their general to await his command. The general was a short, heavy-set guy. His blue uniform had a wide stripe down the seam, dressed up with pins and ribbons from his military accomplishments. He wore a black sombrero—embroidered in red, with several gold sequins around the crown—and tan leather armas.

The general looked at Arabella. "That your husband, señora?"

Arabella nodded. "Yes, and my son."

The general motioned to his sergeant to stand down as Domingo dropped his saddle to the ground and rushed to Arabella's side.

Paying little attention to Domingo as he reached Arabella, the general watched Marcello climb down and tie his horse off to the fence, then make his way toward his mother and father. He then looked at Domingo as he pulled a cigar from his front pocket.

"Surprised you were able to keep a horse in these parts," said the general, lighting his cigar.

"I'm surprised you have too," replied Domingo.

The general smiled as he took his hat off to wipe his forehead. "Well, you will be relieved to know we are going to clear the Apache out of here."

Without taking his eyes off the general, Domingo said to Arabella, "Take the kids inside."

"It was a pleasure to meet you, señora," said the general as he raised his hand in a friendly gesture.

Arabella smiled at the general, then called for Marcello and took Camille by the hand to direct her inside.

Domingo was not feeling very friendly at the moment and simply crossed his arms. "They have been no harm to me or my livestock," he said.

"That's because they don't know you're here." The general snickered.

"I doubt that," answered Domingo. "There's a lot o' ranchero's around here."

The general took another hit from the cigar, then pulled it from his mouth and wagged it in time with his words. "Yes, but none this far north."

Domingo wasn't sure what to make of the general. His first impression was that the man seemed very arrogant, and his intentions were still a mystery.

"The name is General Sanchez," he said, pulling out a piece of paper. "Says here you are Domingo Montoya. Is that right?"

Surprised the general knew his name, Domingo hastily asked, "What is it you want with me?"

The general looked behind him at his men, then back at Domingo. "Calm down, señor. We just need a place to camp for a couple nights."

"Well, it won't be here," said Domingo.

"Oh, yes, it will!" said the sergeant, standing a little behind Sanchez.

General Sanchez turned his head and paused for a moment, then signaled his sergeant to shut up and looked back at Domingo with a smile. "This land belongs to the Mexican Republic."

"This is my home and my land," barked Domingo.

"This land was given to you by the Mexican Republic, by the kindness of our very own Presidente Santa Anna," answered Sanchez.

"I don't want you here. There's all sorts of other Santa Anna land, so go find some," answered Domingo.

The general's smile quickly dissipated. "Are you not a citizen of the Mexican Republic?"

"Of course I am," answered Domingo.

"Are you not willing to help protect your fellow citizens?"

Domingo stood silent and expressionless, gazing at the general and wishing he could say what he really wanted to say.

"Are you not willing to help your country's soldiers defend its people and territory?" asked Sanchez.

Domingo just stared back, unmoved.

"Sir, I will ask you again!" said the general in a very serious tone. "Are you not willing to help your country defend its people and territory? Are you not willing to help protect your fellow citizens?"

"I told you I am," answered Domingo with piercing eyes glaring angrily at the general.

The general took off his hat and wiped his brow with his bandana. "Look, I can appreciate you being upset at coming home just to find Mexican soldiers setting up camp, but the truth is that it's a lot better than coming home to an Apache war party. And that's exactly what you will find unless we clear them out of here! You should appreciate what we are doing. Our mission is to protect the citizens of Mexico. We need to create a safe route to Alta California, and this area will be part of that route." Sanchez put his hat back on and waited for Domingo to reply.

Thinking about his ordeal with the three Indians by the Gila River, Domingo nodded in agreement. He looked around at the soldiers already surveying for a good place to set up camp, knowing he had to go along with Sanchez whether he liked it or not. There was no use fighting it.

"Sorry, General. It's been a long day. I meant no disrespect," said a defeated Domingo as he wiped the sweat from his brow. "You are more than welcome here." He pressed his thumb and finger against his eyebrows, trying to suppress an oncoming headache.

The general paused momentarily, as he could see that Domingo was exhausted from the conversation. Then he walked over and placed his hand on Domingo's shoulder. "Look, we will only be here in the evening, and by early morning, we will be out patrolling and scouting. All we need is some food and water, perhaps some help tending to the horses when we arrive in the evening, and we'll be out of here in a couple days. We will chop our own wood and set up far enough away to not disturb your home or livestock."

"I appreciate that," said Domingo halfheartedly.

"Then, when we are victorious, I'll tell the war department of your hospitality and how it was your wife's cooking that kept us fed while we cleared out the Apache," said a smiling General Sanchez. "Who knows? Maybe Santa Anna will give you a couple more thousand acres in his appreciation." He then turned to his comrades, nodding.

"We hardly have any food. We cannot feed you," said Domingo.

The general looked over at the milk cow in a small fenced-in area. "Looks like she will just have to do," he said. "We'll cook what we need tonight and smoke the rest." He reached into his pocket and pulled out a small pouch of money, then tossed it to Domingo. "Here, señor. I'm sure it's twice as much as you paid for the filthy beast." General Sanchez waved his hand above his head in a quick circular motion, signaling his sergeant to shoot the cow.

Domingo just stared at the general as two gunshots rang out, then he looked over just as his cow fell to the ground.

"It's dinner time, boys!" shouted the general.

There was a low rumble of laughter across the soldiers as a few of them began thanking the general and Domingo. The soldiers were quite hungry, as they had ridden for several days with very little food.

Domingo

Domingo was angry about the cow, but the money was more than fair. He turned away from Sanchez and walked up the porch steps just as Arabella made her way out to see what the commotion was. He grasped her arm and redirected her into the house.

"Well, what do they want? And why were there gunshots?" asked Arabella as she spun on her heel to follow her husband's lead.

"They want to camp here a couple days," replied Domingo, setting his sombrero on the table just inside the door to his left and pulling out a chair to sit down.

Arabella went to the other side of the room, in the kitchen area, to get Domingo a cup of water. Ever curious, Marcello and Camille stood in the kitchen, listening to their parents' conversation.

"They wanted food, and I told them we don't have any, so they shot our cow." Domingo again pushed his fingers against his brows.

Camille rushed to her father's side and wrapped her arms around his neck.

Domingo smiled as he embraced his daughter and thanked her for the hug.

"What gives them the right to come here and do that to us! We needed that cow," stated Arabella. She set the cup of water in front of Domingo and sat in a chair next to him.

"Well, there's not much we can do. They are here to clear out the Apache. As far as they're concerned, we either support them or be considered an enemy as well," replied Domingo. "Let's just go along with it and look forward to them leaving." He leaned toward Arabella, kissed her forehead, and embraced her.

Domingo found himself divided over the unexpected visitors. It wasn't that he disliked General Sanchez, as he seemed friendly enough, but he had moved there to stay away from the corrupt Mexican dictatorship and people in general. The idea of so many soldiers around his ranch over the next couple of days made his skin crawl. He did like the idea of the soldiers clearing out the Apache, especially after running into them on the way back from the river. If the Apache were cleared from the area, it would bring security to his home, family, and livestock. In the end, there was little Domingo could say about it. He knew General Sanchez had been fighting in a land that knew only one law—his—and you were either with him or against him.

Marcello walked from the kitchen to his father as Domingo was just pulling away from Arabella to lean back in his chair.

"Papá, can I go outside to see the soldiers and their horses?" asked Marcello, his eyes wide while bouncing around in excitement.

Camille quickly joined in with her brother. "Please, Papá," they both said repeatedly.

Domingo began to smile and even chuckled a little at his son and daughter. "What a day we're having, huh?"

Arabella smiled. "I think it's kind of nice having visitors," she said.

Domingo's eyes opened wide, as did his mouth. "Oh, you do, huh? What if it was twenty women out there? Would you still feel that way?"

"Better still," she replied with a large grin.

Domingo smiled as Camille began pulling on his arm, still wanting to go outside.

"Okay, okay!" answered Domingo. "Help me gather some stuff first, son. We have a cow to butcher."

The kids jumped up and down and began spinning in circles, holding each other's arms.

Domingo and Marcello gathered up some pliers, aprons, and knives, heading outside. He, Sergeant Balas, and two soldiers butchered the cow while Arabella made bread. Some soldiers roamed about gathering firewood, as others set up tents about a hundred yards from Domingo's home. The general's tent was put up first, with the Mexican flag hanging off the front. Marcello spent most of his time talking with General Sanchez and petting the horses while the general told him the horses' names and their heroic battles. As the sun began to set, the smell of cooking beef filled the air, and the flames of the campfires could be seen across the open fields.

As he washed up for dinner, Domingo thought again about leaving to get more supplies. With Apache in the area, he could not see leaving his family for several days alone. Then he got an idea. If he rode straight through, he could make it to his brother's home in two days and get supplies, a horse, and possibly another cow. There were so many things he needed to get, and this would be a perfect opportunity with the soldiers camped at his ranch. He would have certainly resisted this notion before, but after spending a couple hours with Sergeant Balas and the two soldiers butchering the cow, he felt more comfortable with them around. Domingo remembered the general mentioning staying in the area for two days, so maybe he could get him to leave a few men behind for a couple more days, and Domingo's family would not be alone at all.

Domingo knew Arabella would not be excited about him leaving, but he figured she would understand and eventually agree. He finished washing his hands and made his way to his room for a clean shirt. Then he walked out on the porch, where Marcello was still listening to Sanchez tell war stories.

"We have your plate inside, General. Marcello, you run along and get cleaned up. Your mama will have yours ready soon."

Marcello kicked the ground in disappointment.

"I mean it now, boy. Go get your sister and get cleaned up," added Domingo.

Sanchez put his hat on Marcello's head. "Can I trust you to guard that for a couple hours?"

Marcello grinned and saluted the general while replying enthusiastically, "Yes, sir!" Then he quickly ran off to get his sister.

Domingo watched Marcello dart away with a concerned look.

"Don't worry. That sombrero has seen better days," said the general as he stood next to Domingo.

The two men walked into the house and sat at the table.

Within moments, there was a knock on the door. Arabella opened the door to find a soldier holding several nice-sized pieces of meat on a metal tray. She took the tray and instructed the soldier to wait there. After setting the tray down in the kitchen, she returned to the door with three loaves of bread for the soldier to take to the men.

"*Gracias*," said the soldier. He turned and quickly made his way back to the camp.

Arabella prepared a plate for Domingo and Sanchez, placing it in front of them with glasses of tea.

"Now that looks delicious!" said General Sanchez, rubbing his hands together in front of him.

Domingo

"It really does," replied Domingo. "It's been some time since I had beef. Mostly mutton and fish for us lately." Domingo looked up at Arabella and reached for her hand. "Thanks, beautiful."

"Yes! Thank you very much, Arabella, for your hospitality," said Sanchez, already chewing on a piece of steak.

Arabella smiled and walked back into the kitchen to prepare a plate for the children and herself.

The two men ate in silence for several minutes, enjoying their dinner.

Hearing soldiers outside, talking and laughing, drew Domingo's attention to peer out the window at the campfires and men milling about. Some of the men sang while playing some sort of makeshift drum. He watched Marcello and Camille dance around near the front porch. As much as he had not wanted the soldiers there when they first arrived, he really enjoyed this moment. It had a feel of festivity and safety. He asked Sanchez about his family and his years in the Mexican army, and it wasn't long before the two men were cheerfully discussing many different things while enjoying their meal.

Arabella opened the door and called for the children to come inside to eat. Marcello and Camille came inside and reached for their plates, but Arabella stopped them. "Wash your hands first. They are filthy," she said.

Camille and Marcello both reached for the water and towel at the same time, trying to pull it from the other's hand.

"Stop it," said Arabella. "Give her the towel, Marcello." Arabella reached for the general's hat and pulled it off her son's head. "And give the general his sombrero."

The boy reached for the sombrero, but Arabella was too fast. She knew they were excited to eat and because of their unexpected guests, so was trying to be patient with them as they finally finished cleaning up.

"Take your plate to your room so your papá and the general can eat in peace," said Arabella.

The two children picked up their plates and made their way to their room.

Arabella placed the general's sombrero on a hook by the door and continued cleaning up the kitchen, listening to the men talk while taking a bite of her food from time to time.

As General Sanchez and Domingo finished eating, Sanchez leaned back in his chair and pulled two cigars out of his coat pocket. "I am sorry for all the trouble, señor, but I have my orders."

Domingo lit his cigar from a candle burning on the table, nodded, and took a puff. He hadn't liked Sanchez at first, but now he was finding him much more tolerable, maybe even enjoyable.

"I just want to live in peace with the Apache," said Domingo.

The general laughed, then coughed as he lit his cigar. "Excuse me," he said, shaking his head. "*You* may want to, but *they* don't." Then he took a drink of his tea. "Live in peace," he quipped with a slight smile. "That's very unrealistic, my friend."

"I've done well so far," added a confident Domingo.

Sanchez knocked the ashes from his cigar and said, "Listen, after a few weeks, you won't have to worry about being friends or at peace, because they will be gone."

"With twenty men, you're going to clear the Apache out of this entire region, huh?" said Domingo with a smirk.

Sanchez smiled. "I have many more men at my disposal. We might build an outpost out this way."

"An outpost?" a surprised Domingo said with a concerned and equally disappointed look.

Arabella came back into the room with two shot glasses and a bottle of tequila, then poured a glass each for Domingo and General Sanchez.

"Ah, *gracias*, señora. You are too kind," said the general.

Arabella smiled and again left the room.

"Well, señor, things are getting crazy around here. There are constant raids by the Indians, killing women, children, and families…families like yours, Domingo! They have to be stopped," said the general, a disturbing expression on his face. He sat looking out the window for a few moments before continuing, "Then there are the Americans…"

Domingo puffed on his cigar and waited for Sanchez to continue, but after a few moments of silence, he tired of waiting. "What about them?" he asked.

"They are taking all our land; claiming it for themselves. The land we have fought for!" Sanchez hit his fist on the table, then slammed back his tequila. "The Mexican government has been so kind to those gringos settling in our land, but once you get a group of them together, they claim it for themselves. I believe war between the US and Mexico is an utmost certainty." Calmer now, he set the empty glass down and stared at it.

Domingo wanted to ask if he wanted more tequila but kind of felt like he'd had too much already. He wasn't sure what to say about what the general had just told him. Half of him thought he was just jawing—the tequila talking.

Wishing to lighten the mood, Domingo said, "Well, General, with all that going on, I'm glad you're here after all." He raised his glass to the general.

"You think I'm crazy, but wait and see," said Sanchez.

"Arabella!" yelled Domingo.

Arabella returned to the men at the table, bringing the bottle of tequila with her.

"Thanks, beautiful," said Domingo, not at all surprised that she knew just what he would ask her for.

"I'll just leave it with you, boys," said Arabella, smiling as she set the bottle on the table.

"*Gracias*. You know the way to a man's heart," said Sanchez with a smile.

After Arabella left the room, Domingo realized now was his chance. She would not like the idea, so he wanted to discuss it with the general while she wasn't around. "I have a favor to ask from you, General," he said, leaning forward to pick up the bottle of tequila.

Sanchez watched Domingo pour them each another glass, then said, "All right then, ask."

"My ranch hands will be away for another month, and I am very low on supplies and need to go to Tucson." Domingo looked behind him to see if Arabella was coming. "I could leave tomorrow morning and be back in four, maybe five days, tops," he explained.

"And you want me to wait here for your return?" asked Sanchez.

Domingo leaned toward Sanchez so Arabella wouldn't hear, then glanced behind him to make sure she wasn't coming. "Well, you mentioned being here for a couple days, and I was hoping you could just leave a few of your men for a couple more?"

General Sanchez leaned back while taking a hit off his cigar, then started twisting the ends of his mustache. "I think I can arrange that," he replied, nodding his head. "We're not expecting any action. It's just a reconnaissance mission."

"*Gracias*," said Domingo. "You will leave men who can be trusted? I mean, it's my family."

Sanchez stared at Domingo with his eyes squinted and a slight shake of his head.

"I don't mean no disrespect, General. I just am struggling with having to leave my family for so many days," Domingo quickly added.

"These men may look rough, but they are soldiers and have families too."

Domingo nodded his head. "*Gracias*, General. I will leave at first light." With renewed enthusiasm, he rose from the table. "I must get my things together."

Sanchez chuckled. "Hopefully, a new pair of boots is on your list of supplies."

Domingo looked down at his leather boots and laughed. They were so old and worn out that his feet were exposed. "Yeah, I reckon I could use a new pair," he replied.

Sanchez rose from his chair and grabbed the bottle of tequila, looking at Domingo and then at the bottle in his hand. "We'll call it even," he said with a grin, walking out of the house with the bottle.

Arabella walked into the dining area a short time later, finding Domingo with his hand to his chin as he paced the room. "What are you doing?" she asked.

Domingo jerked his hand from his chin and looked at her. "Hey, beautiful. I need you to sit down for a second."

Arabella pulled out a chair from the table and slowly found the seat while keeping her eyes on Domingo.

"You know we are low on supplies, and I need to travel to town to restock."

Arabella tilted her head in confusion. "Well, okay. Then ride to town."

Domingo rubbed his face with his hand and then nervously continued, "Well, I was hoping to go to Tucson for the supplies and see Vicente."

Arabella crossed her arms and leaned back in the chair. "Then take us with you," she replied sternly.

Domingo smiled while shaking his head because he'd known that was coming. "You're pregnant, Arabella. What are you going to do? Bounce around in the back of an oxcart for four days?" said Domingo reaching for his glass. "That's not an option. Besides, it's too dangerous."

"Leaving us here for a week isn't?" snapped Arabella.

"With the soldiers here, you would be safe. Think about it. This is a great opportunity for me to make that trip." Domingo took a drink of the tequila.

Arabella stared at him, shaking her head. "We have enough to hold us until Luis and Jose return. That's the end of this discussion," she said.

Wide-eyed, Domingo smiled at his feisty wife. "Oh no, it's not," he replied. "I am leaving at first light, and you are staying here."

Arabella quickly stood from the table and walked out of the dining room, heading for their bedroom.

Domingo tilted his head and muttered, "Well, that went better than expected." Then he slammed back the rest of the tequila in his glass and made his way to the bedroom as well.

Domingo

"We will be fine, Domingo," said Arabella the moment he entered their bedroom.

He went to the closet and grabbed a cloth tote, then headed to the dresser and started packing as if he didn't hear her.

"Domingo!" she said with more urgency.

He stopped packing and went to her side, reaching for her hand. "Arabella, my love, I have to make this trip. We are low on supplies. I cannot bring you with me because it is too dangerous. And I cannot leave you behind by yourself because it is equally dangerous. These soldiers will protect you and the children while I am away."

"Why do you think it's so dangerous for us to be alone? And what happened to your horse?" asked Arabella.

Domingo was reluctant to tell her because she had not been a big fan of moving to this area. She would have much rather moved to Tucson near Vicente and Maria. With no choice but to tell her the truth, he downplayed the run-in with the Apaches as best he could.

Worry and animosity grew on her face as he spoke. "Marcello won't be returning to that river," she said abruptly.

"I know. That is why it's even more important that we get supplies now." Holding Arabella's hand with both of his, Domingo lowered his head. "I understand how you feel, but we really must take advantage of the situation." He looked up at her and smiled, then brushed his fingers across her cheek and moved her hair from her face, tucking it behind her ears. "Maybe I can convince Vicente and Maria to come back with me and visit us for a while, or maybe even move here."

Arabella nodded, relaxing under his words and touch only slightly.

Domingo tried to think of ways to cheer her up. "Besides,

when I'm in town, I will find a beautiful dress for the most beautiful woman in all of Mexico."

"I hope you are referring to me, Domingo," replied Arabella with the hint of a grin.

Domingo smiled at her. "How could there be any other?" he asked. He'd always loved her sense of humor. It had pulled them together when they'd first met and remained one of their strongest connections.

Arabella made a playfully mean face and poked him in the chest. "Well, if there is, don't be trying to find her!" She then rolled her eyes. "Oh, and I can't wait to see the dress you pick out!"

Domingo smiled even wider. "Keep it up and see where it gets ya."

"Make sure you keep the receipt," added Arabella.

"Oh, you are in trouble tonight!" he said as he lifted her up, then laid her on the bed.

They laughed together, then drifted closer and fell into a passionate kiss. Domingo ran his hand up and down her leg, caressing her soft skin as he started to undress her.

"No, no, wait, Domingo," Arabella whispered. "There are too many people around, and the kids are still awake."

This had little effect on Domingo, and he continued trying to undress her. "The kids are in their room, and besides, this is a perfect time," he said as he opened her blouse.

Arabella bit down on her bottom lip and closed her eyes as he caressed her breast. "And why is this time so perfect?" she asked, reaching up and unbuttoning Domingo's shirt.

"Because they won't hear you moaning over the sound of that drum," he replied.

They both soon realized the drum wasn't loud enough.

CHAPTER 4
TURQUOISE PENDANT

The Eastern Chiricahua Apache had been fighting Spaniards and other tribes for decades, but it had never resulted in the loss of land. Since the independence of Mexico, their territory had been diminishing as fighting with the Mexicans intensified

Mangas had made his first kill at the young age of fifteen, and he had proudly worn the blood of his enemy on his arms for several days, earning him the nickname of Red Sleeves. He was so good at fighting and strategy that he had recently been promoted to war chief. Having fought together many times, Red Sleeves and Chief Compa had great respect for each other. They were not brothers by relation but were in every other way.

When the Apache hunting party returned to their tribe, Red Sleeves went to see Chief Compa and tell him about running into a Mexican man and his son hunting on Apache land near the Gila. The chief told him they would discuss it with the elders at the gathering later in the evening.

Domingo

Red Sleeves entered his wickiup, nodding to his wife as he stepped past her and the cook fire she was working over to lay down on his buckskin bedding. He stared up at the stick ceiling and thought about the ordeal at great length. There was something about the man he'd met. He could tell the Mexican was a fierce fighter who could have easily shot and killed him. Looking back at it now, he was surprised the Mexican hadn't shot him while he had the chance. It was very uncommon for him to encounter a lone Mexican man and let him survive, but he'd known something was different this time.

Red Sleeves's wife sat down beside him with two dishes of food, and they said a little prayer together before eating in silence. Before they finished, a stick smacked the side of the wickiup, signaling it was time to meet with the chief, medicine man, and elders. He sat his bowl down beside him and kissed his wife on the forehead, then pushed the animal skin flap aside and left the wickiup.

Red Sleeves briskly walked to the gathering around a small campfire just outside the chief's wickiup. Besides Chief Compa, the two elders—Red Elk and Gray Sky—and the medicine man, named Buckskin Hat, sat in a circle looking down at the flames. They all nodded as Red Sleeves joined them.

The chief discussed relocating the tribe farther north—closer to the buffalo—and then traveling to the Santa Rita mountains in the spring, a sacred and spiritual place for the Apache. Compa also told them of his plan to visit the western Apache chief and discuss a possible alliance to protect their lands together. Everyone agreed with their chief; that these ideas were good for the tribe.

Red Sleeves tried his best to sit quietly and not show his impatience to discuss his run-in with the Mexican, but he found it very difficult. He knew Chief Compa was purposely delaying bringing up what Red Sleeves had told him, which was his way of teaching Red Sleeves that all things are important, not just war.

Then Compa finally said, "It seems a Mexican family has taken a home below the Gila. Red Sleeves ran into them while returning from a hunt." The chief waved heat from the fire toward himself with both hands. "The Mexican and his son were hunting on Apache land."

The men sat quietly as they gazed into the fire without expression.

"That land is cursed. We should just leave them be. It's protected by the spirits of the ghost child and the raven," said the medicine man.

"We cannot have Mexicans hunting our land. We must attack and leave them for the buzzards," said the elder, Gray Sky.

"I talked to the Mexican man and told him not to hunt Apache land, and he gave me his horse," said Red Sleeves.

"Is one horse enough for this trespass?" asked Gray Sky.

Red Sleeves looked across the flames at Gray Sky, then turned to his chief. "He will give us nothing else," he said.

"The man you met—did he have any visible scars on his face?" asked the medicine man.

"None I can remember, although he looked to be of a fighting type," answered Red Sleeves.

"In my visions, I have seen a man with a great scar on his face. I have seen great suffering of our people at the hands of this man," said the medicine man.

"I remember many moons ago, when the first family made a home near the Gila," said Red Elk as he coughed and pulled a blanket around himself. "We gathered much like we are now, and one of the elders was asked what we should do about them. He said not much would happen if they stayed, but he feared what might come if they were removed." The elder coughed again and wiped his mouth. "We decided to attack the family the next day, killing many of them and taking all they own."

Red Elk warmed his hands, staring into the fire as the group waited for him to continue.

"Shortly after, many of our men and women were scalped for bounty money that Mexico placed on all Apache."

There was a long silence as the chief nodded to Red Elk and then looked at Red Sleeves.

Red Sleeves returned his chief's gaze with a look of uncertainty and deep thought, not convinced either way. He then fixed his eyes on Gray Sky, who stoically stared forward, unaffected by Red Elk's story.

"I have heard enough, and I have made my decision," said Chief Compa. "I also was there when we brought war to the family that Red Elk speaks of. We lit the home on fire and waited for them to come out. Two men were the first out. One with a gun, and another carrying a woman."

Gray Sky interrupted the chief. "It's not good to talk of these things among our people. Let us go to the cliffs in the morning to talk," he said.

Chief Compa could have continued the story, but out of respect for the other elders, he simply nodded at Gray Sky. Then he sat still, staring into the fire before looking up at the group gathered around him. He raised his arm, motioning toward Red Elk. "Red Elk is right. We gained nothing from killing them. But Gray Sky is also right. They cannot stay." The chief turned toward Red Sleeves. "Tomorrow, Red Sleeves, you and your warriors will ride to the home, destroy it, and take all they own. But try to do this without killing them." Compa then looked to the medicine man. "But if one should die, they all will die," he quietly added. Reaching for his necklace, he grasped the piece of turquoise attached to it. "I will also ride along and cast this turquoise stone into the fire to protect us from the spirits." He reached for his pipe. "Now, let us smoke and find peace within ourselves."

CHAPTER 5
RAVEN

As dawn announced another rather cool morning, General Sanchez was in his tent, going over maps for his northward ride into Apache territory. He called for sergeant Balas and major Juarez, and the three men stood at a table the soldiers had constructed the night before to go over their plan of action.

Sanchez was hoping to pinpoint the Apache's whereabouts and look for a strategic place to surprise attack; however, if they found an Apache force they could overtake easily, they certainly would without any strategic planning. Sanchez had requested more troops but knew that with the mounting tension between the United States and Mexico, his superiors were not likely to send additional men anytime soon. The general's task was to severely cripple the Apache tribe, driving them north to allow a safe gateway for Mexican civilians moving into the mostly unpopulated Alta California Territory. Although outnumbered by the Apache, Sanchez felt confident he could do it with the small force he had.

The general listened to his men and their ideas. They all agreed they would reach the Apache tribe just north of the Gila River, camp out a mile short of it, and send out scouts to locate the enemy. If the Apache were not spotted, they would ride east in hopes of finding them there. As the general went over his map with the major and Sergeant Balas, he informed the sergeant that he and two other men would stay behind.

"Sir," said Sergeant Balas as he turned away from the map and looked at General Sanchez. "I understand you would like me to stay behind, but sir?" He looked at the floor for a moment and shook his head, then looked at the general. "I do believe any fighting we might have would occur by the time you return this evening." Sergeant Balas then pointed to the map. "That position is no more than a couple hours of riding from here. We should all ride out together, sir."

General Sanchez grinned and placed his hand on the sergeant's shoulder. "Don't worry, Sergeant. There won't be any fighting until we all ride out together in a couple days. Once we pinpoint the enemy's whereabouts, we will plan our attack and hit them so hard, they won't come this far south for generations."

Sergeant Balas shook his head and tilted it to the side, showing he was still not in agreement. "Forgive me, sir, but if we are no more than a couple hours' ride—"

"It's not just the ranch you are protecting, Sergeant!" said the general sternly.

The sergeant quickly stood at attention, looking straight ahead with his hands by his side as the general stared angrily at him.

Domingo

The general took a deep breath and slowly raised his hand to acknowledge the sergeant's feelings on the matter, then bowed his head a bit and began nodding. He looked up at the sergeant, still standing at attention, and calmly stated, "This is our camp, Sergeant. Our tents, gear, ammunition boxes, and food are right here. If this was lost, what would we do?"

Sergeant Balas stayed tight-lipped as he nodded.

The general walked past the sergeant and major, making eye contact with them both as he did, then placed his hands behind his back before coming to a stop.

The two soldiers turned to face their general.

"Men, we plan to be in these parts for some time, and this ranch will become a useful resource." Then the general turned and faced his men while pointing to the ground. "This ranch sits perfectly between the citizens we need to protect and the Apache savages on those rocky cliffs," explained Sanchez, pointing north.

"Yes, sir," replied the major.

"Yes, sir. I understand, sir," replied Balas.

"Good," replied the general with a quick nod. Looking at the major, he said, "Now, ready the men, and let's head out within the hour."

"Yes, sir!" The two men saluted their general and made their way out of the tent.

While the soldiers mounted their horses, Chief Compa, Red Sleeves, and the Apache warriors prepared to head south toward Domingo's ranch. Always more than ready to fight, Red Sleeves did not want to kill Domingo and his family, but he had finally agreed they must go.

The Apache warriors painted their faces while other members of the tribe decorated their horses. Then the warriors gathered in the center of the camp with the rest of the tribe surrounding them.

Red Sleeves wife put a necklace she had made for him around his neck. He touched his hand to her face with a proud expression as he looked at her and his boy. Next, he went to his horse, and his son followed. The boy placed his hand on the neck of his father's white and brown-spotted appaloosa, making a yellow handprint. Red Sleeves put his hand to the horse's cheek and placed his forehead to its muzzle.

"Carry me safely, Whom'tu," said Red Sleeves.

The horse's Apache name meant White Thunder, and sometimes he would spend an hour talking to him before a battle. Today, Red Sleeves did not foresee any major fighting. He jumped onto his horse and rode slowly to his men. As he reached the war party, the chief raised his spear, which was decorated with paint and white feathers.

The warriors cheered, then fell silent.

"Today is a great day. The sun god is with us and will bring us to victory," said Compa.

The men cheered again until moments later, Red Sleeves raised his spear and silenced them.

"Our great Chief Compa rides with us today, and our lives will end before even a single drop of his blood is shed," shouted Red Sleeves.

The men raised their fists in the air as their war cries echoed in the valley.

The chief looked around at each of them and said, "It's true. I ride with you today, and as much as it hurts me to say,

Domingo

I am now an old man. Too old to fight. I will not lead you today, but rather ride behind the great War Chief Red Sleeves."

The Apache warriors yammered and yelped, raising their rifles in the air to honor Chief Compa.

Red Sleeves and Compa reached out, locking arms at each other's biceps. He nodded to his chief, then led the twenty-six warriors south toward the Gila. The entire Apache tribe watched them go, beating drums and singing as their warriors rode into the distance and eventually out of sight.

Sanchez and his men rode straight north, toward the Gila, following the trail Domingo and Marcello had made. It would be about a two-hour ride to reach the area they had circled on the map, about one mile south of the Gila River. Sanchez would keep his approach toward the Gila slow, letting the scouts ride ahead and report back.

Their horses twisted and turned up the narrow path, through several different terrains ranging from rock, sand, grass, clay, and a lot of dried-up water spots where the ground was cracked and brittle. The brush was so thick in certain areas, it became difficult to see ahead. After the men rode for about an hour, the general stopped to study his compass. He looked in front of him at the valley ahead, then decided to head east. As the soldiers continued, the terrain became even more difficult. After a while, the general ordered his men to stop for a water break. He pulled out his canteen, sitting under a palo tree to study the map after sending two men ahead to scout the area for signs of Apaches. He then placed his sombrero down over his eyes to relax.

Only a few hundred yards from the Gila, Red Sleeves jumped down from his horse and searched the ground for tracks. Every fifteen to twenty feet, he picked up some dirt, then crumbled it in his hand and released it. He continued toward a heavy brush-covered area and disappeared into it, walking about another fifty yards toward the Gila until it came into sight, then quietly watched and listened. He spotted a couple mule deer drinking from the river—a good sign that no one was close by. Walking back to his warriors and chief, he jumped on his horse and led the way to the river.

Once they reached the river, Red Sleeves led Whom'tu to the water. The other warriors did the same with their horses, then they sat next to the chief on their riding blankets. They talked briefly about the river, which seemed to be low these days. Compa talked of the Apaches who had lived on the river many lives ago, long before they became a nomadic tribe. Compa was the son of a chief and brother of a medicine man, so his knowledge of their history ran deep. Red Sleeves had lost much of his family when he was young and enjoyed hearing the stories of those who knew his parents. His father was buried in the Santa Rita Mountains, a resting place for the Apache. Red Sleeves used to go there quite often with Compa before he became chief.

Red Sleeves was really enjoying this day with the chief, as it felt like some time since they had been away from the tribe together. He decided to ask Compa to finish his story about the Mexican family Red Elk had spoken of the night before.

Compa nodded his head and began, "As the family emerged from the home, we cut them down while they tried to flee. The home burned, and we figured anyone left inside was dead. Surprisingly, a short time later, an elderly woman—holding hands with a young boy—emerged from the house. The sight of it was chilling. Most of the warriors just froze where they were, unable to react. The woman's hair was on fire, and although both the woman and child were badly burned, they didn't seem to feel their wounds."

Compa shook his head. "With their clothes and faces mostly black, they just stood there laying eyes on us. Not frightened, not angry…completely emotionless. Even with their family's butchered bodies lying in front of them, they only looked at us."

"Must have been in shock," said Red Sleeves.

Compa nodded. "Buckskin Hat and many others got on their horses and started to leave. I approached the old woman and young boy. They didn't look at me. They just kept their eyes fixed forward. It seemed their spirits had left their bodies, and they were dead and alive at the same time. As I began to turn away, I saw the old woman's hand move toward me. She had a necklace in her hand with a blue turquoise stone."

Compa reached for the necklace around his neck. "This stone." He stretched the chain closer for Red Sleeves to see. "I don't know if she was trying to give it to me, but I took it. As I climbed back on my horse to join the others, I saw a raven land in a tree near them. The bird made such loud screeching cries that I turned from it and rode away quickly. I can still hear the birds cry, and it is something I will never forget. As we were riding away, I looked behind me several times and only saw smoke climbing into the clouds behind us."

Visibly upset, Compa sat quietly for a moment before continuing. "After some time passed, I returned to the home.

The bodies were gone…I suppose dragged off by lobos or coyotes. I looked inside the mostly collapsed home, and there was nothing inside. As I got on my horse and started to leave, I looked to the sky and saw a raven approaching. A chill ran through my body as I kicked the horse and rode as fast as I could to get back to the tribe."

Red Sleeves now understood why the medicine man called it cursed ground and why Gray Sky didn't want to talk about it.

"I have heard stories of a man named The Boy, who survived after his family was attacked by the Apache. His story sounds eerily similar to that of the family we killed near the Gila many years ago. They say his face and body are burned, and he wears a necklace lined with raven feathers," said Compa.

"The boy could not have survived on his own," said Red Sleeves. "How would he eat?"

Compa looked across the river, taking a deep breath. "They also call that man The Cannibal."

Red Sleeves gave his chief a bewildered look, then quickly rose to his feet when he caught a glimpse of something moving up the ridge. He stood on a fallen tree nearby to get a better look, but it was gone.

"What do you see?" asked Compa.

"I saw something move up there," said Red Sleeves, pointing to the ridge in the distance. "Could have just been deer."

The chief stood and looked over to where Red Sleeves was pointing but saw nothing.

"I will ride up there," said Red Sleeves. "It's possibly the Mexican."

The chief continued looking in the distance. "Well, if it

is, he will be riding home. We will meet him there," replied Compa.

Red Sleeves looked at his chief and nodded. "We should move quickly so he has little time to prepare."

Red Sleeves climbed on his horse, as did the chief and warriors, and they set a quick pace south.

General Sanchez and his men climbed back on their horses to continue their drive northeast as one of his scouts rode toward him in great haste.

"Sir!" he said to General Sanchez, breathing heavily.

"What is it, soldier?"

"Apache, sir! Coming this way!"

"How many?"

"Fifteen, maybe twenty of them. Two miles tops," answered the soldier.

"Were you seen?" asked the general.

"No, sir," replied the soldier, still catching his breath.

Sanchez turned to the major standing to his left. "Get the men ready. Let's take cover right here on this hill and surprise them."

"Yes, sir," replied the major.

"You men, gather the horses and tie them up out of sight, but close where we can still get to them quickly. Now I want to form a line right here," said the major, pointing to the ground in front of him. "And a second line right there," he said, pointing to his left. "We'll use the low brush as cover!" shouted the major as the men began scrambling to their positions.

The general believed having his men on the ground, taking cover in the brush, would give them a huge advantage. As the men began fortifying, he led a few soldiers on horseback to the rear with him, on the other side of the hill, with plans to pursue retreating Apache. The general wondered why the Apache were coming this way, then he realized they were probably on their way to Domingo's ranch.

The major watched the soldiers dig a quick bunker in the dirt, looking in the distance for any approaching Apache. "You men wait until the last possible second to fire. We have the advantage of surprise, so let's keep it!"

Riding to General Sanchez's position on the other side of the hill, the major stopped briefly to survey his men and surrounding landscape. Seeming pleased at the position of his men, he then made his way to his commander, who was still on horseback and looking over a map.

"Sir, we have formed two lines, and the men are hunkered down and waiting for them," the major said to General Sanchez.

Sanchez nodded to the major, finished looking over his map, then folded it up and put it in his pocket. "Well, I don't think we'll have much to worry about here. I expect them to run after the first round of shots, then we will pursue." He then turned to a soldier standing nearby. "So have the horses ready!"

"Yes, sir," replied the soldier.

The major climbed down from his horse and handed the reins to a soldier standing to his right, then he turned back toward the general, stood at attention, and saluted his commander.

General Sanchez saluted him back, then smiled at his old comrade and friend. "You be safe out there, Pablo."

The major smiled up at Sanchez. "Will do, sir." The two men shook hands, and the major quickly made his way to the soldiers on the other side of the hill, taking cover behind some brush.

The Apaches steadily rode south, and Red Sleeves in the front, watching and listening. He was a little unnerved after seeing something at the river. He wasn't sure who it was, but he really didn't think it was the Mexican he'd run into the day before. Why would the Mexican return so soon after running into him? He would be crazy to do that. He thought maybe it was the mule deer, but whatever it was, he was going to keep his senses on high alert.

He led the warriors through a thick group of pine trees and brush, where the trail made a sharp turn to the left, then slowly curved to the right. There he stopped, overwhelmed by the feeling that they were being watched. This was a bad place to be if they were attacked. He surveyed the area in all directions.

The chief looked around, then at Red Sleeves. "What is it, Red Sleeves? Do you see something?"

"No, I just have a strange feeling," he replied, still looking in all directions. He listened carefully for several moments, then said, "You should turn back."

Compa looked confused. "Take another way, you mean?"

Red Sleeves looked at the chief. "No, me and the warriors will follow this path. I ask you to return to the river and wait for us until we know it's safe."

Compa looked around and said, "I may be too old to fight, but I'm not afraid to fight. I will carry on with you."

Red Sleeves nodded to his chief. "Will you stay towards

the rear? Make for the Gila if a fight breaks, then head back to the tribe?"

Compa looked at Red Sleeves and smiled. "I think you worry too much when I am here. If I was not with you, you would have already passed through the thickets."

Red Sleeves nodded. He would have already been to the Mexican's home by now. Still, he had a gut instinct, and it wasn't just because the chief was there. He rode ahead, and the chief waited until ten warriors passed before he rejoined the group.

They made it through a couple more turns, then came to a clearing in the land. Red Sleeves studied the ground and surveyed the area momentarily, then continued. Upon seeing hoof prints, he realized it was probably a horse he'd seen on the ridge at the river. Whoever it was must have been heading back toward the Mexican's home, and by the looks of the tracks, at a very quick pace. He studied the landscape in front of him, then told the warriors to prepare for a fight. He took off at a fast pace, the men following, and went about a hundred yards before stopping again. Up ahead was a hill and another group of trees with more thick brush. Thinking that was a good place for a surprise attack, Red Sleeves watched the tree line and studied the brush, but he did not see any movement. Then he noticed some of the brush on the hill was matted down.

He turned toward his warriors and chief. "They are up there," he said, pointing up at the hill in the distance. "We move in quickly. They are off their horses."

The chief looked at the tree line and hill where Red Sleeves pointed. "Who's out there?" he asked.

"Not sure who exactly or how many," answered Red Sleeves as he gazed into the distance, still looking for any movement. "But we will find out soon enough." Then Red Sleeves turned toward his chief. "Wait here as we move up the trail, then charge up the hill. Let us see exactly what's up there. If you see us racing back down, make your way to the Gila."

The chief and Red Sleeves locked arms as they always did and quickly nodded to each other.

Red Sleeves rubbed Whom'tu on the neck, then he spun the horse around a few times, kicking up dirt and dust. He locked eyes with each of his warriors, then raised his rifle and belted out a war cry. Kicking his horse while smacking the reins, Red Sleeves quickly headed down the trail. The warriors simultaneously turned and charged down the trail, past the thickets, and hastily up the hillside, following their war chief.

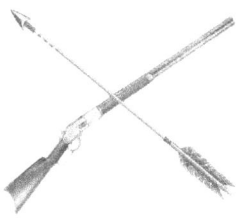

CHAPTER 6
BLOOD AT THE GILA

Confused by the thundering of hooves approaching, Sanchez's men became jittery. They'd been sure they were not spotted, yet the Apaches were coming at them as if they knew exactly where they were. The rumble grew louder and louder as the Indians closed in.

Kneeling down behind some brush, but still visible to his men, the major called to his soldiers, "Steady, men! Don't give away your positions. We have the advantage." He noticed one of the soldiers shift in his position, hunkering farther down and to his right a few inches, and shouted, "Hold your ground, goddamnit!"

The Indians bellowed out a war cry that was easily heard over the thunderous hoofbeats, now less than fifty yards away.

The major lifted his hand and brought it down quickly. "Fire!" he shouted.

A round of gunfire rang out from the hillside, then the firing soldiers bunkered back down to the ground as five Apache warriors fell off their horses.

The major yelled to the second line of soldiers to his left, "Fire!"

Another round of bullets sprayed through the brush, hitting three more warriors.

The lead warrior was hit in the left arm, just above his elbow, but it didn't slow him down. He fired into the thicket, hitting a soldier in the chest, as the other warriors fired all around him. Reaching the brush line, their horses charged right into the line of soldiers. Some of the soldiers were trampled, while those who tried to run back for their horses were quickly run down and shot by the charging Indians.

Farther up the hill, using his field glasses, Sanchez watched in disbelief as his soldiers were pummeled by the Apache warriors. Realizing the scout's report had been wildly inaccurate, he shouted angrily, "Fifteen to twenty men? More like thirty!" Turning to the two soldiers next to him, he pulled his sword and pointed it toward the fight below. "Charge!"

Sanchez and his mounted soldiers raced straight at the Apache warriors.

A shot to Whom'tu's rump caused the horse to lose his balance, throwing Red Sleeves to the ground. Red Sleeves jumped up with his spear and stabbed the closest soldier in the chest. While still holding his spear in his left hand, he grabbed his tomahawk with his right and delivered a blow to another soldier's head. He took several steps forward and threw his spear, hitting a third soldier in the side just before the soldier could shoot one of Red Sleeves's brethren.

Domingo

Something slammed into his back, sending Red Sleeves to the ground. He rolled and looked up, ready to defend himself, as another warrior on horseback charged the soldier who was holding his rifle like a club and standing over Red Sleeves. The soldier turned to avoid the charging horse but lost his footing and fell to the ground. Red Sleeves jumped up and brought his tomahawk down on the soldier's throat. Blood squirted up, covering Red Sleeves's face. He jumped back on his injured horse and yelled for his warriors to retreat.

The warriors rallied and charged back in the direction from which they'd come. Although Red Sleeves had asked Compa to head to the Gila, the chief had waited for them to return. Joining their chief about a hundred yards beyond the bottom of the hill, the men formed a circle around him and their war chief to keep watch.

Beginning to feel the wound to his left arm, Red Sleeves wrapped a piece of cloth around it and pulled it tight. "Mexican army," he said to the chief.

"I will return to the tribe and prepare them to move north in case there are more," said Compa.

Red Sleeves nodded his agreement. "We will hold them here, maybe make one more attack. The advantage is ours."

The chief looked up the ridge toward the Mexican army. He could see them rallying in preparation for the Apache to make their next move.

"You are the war chief, Red Sleeves. The decision is yours." The chief climbed on his horse and turned toward the Gila, trotting down the trail.

Red Sleeves moved around the circle of his warriors, taking inventory. He had lost ten, most falling on the initial charge toward the soldiers' fortified position. There were sixteen warriors remaining, and although many of those had injuries, including Red Sleeves, they were all capable and eager for another attack. Knowing that to retreat now would lead the Mexican soldiers straight to the tribe, he decided to charge the soldiers in hopes of making them flee.

To honor their fearsome war chief, a few warriors who noticed his wounded arm shouted, "Red Sleeves!"

Red Sleeves raised his rifle with his bloody arm, yowling in celebration and determination.

The warriors followed his lead, raising their rifles and letting out a fierce war cry in preparation for another attack.

Unwilling to retreat or advance, Sanchez decided to hold his position. They'd suffered eight casualties, and five soldiers were injured—two of them critically. The able-bodied soldiers helped move the wounded farther up the ridge, leaving the dead where they were. The remaining eleven men got on horses or formed a firing line farther up the ridge than the original line, preparing for the next attack.

The soldiers went silent as they heard Indians at the foot of the hill chanting, "*Ko Kun Noste! Ko Kun Noste!*"—Red Sleeves! Red Sleeves!—followed by a war cry and the thundering of horses' hooves.

"Ready up, men! They're coming again!" yelled Sanchez, watching the Indians through his field glasses. He watched the lead warrior spin his horse around three times and let out another war cry. "Red Sleeves."

"Who, sir?" asked the major.

"Red Sleeves," replied Sanchez, looking across to the Apaches heading back up the hill. "He stopped General Pico and his men a couple years back. He's a murderer, thief, pillager… He's done it all." Turning to his men and pulling out his sword, he shouted, "All right, men! They're coming! This is it!"

Sanchez watched Red Sleeves lead the Apache hastily up the hill for another moment, then yelled, "Okay, men! *Charge*!"

The Mexican soldiers charged down the hill, meeting the Apache in what became an open battlefield just above their original line. Horses collided, dumping several men to the ground. Some of the men were trampled by their own comrades' horses. Red Sleeves jumped from his horse at a soldier on horseback, dropping them both hard to the ground. Reaching for his rifle, the Apache warrior fired point-blank into the soldier's head, then reached for his tomahawk. Sanchez watched the major charge at the Indian, but Red Sleeves grabbed him from his horse. The two rolled around on the ground, punching and kicking. As their ferocious hand-to-hand combat ensued, Red Sleeves managed to get his knife out and stab the major in the side. The major squealed, writhing around on the ground in pain, as Red Sleeves took out his blade and scalped him.

Sanchez watched in horror as his longtime friend took his last breath while Red Sleeves rushed toward another soldier, then rage took over, and he pushed his mount to charge right toward the Indian war chief. Before the horse took its second stride, Sanchez was shot in the leg just above the knee. Grabbing his leg, he pulled back on the reins and scanned the battlefield. The battle was lost, and retreat or death were the only options.

"Retreat!" yelled Sanchez to what was left of his soldiers while glaring at Red Sleeves. "Come on, men! Let's go!"

Sanchez held pressure to his leg to slow the bleeding as he and eight soldiers hastily headed south in retreat. Glancing back when he could, he saw Red Sleeves and his warriors pull two more soldiers from their horses, delivering blows from their tomahawks until the last rider was out of reach.

The Apache walked through the bodies scattered about the ground, stabbing and scalping any wounded soldiers still trying to get to their horses. They scalped every man left behind before celebrating their victory. The blood of the Mexican soldiers covering Red Sleeves's arms inspired the warriors to cheer his name again.

"Red Sleeves!" they shouted, circling their war chief and pumping their tomahawks and rifles in the air.

After celebrating their victory for several minutes, they began helping their injured warriors onto their horses. Red Sleeves was not about to let his dead warriors lie on the ground for the wolves and coyotes. It took over an hour for the able warriors to collect their dead, lying their bodies across the horses and then leading them on foot to the Gila. When they reached the river, Red Sleeves lay in the water and watched it turn red around him.

General Sanchez and his six remaining men rode south for about one mile, then they stopped to tend to their injuries. The healthiest men stood guard in case the Apache war party was pursuing them.

Sanchez had lost a lot of blood and needed to get the bullet out. He had one of his men grab the bottle of tequila from his side saddle and took three large swigs. Putting a stick in his mouth to bite down on, he nodded to his would-be surgeon. The soldier used a knife to dig into the general's leg and removed the bullet. Sanchez was about to pass out from the pain before the bullet finally came out, then he took another long swig of tequila as they bandaged him up.

Surprised by how hard the Apache had fought, Sanchez sat resting against a tree as he pondered their next move. It seemed the Apache were not willing to retreat, even when his army had the initial advantage. He thought of Red Sleeves, who had fought with such skill. He alone had killed at least five of his men, including the major. Sanchez lay back on the ground, covered by a blanket his men placed over him, then placed his sombrero over his face.

"Sir?" said one of his men. "Is there anything you need?"

Sanchez lifted his hat with a look that said, "dumb question," then he put it back over his face. "Not a damn thing, but thanks anyway," he said.

"Of course, sir. I'll be back to check on your wound in a bit."

"I'll be fine," the general grumbled. "Just need some rest."

"Yes, sir. Oh, and sir, we just lost another man. Rico was hit in the stomach."

The soldier waited for a response, but none came.

"I'll brief you later, sir, on the men's injuries," said the soldier before his footsteps told Sanchez he'd gone.

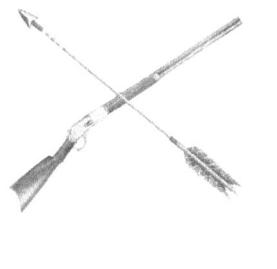

CHAPTER 7
HEADING SOUTH

Making good time on his way to Tucson, Domingo decided to rest for a few minutes on the back of his oxcart. He drank from his water canteen while cleaning the dirt out of his ragged boots. Looking up at the sound of hoofbeats, he saw two riders approaching from the south. The route he was taking to Tucson was known to be a pretty safe one, so he was not alarmed by the approaching men. He watched for a moment, trying to see if they were Indians, but they were still too far away to tell. Even if they were Indians, Domingo was not too concerned. With just two of them, he knew he had a good chance if things got heated.

He closed his canteen and reached for his rifle, dusting it off and checking the load as he waited for the riders. Soon he could see they were not Indians, but they looked like Mexicans wearing bandoliers. Probably outlaws or drifters. The men slowed their mounts to a walk as they neared Domingo, still sitting on the cart with his rifle beside him. One of the riders was a tall, thin man in a gray suit with the leather bandolier across his chest. He had rather large ears, a boney face, thick mustache, and a white hat that looked like something a plantation boss would wear. The other was much tougher looking in a dark overcoat, pants, a two-rig belt, and a rifle in his hand. He had very dark hair and mustache and wore leather armas.

"Hello, señor," said the thinner man in the white hat.

"Hello," said Domingo, squinting against the sun.

Just ten feet from Domingo and his cart, the two strangers looked at each other, then back at Domingo.

"The name's Santos," said the thinner man. "And this gentleman here is Diego."

Domingo nodded, never taking his eyes off them as he watched for any sudden movements. "Domingo," he replied.

Santos looked around and up at the hot sun almost directly above them. "We've been riding for some time, amigo. We are very thirsty. Would you mind?" The man pointed to Domingo's canteen.

Domingo sensed they were up to no good, but he tossed the man his canteen anyway.

"*Gracias*," said Santos. He took a quick drink and handed the canteen to his comrade. "Where are you heading, señor?" he asked, turning back to Domingo.

Domingo was about to answer when he noticed the quieter man pretty much kill his canteen of water. He had more but didn't take well to rudeness. "Hey, chico," he said.

The man slowly took the canteen from his mouth.

"You better be handing that back now," demanded Domingo, reaching out his hand.

Diego gave Domingo a sour look and didn't move to return the canteen.

"Give him his water, Diego," Santos said, then he grabbed the water and tossed it to Domingo. "I'm sorry, señor. He was not raised among civilized people like yourself."

Domingo looked back at him and said, "You don't have to be raised among royalty to have manners."

Santos removed his hat and wiped his brow. "So, where ya heading?" he asked.

"What's it to ya?" replied Domingo.

"Well, it's not the safest area. Maybe we could ride together?" Santos said. "I mean, if you're heading the same way and all."

"Where you all riding from?" asked Domingo.

"Deep Mexico. We came up here to do some ranching," replied Santos.

Domingo looked them over for a second and smiled. He knew he couldn't trust these two men. The one guy who talked a lot wasn't too bad, but the other had a chip on his shoulder. Figuring they were probably bank robbers or cattle thieves, he couldn't risk them taking off with his oxcart and water, or maybe even killing him when he fell asleep.

"Don't look like ranchos," said Domingo. "Look more like you been running from someone."

The men looked at each other, and Diego shook his head as if annoyed with Domingo.

"Aw, señor. What about those manners you spoke of?" asked Santos. He looked at his comrade and smiled.

"If it's all the same to you, I think I'll be heading out alone," said Domingo. "Now, I'll give you men some water, enough for a day's ride. That will get you to the San Rico River about fifteen miles west." He wanted the men to go west because he was heading north, and his home was to the east.

"We're not heading west, señor," replied Santos.

"I can't help you then," said Domingo.

"Oh, but we think you can," said Santos with a smile.

Diego put his left hand on his pistol.

"Left-handed are ya, chico?" said Domingo, glaring at Diego.

Diego returned the glare, unflinching.

Santos looked at the rifle resting on Domingo's lap, the barrel pointing toward Diego. "We don't want trouble, señor," he said.

"Then start riding," said Domingo.

"We tried to be civil and have manners, but the truth is that we need something, and I think you have it," explained Santos.

"You thought wrong," replied Domingo. He looked back and forth at the men, watching their movements. He just had to move his hand a little bit to pull the trigger if it came to that.

"Don't even think about it, señor. An oxcart ain't worth dying for," Santos said, putting his hand on his pistol. "Now move away from that cart."

In a tough spot now, Domingo wished he had just shot them as they approached. Even outnumbered and outgunned, he was glad it was going this way so he could kill them without feeling bad about it. He raised one hand and smiled. "Okay, listen, amigos. You are right. One oxcart is not worth dying for. However, I really need this particular oxcart because I have to get supplies for my boss, ranchero Juarez. Now maybe you heard of him?"

Santos looked over at Diego then back to Domingo. "No, amigo. We have not, but please continue," he said sarcastically.

"Well, if I return with no supplies and no oxcart, I am likely to be labeled a thief," said Domingo.

"Would you like us to write a letter to your boss saying we took the cart, so you won't get in trouble?" asked Santos with a chuckle.

"Well, as nice as that offer is, I don't think it will be enough," replied Domingo.

"So, what do you propose then, señor?" asked Santos.

"Here is what I am proposing, amigo. Leave the cart, and I'll pay you," replied Domingo.

Santos and Diego looked at each other, then back at Domingo and smiled.

"Then show us the dinero, señor," said Santos, rubbing his fingers together.

Domingo reached inside his vest.

"Careful," said Santos. He pulled out his pistol and pointed it at Domingo.

"Easy, señor. It's right here." Domingo pulled the money pouch he'd gotten from the general from his vest pocket.

"Toss it here," said Santos, putting his pistol back in the holster.

Domingo tossed Santos the pouch, the coins jingling as the man caught it.

Santos took a quick peek inside. With a smile, he said, "Not bad. Well, I think I'll let you live!" Raising his head, he looked at Domingo, then pointed at Diego and said, "But that's not up to me. It's up to him." Turning to his partner, he smiled and asked, "What do you think, Diego? Should we let him live?"

Diego stared straight at Domingo and shook his head.

"Aw, shucks," said Santos. "And I really liked you too."

Domingo

Domingo raised his hands and said, "Wait. I have a little more. If I give you that, will you let me go?"

Paying great attention to Domingo's movements, Santos asked, "Where is it?"

"It's right here," replied Domingo. He patted the other side of his vest.

"Well, give it here, and we will see if you can go," said Santos, looking into the money pouch again.

Diego kept his hand on his pistol, his glare fixed on Domingo.

Domingo reached inside his vest, this time grabbing his throwing knife. Like a flash, he pulled the knife out and threw it at Diego, hitting him in the neck.

Blood poured from between Diego's fingers as he desperately grasped at his throat. He then fell backward, off his horse, causing the animal to jump forward and startle Santos's horse.

Santos dropped the pouch and went for his pistol, but Domingo pounced first and pulled him down from his horse. As soon as Santos hit the ground, Domingo punched him hard in the face three times, knocking him out cold. Domingo went over to pull the six-shooters from Diego's belt. As he knelt beside Diego, he could see the man was no longer a threat.

"Hmmm, let me see. Should I let you live?" asked Domingo, pulling his blood-covered knife from Diego's neck before wiping it clean on the dying man's shirt.

Diego made gurgling noises as he tightly gripped his throat.

"What's that?" asked Domingo. "I am having a hard time understanding you, chico." He leaned closer and looked the dying man in the eyes.

Still grasping his throat while staring directly back at

Domingo, Diego's eyes filled with fear. He took a few more gasps of air, and his hands slowly released their grip. The blood poured onto the ground around him. His arms fell to his sides, and his eyes rolled slightly back, then began to cross.

As the man died, Domingo remembered them saying they were not heading west and muttered to himself, "Which way are you heading now, chico? South?" He shook his head as he returned to his feet, looking over at Santos to make sure he wasn't moving.

Domingo led Diego and Santos's horses over and tied them to the oxcart, then he went back to Santos, taking his pistol and the money pouch lying on the ground beside him. He searched both men, taking the little money they had on them. Sitting back on the oxcart, he lit a cigar and looked both ways to see if anyone else was coming, but it was clear in both directions. As he enjoyed his cigar, he thought about what to do with the men. Diego was dead, but Santos would be coming around shortly. He figured he could tie them to their horses and bring them to Tucson with him, but he didn't feel like going through the trouble.

Domingo got down from the oxcart and pulled the two men away from the road. He knew the men had done plenty of bad things in their day, and the world would be better without them. He was more concerned about getting home as soon as he could, and if he took Santos and his dead companion to Tucson, there was no telling what time would be wasted.

"I guess this would be the best way to go." Domingo pulled his pistol from the holder and pointed it toward Santos's head. "While you're sleeping."

Bang! The shot echoed through the nearby canyon.

Domingo stood and wiped blood spray from his hand and

face. Walking to Diego lying nearby, he lifted the dead man's leg, pulling off one of his boots. He kicked one of his own boots off and tried on Diego's. "Damn, you have little feet for a big guy," he said, kicking the boot away. He then looked at Santos's boots, but they were clearly too small. "Man, what were you guys? The baby foot banditos?" He chuckled as he covered the men up with nearby brush and sticks.

After Domingo made his way back to the horses and oxcart, he put out his cigar and climbed on Santos's horse. He led the ox and Diego's horse away at a fast pace to put some distance between him and the dead men. After about forty minutes, he stopped and climbed down from the horse, relit his cigar, and sat on the oxcart. Cigars seemed to relax him when he got worked up, so he finished it and took a couple drinks of water from his canteen before starting out again.

As Domingo rode along, he thought about the ordeal so much that he almost forgot he was even riding. He thought how lucky he had been with the knife. He was good with his throwing knife but had never really practiced pulling it from his pocket like that before. And he'd been aiming for Diego's chest but got him in the throat, which was better still. He felt bad for killing the two outlaws, but he knew they were going to kill him if he hadn't. He asked God to forgive him, as he had done many times before, though he felt he'd been doomed to Hell long ago.

If the world were different, I would be different, he sometimes thought, but the world was a tough place. All he could do was survive.

Domingo rode on, keeping a careful eye behind him to make sure no one else was coming. He soon realized he was almost halfway to Tucson with a couple hours of light left. The new horse was making his trip much quicker and a lot easier.

He smiled and spurred his horse forward, saying, "How lucky I am that those nice fellers gave me these horses."

CHAPTER 8

A STIR FROM THE BRUSH

AFTER ASSESSING HIS INJURIES AND finding only a two-inch laceration from a bullet grazing him, Red Sleeves lay back against a somewhat comfortable dirt formation by the edge of the river and closed his eyes. He thought of how this day was supposed to be just a small skirmish, but it ended up being a tough-won battle against the Mexican army. If only he'd known of the impending battle, he would have brought more warriors for a less costly and more decisive victory. Then he thought how lucky he was to have as many as he did. Normally, only six or seven warriors would have made that trip, but since the chief had been there, more protection had been required. Red Sleeves figured the man he'd met the day before had told the Mexican general where he'd seen them, and that was why they were heading that way. He thought things over in his mind and began to wish he'd pursued the fleeing army, even if it meant his own death. He knew the

Domingo

Mexican army and its general would be back, and next time, with more men and a personal vendetta against the Apache.

If only I had killed him, thought Red Sleeves of the Mexican general. *I was so close.*

Red Sleeves figured many more battles would be needed to keep the Mexican army out of Apache lands. He agreed with Chief Compa that the tribe would have to move farther north to keep them safely away from the fighting. Driving the Mexican family out would now have to wait. If he drove them out now, he risked running into Mexican soldiers and losing more warriors that his tribe couldn't spare.

After resting for about fifteen minutes, Red Sleeves stood and went to assess Whom'tu's injury. The bullet had grazed across the horse's rump about eight inches before settling about an inch deep. Although there was plenty of blood coming from the wound, Red Sleeves knew Whom'tu would heal fine if he just got the bullet out. He pulled out his knife and rubbed Whom'tu on the back and side to comfort him, then pushed the knife inside the wound until he was behind the bullet and could reach it with his fingers. Whom'tu showed little signs of discomfort other than a couple snorts while turning his head to look back at Red Sleeves. After tossing the bullet away, Red Sleeves chewed some yarrow plant, rolled it in a ball, and packed the horse's wound before his own.

Sergeant Balas called for the two soldiers left with him at Domingo's ranch to join him in his tent. Moments after Private Gil Yorba and Private Mannie Cota came in, the sergeant informed them he planned to head out directly.

"Sir, the general just left an hour ago. Aren't we supposed to wait here for him to return?" asked Private Yorba.

The sergeant took a hit off his cigarette and glared at the soldier. "We're soldiers, not babysitters. We are going to ride out and do our own reconnaissance. We will only be gone for four or five hours, if we move quickly."

"Yes, sir," replied Yorba.

The sergeant took another hit from his cigarette and tossed it on the ground, then spread a map out on the table to show his men. "Now, the general went north and then will head east to right about here before returning to the camp. We're going to head northeast and cross the Gila somewhere along this area here," said Balas, pointing to an area on the map. "Once we get across the river, we ride for a couple miles east and see what we find. I do believe the tribe will be in this area." He again pointed to a spot on the map northeast of the Gila. "We are not going to engage them or even be seen. We'll just mark their location and make our way back." Sergeant Balas looked at the map a little closer, examining it in fine detail. "Then we will cross back over the river through here and make our way southwest, right back to the camp."

Tapping on the tent and a woman's voice made the three men looked toward the tent's opening as Arabella entered, carrying a small pot of beans and some bread.

"Would you men like some beans and bread?" she asked.

"Oh, yes. *Gracias*, señora," replied Balas. "That is very kind."

Arabella nodded and approached the table they were gathered around. As she set the pot of warm beans and bread on the table, Private Cota fell under the spell of her beauty and stared at her wistfully. She noticed his gawking and turned away, then quickly exited the tent.

Private Cota moved to follow her.

"Private Cota, you are not dismissed," said Sergeant Major Balas.

Head down, Private Cota turned around. "Yes, sir," he replied.

After the men quickly finished their food, they grabbed their packs and rifles, climbed on their horses, and rode away from the ranch.

Sergeant Balas and his men rode northwest at a fast pace for a little over an hour. They came upon a lone Indian leading his horse down a ridge in the distance. They wondered if he was an Apache retreating after a skirmish with General Sanchez and the rest of the soldiers.

"His horse must be injured," said Yorba. "Maybe he is too."

"Well, there's no use letting him get away. Might be the only action we see for a while," said Balas. He glanced around the area and focused in on the Apache, realizing he was an older man who looked unharmed, though his horse was clearly favoring its front leg.

Chief Compa noticed three soldiers approaching him but showed no reaction. He first hoped the men would pass by without engaging, but within moments, he was certain they were coming for him. Even though he knew this land like his own hand, he could not outrun the soldiers on an injured horse. There was only one way out, and that was to fight.

The chief purposely kept his head opposite of the soldiers

while observing them from the corner of his eye. His rifle was already loaded, and he pulled it from the sling, keeping it down along his leg to conceal it. Once they were in range, the chief stopped his horse, got down to his knee, and pretended to check out the horse's injury.

The Indian examined his horse's leg while Sergeant Balas and his men quietly made their way up the rocky slope. The soldiers stopped about fifty yards from the Indian, hiding behind some high brush and a group of pine trees.

"This might be our lucky day, señors," said an excited Balas as quietly as he could.

"Sir?" said a puzzled Cota.

"Well, look at how he's dressed. He must be of some importance because of the way he is all decorated. That might be the damn chief," explained Balas, handing Cota his field glasses.

The private raised the glasses to his eyes. "Yeah, I think you are right, sir." He handed the sergeant back his field glasses.

The sergeant placed the glasses into the pouch alongside his saddle, then pointed in the distance. "Private Cota, you head behind him over that way, and we'll go straight at him."

"Yes, sir," replied the soldiers.

"He won't be getting away from us," added Balas, peering through the brush at the Apache still knelt beside his horse.

Just as Cota turned his horse, Balas and Yorba emerged from the brush. They barely noticed how quickly the old man lifted a rifle.

Bang!

Before Sergeant Balas had a chance to react, the round hit

him right in the chest. The two soldiers looked on in horror as their sergeant fell off the rear of his horse. Sergeant Balas hit his head on the rocky ground and fell unconscious.

Yorba and Cota quickly looked at each other and then back to the Indian who was now reloading. Giving him no time to get off another shot, the men charged their horses straight at the Apache as he dropped the rifle and pulled out a knife. Cota jumped from his horse when he got close enough, but the Indian moved at the last second, and the soldier fell to the ground with a loud thud. The old Indian jumped on Cota and stabbed him through the hand as the soldier raised them to protect his chest from the blade. The two men rustled around, fighting for the knife until Yorba jumped from his horse and hit the Indian on the head with the butt of his rifle, knocking him unconscious. Yorba raised his rifle and fired into the old man's chest, killing him instantly. Cota grabbed the knife from the dead Indian's hand and scalped him.

The badly shaken soldiers rushed back to where Balas had fallen and knelt next to their comrade to see if he was still breathing. The blood from the sergeant's chest and head was slowly running down the dirt slope. The sergeant's horse stood within thirty feet, pawing at the dirt and snorting. After a few moments with no sign of breathing or a pulse, Private Yorba pulled off his hat and gripped it tightly in front of him.

"Goddamn Indian savages," said Yorba, rubbing his head in frustration.

Private Cota also removed his cap and sat quietly, shaking his head in disbelief. "What do we do?"

"I don't know. Probably get back to camp," answered a tearful Yorba.

"What about General Sanchez? Should we look for him?"

asked Cota, nervously looking around in all directions. "I mean, what if more come through here? There's only two of us."

"Get me the sergeant's field glasses," said Yorba, wiping his face with his hand.

Cota quickly got to his feet and went to the sergeant's horse. "Calm down, boy. It's all right now," he said. He rubbed the horse's neck while reaching into the saddlebag.

Returning to Yorba, who still knelt by the sergeant, Cota held out the field glasses as Yorba got to his feet. The soldiers scouted the area for a few minutes, looking in all directions for more Apache, but they didn't see anyone else coming.

"Let's head back to camp and wait for the general to return," said Yorba, removing the field glasses from his eyes. "Help me lay the sergeant across his horse and tie him to it so he doesn't fall off."

"What about the Indian?" asked Cota.

"Hell with him. We're moving out."

The two men got on their horses and rode side by side, leading the sergeant's horse and his lifeless body along as they started back toward camp.

"The general will be none too happy about this," said Cota.

Yorba looked over at his comrade, drew a deep breath, and shook his head. "I suppose he won't."

After laying Rico over his horse and securing him to the saddle, General Sanchez and his five remaining men rode south toward their camp at a slow pace. Corporal Munoz noticed Sanchez was leaning so far forward in his saddle that his head nearly touched the horse's mane. Afraid the general would fall from the horse, Munoz told the men to stop.

Lethargic, the general barely responded to the men as they talked to him and secured a new bandage to his leg. With what little strength the injured soldiers had in them, they secured the general to the saddle with rope and placed a blanket between him and the saddle horn so he could lean forward more comfortably. Then they tied the general's horse to Private Loupe's horse, as he was the healthiest man of the group with just a cut below his left eye and two broken fingers on his left hand.

Taking note of the general's weakening condition, Munoz hobbled his way to Loupe, who was already in his saddle and set to leave. "Move fast, Loupe. Get him to camp as quick as you can. Sergeant Balas is there. He will know what to do," said Munoz, grimacing in pain. "After you take care of the general, grab Private Cota or Yorba and come back here for us with medical supplies."

"Yes, sir," said Loupe, then he spurred the horse and rode off at a quick pace.

Corporal Munoz turned around, facing the two soldiers sitting on the ground and tending to their wounds. He hobbled over to their horses—about thirty feet away—and grabbed the canteens, then sat down next to his comrades. After about twenty minutes of taking drinks of water and cleaning their wounds, the three men pulled their hats over their eyes to rest.

A stick cracking and a shuffling noise from the nearby brush caught Munoz's attention, and he slowly lifted his cap and looked in the direction of the sound, but he saw nothing. After a few moments, he began to relax again and pulled his cap back down. Moments later, he heard the noise again. He raised his cap and saw nothing. Over the next half hour, he heard the noise several more times. Lifting his cap each time, the corporal finally caught a glimpse of a dark coat and bushy tail moving through the brush. He continued looking for the animal, without luck. His heart jumped, and great fear came over him as his eyes fixed squarely on a set of eyes, which stared directly at him from the low brush no more than forty feet away. The animal's head was low to the ground, and its piercing eyes brought a chill up the corporal's spine.

"Hey, fellas! Get up!" he said, shaking his comrades awake without taking his eyes off the beast.

Private Lanza and Santoyo quickly removed their hats and looked around, then at Munoz.

"What is it?" asked Lanza.

"Damn lobos," replied Munoz. "Right there." He pointed toward the brush.

The soldiers looked to where Munoz was pointing for a few moments.

"I see 'em," said Santoyo, lifting his shaking hand to point toward the brush.

"Oh yeah, there he is," said Lanza quietly.

"Probably after Rico or the horses," said Munoz. He slowly got to his feet and staggered toward his horse for his rifle, which was still in the sling.

There were several loud cracks of sticks and brush moving around them, followed by a whinny from the horses.

Munoz watched helplessly as the frightened horses kicked frantically at several wolves emerging from the brush, immediately attacking their hindquarters, necks, and muzzles. One wolf had Rico's lifeless hand and was pulling him off the saddle.

"Shit!" yelled Munoz, hobbling toward the pack. "Get out of here! Go! Git!" he yelled.

A couple wolves turned toward him, standing their ground.

Munoz turned to see where Santoyo and Lanza were, finding the two soldiers on their feet, in obvious pain. They had no intention of approaching the beasts. As Munoz looked back toward the pack, the strap securing Rico's horse to the tree broke. The horse took off, dragging Rico along beside it.

"Goddamnit!" yelled Munoz. He charged toward the wolves and horses.

The wolves darted after the fleeing horse, gone in a flash.

Munoz reached his horse and tried to pull the rifle from the sling, but the horse was panicked and wouldn't hold still enough. He reached for the horse's reins in an attempt to calm him down, but the frightened horse bucked, kicked, and squealed as Munoz struggled to keep the reins in hand.

After a few moments, the remaining horses calmed down, and silence fell over their camp. The three men looked in all directions, then stared at each other while listening. The fleeing horse's hooves pounded into the hard ground as the sound of snapping branches and rattling brush filled the air again. The sounds seemed to be getting closer, then moved farther away, followed by squealing and groaning. Seconds later, it was quiet again.

"Let's get the hell out of here!" shouted Munoz, frantically waving the injured soldiers along.

Without hesitation, Lanza and Santoyo rushed to the horses. Lanza dragged his leg behind him, holding his side. Santoyo climbed on his horse as Munoz helped lift Lanza onto his. Then Munoz hopped up on his horse and led the soldiers at a steady, quick pace toward Domingo's ranch. As they fishtailed through the tall brush, they could hear the howls of the pack behind them, echoing through the cliffs before fading into the canyon.

Even though Whom'tu's injury would heal fine, Red Sleeves decided to use another horse so the bleeding wouldn't start again. After looking for signs of injury—on the mounts of his warriors and several of the Mexican army's mounts that they'd commandeered from the battle—Red Sleeves led one of the horses over to his warriors grouped by the edge of the river. He looked around at his fourteen remaining warriors, knowing they had little fight left in them. Many were injured, some severely.

"I'm heading the way of our chief. Wait here and tend to your wounds, and I will return as soon as I can. If I'm not back by this time tomorrow, make your way to the tribe through the canyon to avoid detection. Those of you who are able, take down some of these small trees we will need to make several travois to take our dead to the burial ground. The tribe will be moving north and have none to spare. I will bring back a few men to help and bring some possessions of our dead." The Apache always buried their dead with some of their belongings, feeling it protected them from their spirits.

The warriors looked at their war chief and nodded.

As Red Sleeves turned his horse, one of the more severely wounded warriors called for him.

"Red Sleeves," said Little Feather, his hand over an injury to his abdomen as blood ran between his fingers. "Today was a good day to die. It was a good victory."

Domingo

Red Sleeves stared at his warrior with a grin. "It was a great victory, Little Feather. A great day to die." He pointed to the yarrow plant on the ground. "Push that into your wound, Little Feather." He looked to the sun, taking note of its position in the sky. "When the sun rises again, I will be here before its light shines above the trees." He looked back at Little Feather. "I will look at you, Little Feather, and you will be looking back at me."

Red Sleeves rode off, worry that something had happened to his chief eating at his gut. He rode for a good half hour, thinking he was sure about the way the chief had taken and growing more concerned at no signs of his tracks. Reaching a high spot on a ridge, he stopped and looked around. In the distance, riding in the other direction, he saw two men that looked like Mexican soldiers. He studied them and their third horse—with a man lying over its back—until he was sure they were Mexican soldiers and not Chief Compa they had with them. He was careful not to be seen as he moved on through the brush to continue his search.

After about another half mile, Red Sleeves saw buzzards circling in the distance. He picked up the pace, heading straight for them. As he approached, the birds backed away and then flew off, revealing Chief Compa lying on the ground where they'd been feasting. Red Sleeves jumped from his horse and ran to the fallen chief, sliding to a stop on his knees by the man's side. He cried out in grief at the loss of his chief and old friend. He held his chief in his arms for several minutes, rage flooding through him.

The men he had seen were responsible for this, and he wanted to set off after them. Already injured, Red Sleeves took deep breaths to clear his head. He could not abandon his chief, or his tribe, or his warriors at the river still awaiting his return. The burial grounds were back the way of his warriors at the river, so he decided to return to the tribe first and prepare them to move north. He loaded his chief's body onto his horse and quickly went on his way.

As Red Sleeves reached his camp, the men and women of old and young gathered around him. He lifted the chief's lifeless body from the horse and laid him on the ground. The tribe passionately mourned their chief. Many began prayers and rituals as others waited anxiously for Red Sleeves to tell them of who died and who was waiting at the Gila.

Red Sleeves wanted to take a few warriors and track the soldiers who had killed Compa; however, he also knew it was dangerous to leave the tribe and risk losing more men. He simply told his tribe to get ready to head north in the morning.

Red Sleeves's wife embraced him, then walked with him to their wickiup to tend to his wound.

When morning came, the tribe started preparing for its migration north.

Red Sleeves, however, headed back to the Gila where his warriors were waiting for him. He pulled his chief's lifeless body behind him on a travois to take him into the Santa Rita Mountains' sacred burial ground. Two boys of twelve and thirteen years of age followed Red Sleeves to help with the wounded and dead at the river.

When Red Sleeves reached his warriors at the river, they mourned their chief's death together. The warriors had assembled several travois to carry the dead. After spending a few moments talking to his horse, Whom'tu, and a couple more checking his wound, Red Sleeves climbed up on his horse and rubbed its neck repeatedly, then he slowly headed west. Eight warriors who were physically up to it followed Red Sleeves as the boys brought up the rear, heading toward the burial grounds with Chief Compa and their twelve dead warriors, who had fought so bravely the day before. The remaining warriors limped their way back to the tribe that was already moving north. Up in front, Little Feather led the injured party along while wearing a Mexican army cap on his head that he had taken from one of the soldiers he killed.

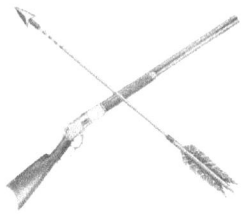

CHAPTER 9

MAN'S BEST FRIEND

As Domingo reached Tucson, he couldn't help but notice all the people dressed in fine clothes and the many high-quality horses with shiny saddles, fancy horns, and silver stirrups. Several carriages whisked past him, more luxurious than he had ever seen. Most were one-horse and two-horse carriages, with a few four-horse carriages, and even some with retractable tops. The carriage horses were as decorated as the carriages, and the coachmen wore fancy suits.

Domingo climbed down from his horse to lead his caravan through town. He strolled down the street, taking time to look at every building he passed while keeping an eye out for Vicente's blacksmith shop. He passed a bank, barbershop, gunsmith, saloon, tailor, jailhouse, hotel, bakery, general store, clothing shop, outfitter, and butcher, wondering if it would ever end. Most buildings were brick and adobe style, but they had many different shapes and colors. There were also a few wood buildings, like the saloon and jailhouse. He couldn't figure if the town had changed a lot since he last saw it, or if it had just been so long since he'd been to a big town. He was surprised by the amount of white folks there were—it seemed like there were more of them than Mexicans. He began to feel out of place, rolling through town in ragged clothes while leading his oxcart. Some folks looked at him and quickly moved aside or turned the other way. Once he reached the Santa Cruz river, he led his ox to the side. Taking in the scenery for a few minutes, he opened his canteen and took a couple large gulps.

As Domingo lowered the canteen from his mouth, he noticed there was a dog chewing on a stick to his right, lying under a tree. The dog looked homeless and hungry, maybe an old coach hound. He threw the hound a piece of jerky he had in his pocket. The dog swallowed it without chewing.

"Easy there, fella," said Domingo.

The dog started hacking the jerky back up.

"Goes down easier if you chew it first."

Domingo put away his canteen and picked up the leader to his ox. Having to time his caravan's entrance back onto the congested street, he continued on. It wasn't too long before he noticed the dog following behind him.

Stopping, Domingo yelled at the dog, "Go on now. Git!"

The dog stopped and turned away, but when Domingo started moving again, the dog started following along. After a few attempts to run the dog off, Domingo noticed the dog was limping on a hurt leg. He stopped and stared at the dog, and the dog stared right back.

"I knew I shouldn't have fed ya," said Domingo, wiping sweat from his brow. "Well, you're gonna have to pick up the pace if you're coming."

The dog was nothing special—just a knee-high, multicolored mutt with a bad leg—but Domingo liked him for some reason, which was strange since he really didn't care much for dogs. He'd always felt like they were just another mouth to feed. As he continued down the street, finally getting past the downtown area and into the more residential sections, he watched the dog struggle to keep up. Stopping again, he walked around the oxcart and approached the nervous dog, holding out another piece of jerky. When the dog came close, Domingo picked him up and sat him in the oxcart, then poured some water onto the cart in front of the dog.

"There, boy. Best I can do for ya," he said.

The dog lapped up the water as Domingo lifted himself up in the saddle. Domingo was kind of glad to have someone with him after a long, quiet journey, even if it was a dog.

"Not a bad day for ya, huh?" Domingo looked back at the dog. "Free food and water." He looked forward again, then quickly back. "*And* a free ride!" He shook his head with a smile. "Well, you fared a lot better than a couple guys I met a ways back." He looked back at the dog in the cart, finding him sleeping. "After all I've done for ya, you can't even stay awake to hear me bellyache?" He shook his head again and laughed. "God, I'm getting delirious. Must be the heat."

Domingo thought about Arabella. He always felt better when he thought of her, but he was really beginning to miss her. He hoped she and the kids were getting along okay without him. He didn't like leaving them alone, but he felt he could trust Sanchez and his men. Besides, he'd really had no choice.

Domingo knew he was very close to Vicente's home, but it was going to be difficult to find because they all looked the same, clustered together and equally run down, and it had been many years since he last visited. Vicente and Maria had moved there fifteen years ago, and Domingo had only seen his brother a handful of times since they'd left Guadalajara. Domingo and Vicente kept in touch by writing to each other when possible, and Maria and Arabella also wrote to each other now and then—mainly talking about the kids and things they had recently made. Both women enjoyed making clothes, blankets, and pottery, and they had grown to be like sisters over the years. Vicente had three children, and Domingo had only seen two of them as babies, but the oldest son, Raul, had always admired his uncle Dom.

As Domingo made his way down a dirty street, some children that were playing stopped and watched him. Thinking one of them could be Vicente's children, he asked, "Hey, you kids know Vicente and Maria Montoya?"

The kids ran off, giggling and looking back at Domingo like he was a creepy stranger.

Domingo looked around to see what they were laughing about, but he instead saw a man walking toward him. As the man got closer, Domingo thought he recognized him, but it was not Vicente. The man was close to Domingo's age with a good build and handsome face. When the stranger was only about twenty feet away, he seemed to recognize Domingo as well.

Domingo nodded to him, still struggling to figure out why he looked familiar.

"Hello, Domingo," said the stranger.

Domingo now knew he had certainly met this man before, but he still could not place when or where. He stopped his horse and took off his hat, then leaned toward the stranger. "Domingo is right, my friend, and what would your name be?" he asked.

The man had stopped only a few feet from Domingo and stared up at him without much of a facial expression.

Domingo kept looking at the stranger, but he was starting to get irritated. He was just about to say something rude to the man when he spoke.

"You should never forget the face of a man after you steal his woman, especially one as pretty as Arabella," the man stated.

Domingo stared blankly back, stumped as he looked the man over more closely. "Pedro?" he whispered.

"Ha! Got it on your first try," said Pedro with a smile.

"Wow, I barely recognized you with that beard, and you finally gained some weight," replied Domingo. His mind ran to a time fifteen years earlier, then he shook it off, sure Pedro wouldn't hold a grudge that long. "Well, you're right about one thing," he quipped with a small smile. "I shouldn't forget a face that ugly."

Pedro smiled and shook Domingo's hand. "Climb down, old friend. I'll take you to Vicente. He should be quite surprised to see us walking in the house together."

Domingo nodded. "Yeah, I suppose he would." He then climbed down from his horse and walked alongside Pedro, leading his ox and caravan behind them.

"Vicente tells me you were wanting to start a ranch near the Gila," said Pedro. He added with a grin, "Ranchero Domingo."

"Already happened. We've been there for several months now."

"Wow, señor. You don't waste any time, do you?"

"I wasted enough, I guess," answered Domingo.

"How are Arabella and the kids doing?"

Domingo

Domingo looked straight forward as he replied, "She's good." He didn't want to talk about that too much, so he changed the subject quickly. "What are you doing here in Tucson?"

"I live here now," said Pedro. "Right next door to Vicente. Been here for almost two years," he added.

"Funny, Vicente never mentioned that in our letters to each other," said Domingo, somewhat disappointed. Vicente might not want to move out to the ranch and leave his best friend behind, and Pedro *could not* come along.

"Well, Vicente probably still does his best to keep us away from each other," said Pedro. "Even though that was so long ago, and there are no hard feelings. I am glad to see you well, Domingo. I truly am."

"Same here," replied Domingo.

"Ah, well, here we are," said Pedro.

As Domingo looked at the house, he realized it would have been near impossible to find had he not bumped into Pedro. The house was in much better shape than he remembered, and it now had a nice porch on the front with an awning held up by four wood pillars. There were a few rocking chairs, and a large pile of firewood was stacked to the right of them, almost all the way to the awning. It looked much nicer than the two rundown shacks next to it, though Domingo didn't mention that, figuring one of them was probably Pedro's.

"Looks like Vicente has been busy working on this place," said Domingo, tying off the horses and oxen. He followed Pedro down the dirt path that led to the side door.

Pedro knocked once, then entered.

Maria stood across the kitchen about twelve feet from them, stirring a pot of stew over their wood-burning oven, as

Domingo followed Pedro inside. Her back was to them, and she quickly turned around at hearing the door open. "Hello, Pedro," she said, looking back at the stew.

"Hey, Maria. I brought company with me," said Pedro. He stepped to the side, leaning against the back of one of the dining chairs.

She removed the spoon from the pot and set it down on the table, then turned around to see who he'd brought. Her eyes opened wide, and a huge smile spread over her face as she squealed, "Domingo!" She rushed to embrace him.

"Maria! As beautiful as ever, I see," said Domingo, returning the embrace.

She then ran to the window and yelled, "Vicente! Hurry, come see!"

"What is it?" he shouted back, not looking up from the horse's hoof he was shoeing.

"Hurry! Come see!" said Maria.

Moments later, Vicente entered through the back door. "Domingo!" he said cheerfully.

"Hello, brother!" replied Domingo as Vicente crossed the kitchen to hug him.

"What a great surprise!" Vicente said, placing both hands on Domingo's shoulders and embracing him again. Then he looked from Domingo to Pedro and back again with a big grin.

"So good to see you, Vicente," said Domingo.

"Where is Arabella? She with you?" asked Vicente.

"No, it's only me this time," replied Domingo. "Oh, and a dog I found. Where are your kids? Maybe they would like to play with him?" He looked at Maria and then back to Vicente.

"A dog?" asked Vicente. "Where is he?"

"In the back of the oxcart, I reckon. Unless he ran off," replied Domingo.

"They will be back soon, and we will have them go out and feed the mutt," said Vicente. "Come, let's step out back and have a cigar. Maria, will you bring us a drink? Domingo must be dying for a drink after that hike."

"Of course," replied Maria with a smile. Then she walked to Domingo and took his hand in hers. "It's so great to see you. I am so glad you are here." She turned back toward the kitchen, calling over her shoulder, "And don't start talking until I get outside with the drinks. I want to hear what you and Arabella have been up to!"

Domingo, Vicente, and Pedro made their way out the door to a nice wood table, which was set up under a tall tree that provided excellent shade. As the three men found their seats, Domingo glanced at Vicente's small barn, including two horses at the fence and another horse inside the barn. Vicente looked across the table at Domingo as if asking approval of Pedro's presence while handing his brother a cigar.

Taking the cigar, Domingo raised it to his nose and took in the smell of tobacco, making a slight gesture only brothers would know, signaling it was fine.

"So, tell me. How're Arabella and the kids?" asked Vicente while handing a cigar to Pedro.

Pedro pulled his chair a little closer to listen in, then slid the ashtray to the middle of the table so everyone could reach it.

Domingo removed his hat and set it on the table, then started lighting his cigar as he replied, "They are fine. Marcello is quite the fisherman, and Camille is so beautiful, just like her mother."

"Well, to say the least, brother, your presence here is a big surprise. You made a long journey, so now I'm afraid there is something wrong," said Vicente, squinting his eyes.

Domingo smiled at Vicente. "No, brother. Everything is fine."

Vicente exhaled in relief and smiled back at his brother.

"Besides," said Domingo, "it was not *that* far."

"Not far. Yeah, right," said Vicente with a chuckle. "You run into any trouble on the way?"

Domingo raised his cigar for another hit. With a grin, he said, "No…no trouble. No trouble at all." He exhaled, leaning back in his chair and swallowing his laughter.

Maria appeared through the back door carrying four drinks. "I told you guys to wait until I was here," she said with a mean face. "Now start over!" she added with a playful look, then sat down next to Domingo.

Domingo smiled at Maria. "I swear we just started." He reached for his drink. "You remember when I wrote you about the land grants?"

While Vicente was in the middle of taking a drink, Maria quickly answered, "Yes."

"They ended up giving me three thousand acres right off the Camino Real, about sixty miles north of Janos."

"Wow!" said Vicente. "So, is that where you're living now?"

Domingo leaned back in his chair again, extending his arms out. "Yes, brother. It's all mine."

Vicente and Maria both laughed as Vicente clapped his hands together.

Maria beamed as she said, "We're so happy for you! I know you've always dreamed of starting your own ranch."

Domingo

"You are so crazy. How long have you been there?" asked Vicente.

"About eight months now," replied Domingo.

"Arabella and the kids there?" asked Pedro.

Domingo looked at Pedro, taking his time to answer. "Yes, Pedro, they are."

Pedro looked at Vicente, then back at Domingo. "A lot of Apache through them hills and valleys…among other things." He then gave Vicente a concerned look.

Domingo slowly sat his drink down as the smile disappeared from his face.

The table fell quiet until Vicente jumped in. "Brother," he said, reaching over and putting his hand on Domingo's shoulder. "It's true. That is a dangerous place for a woman and two kids."

Domingo nodded at Vicente. "That it is, brother. Dangerous for a pregnant woman and two kids," he said with a smile.

Maria threw her hands up wildly, then wrapped them around Domingo. "Oh, my goodness. Why haven't you written us to tell us any of this? How far along is she?"

"About seven months now," replied Domingo, still grinning from ear to ear.

"That is wonderful," replied Maria. "Just wonderful. I will come down there when she gets closer to her due date. You know I was a midwife for many years here."

"That would be fantastic, Maria. *Gracias*," replied Domingo. He leaned over and kissed his sister-in-law's cheek.

The concern on Pedro's and Vicente's faces had only grown more evident as Domingo shared the news. Domingo knew his family was safe with the general's men there, but he hesitated to mention that to Vicente because he needed his help. He felt Vicente's worry for Arabella might be enough to convince him.

"I had no choice but to come. We are low on food and supplies. We would starve if I did not come," replied Domingo.

"You would not starve. You would move here and stay with us," replied Vicente. "Besides, there are plenty of towns much closer to your ranch than Tucson." He took a drink, then squinted his eyes and tilted his head slightly while staring at Domingo. "So…when are we to leave?" he finally said with a grin.

Domingo laughed, then put his cigar to his mouth and took a puff. "You were always the smart one, Vicente." He put down his cigar and pulled the coins out that Sanchez had given him. "As soon as I can get a couple steers, supplies, and a dress I promised Arabella."

Vicente put his cigar down and took a drink of his tequila. "How about some new boots?" he said, looking at Domingo's feet and shaking his head.

"If it's in the budget," replied Domingo.

"Well, I can help with the steers and supplies," said Vicente.

Pedro sat his drink on the table, about to say something, but Maria spoke up first.

"And I can help with the dress!" she said, turning toward Vicente. "Of course, I'll be needing some money just in case I find one I like."

"Oh, of course you will," said Vicente with a smile, shaking his head.

Pedro chuckled at his bickering friends, then he placed the cigar back in his mouth.

Maria jumped up and headed back inside, but she turned

and looked back at Vicente as she reached the door, making sure he wasn't talking about her.

Vicente gave her a big smile, then jokingly showed his guests a look of disgust after she turned around and headed inside.

"Don't worry," said Domingo. "I'll pay for the dress and your help."

"I've heard that before," said Vicente with a chuckle.

Pedro said, "I'd like to ride along with you to get the supplies and steers, if that is all right?" He cocked his head to the side. "Shoot, I been looking for a reason to take a day off work anyway," he said with a smirk aimed at Vicente.

"That's much-appreciated, Pedro," replied Domingo.

Vincente smiled, then raised his glass of tequila high in the air and said, "A toast to my brother the ranchero! And his long journey!"

The three men touched glasses as Domingo smiled and drank his tequila down.

Vicente then stood up and said, "Let's make our way inside. All this talk of cows and dresses is making me hungry." Then looking over at Pedro, he joked, "You know a little about cows in dresses, don't ya?"

Domingo thought of the girl Pedro had dated right after Martina and burst out laughing with Vicente.

Pedro stared dumbfounded for a moment and then joined in with their laughter when he finally got the joke. "Yeah, I guess I do. I did date your sister for a while," he replied.

Domingo and Vicente stopped laughing, looked at each other, then burst out laughing even harder than before. The three men entered the house, still laughing.

"What are you boys doing?" asked Maria with a confused

look. "Take off your hats and sit down and quit acting like heathens."

Domingo quickly looked at Vicente and said, "Seems like you're the one wearing the dress around here."

They all started laughing again.

"Get out of my kitchen!" barked Maria playfully while pointing the spoon toward the dining room just off the kitchen.

The small dining room had a square table in the middle and several pictures and crosses on the walls. A rosary hung from one of the crosses, and on a shelf sat the bible.

Domingo was about to comment on all the religious stuff when the front door blew open, and three kids came running inside.

"Ah, there they are!" said Vicente with a wave of his hand. "Hey, look who's here!" he said, pointing toward Domingo.

The children stopped and looked up at Domingo for a few moments. The youngest were much too young to remember him, so they just stared, unsure of the stranger at their table.

"Who is he?" asked Milo.

Pedro chuckled.

"Uncle Dom!" said Raul, the oldest, as he rushed toward his uncle.

Raul always enjoyed his somewhat eccentric uncle, who he thought was so tough. Domingo and Raul didn't see each other much, but when they did, they were hard to separate. They had bonded quickly, both having an energy that was hard to contain. Domingo taught Raul how to throw knives, and although the boy never really caught on, he was most impressed with Domingo's ability to throw. Domingo had always been that tough uncle who Raul tried to imitate.

Domingo

Domingo stood, and Raul gave him a hug.

"My goodness, boy. You have grown," said Domingo, shaking his head. "How old are you now?"

"Thirteen," replied Raul. He started wrestling with Domingo's arm.

Vicente's two other children—Milo, who was eight, and Cily, who was six—greeted their uncle. They stood back, watching him interact with their older brother before finally joining in.

Maria came out of the kitchen with bowls of stew, beans, and bread. "Go clean up, children," she said, setting the food on the table.

"I'm sitting next to Uncle Dom," said Raul as the three children hurried into the kitchen.

When everyone returned to the table and found their seats, Vicente said a short prayer, and they began to eat. Looking at Domingo, he asked, "Will just us be enough to make this trip?"

Domingo glanced up at Vicente, then back down as he scraped his fork across his plate, gathering beans. "I think so. Maybe Raul could come?" He tilted his head toward the young man sitting next to him.

Excited about the idea, Raul beamed his best "yes, please" expression at his father.

"Hmm. Not sure he's old enough for that yet," said Vicente, shaking his head.

"Please, Papá!" said Raul.

"I'll go if needed," said Pedro, looking down at his plate and gathering a spoonful of beans.

Vicente stopped eating and looked at Domingo.

Domingo kept his head down, eating until the quietness

forced him to look up and answer. "That's mighty kind of ya, Pedro. I'd appreciate that," he replied.

Pedro looked at Vicente, then to Domingo. His expression betrayed that he was completely surprised Domingo had agreed.

"I'd like to see—" said a stumbling Pedro. His smile settled into a comfortable grin, and he tried again, speaking carefully. "I'd like to see this ranch you have."

Domingo reached for another piece of bread and looked over at Pedro. "Well, it's not much to see now. But it will be someday," he answered, looking back down at his plate.

Having waited patiently on perched elbows for a break in the adult conversation, Raul quickly said, "Papá, I want to go."

Vicente looked at Domingo as if to say, "Thanks for suggesting it in the first place." He turned back toward his son. "Boy, your mama needs you here."

Domingo put his hand on Raul's head and turned his face toward him. "It's all right, son. Next time you will come. I promise."

Raul's disappointment clearly showed on his face as he sat back from the table, head down and arms crossed.

Domingo licked his fingers and shifted in his chair toward the boy. "Tell you what. After we get back from the market, we'll step out back and throw some blades," he said.

A smile returned to Raul's face as he replied, "Okay, Uncle Dom."

"That's a good boy," said Domingo, then he turned away and continued eating.

After dinner, Domingo gave Maria a few coins, and she set out to buy the dress. Raul stayed with the younger children as Domingo, Vicente, and Pedro left for the market. They got supplies and went to see a rancher where Domingo bought two steers, six woolies, and some grain. The men also stopped by Vicente's blacksmith shop to grab a shovel, some nails, and a mallet. After stopping at the mill and general store, the three men went back to Vicente's and packed the oxcart full. Shortly thereafter, Domingo and Raul went out back and threw some knives, just as Domingo had promised. Maria arrived a short time later with the dress and a few things for herself.

"I hope this fits her," said Maria as she held the red and black garment up for Domingo to see. "I know she is pregnant, but this material has some give, and she can draw it in later," she explained.

Domingo quickly envisioned the dress on Arabella and began to smile. He came in for a closer look as Maria noted some of the features like the lower cut, tie on the back, and how it went over the shoulders. His eyes beamed as his smile grew, then he gave Maria a big hug to thank her.

That night, they all stayed up late talking about old times. The children played with the dog Domingo had found, and the dog scratched so much that the kids started calling him Scratchy. Maria wanted to go with them but knew she had to stay back with the children. Domingo told Maria and Vicente of his desire for them to move to the ranch, and they seemed to take the invitation seriously. Vicente's shop was doing well, but he wanted to see his brother much more often than he had the last fifteen years. As the night wound down, Maria gave Domingo a long hug and wished him a safe journey home, reminding him that she would be coming down soon.

Vicente disappeared into the back rooms but soon returned with a pair of boots in hand. "Here, brother. I figure you can use these," he said, tossing the boots to Domingo.

"Thanks, brother," said Domingo. "But you know I don't accept handouts, so I will trade mine for these."

Then the brothers both laughed and hugged.

The next morning, the men set off for Domingo's ranch. Pedro and Vicente rode horseback on either side of the small herd of sheep, which followed behind Domingo as he led the ox through town. They had tied the cattle and the horses off the rear of the oxcart, and Scratchy lay on a couple bags of rice in the back. On the outskirts of town, Domingo unhooked a horse from the back of the cart, climbed up, and they continued.

They rode for several hours, passing from the civilization of Tucson and its rural homes into the open plains, where the wind picked up and blew dust across their path. The men made good time, even stopping for water and to let Domingo switch between riding and walking as his back ached from being in the saddle too long.

Domingo eventually told Pedro and his brother about Sanchez and the Apache. He also told them how a couple soldiers had stayed back to watch over his family while he was away. Vicente and Pedro looked at each other in relief as smiles spread across their faces.

After a long day's ride, they found a nice place to camp for the night alongside a little creek that had very little water, though just enough to clean up and water the animals. The men removed their saddles and fed the animals before laying out their bedrolls to get some much-needed sleep.

The next morning, the men had a quick bite of beans and jerky, packed their gear, and continued on. Within a couple hours, Domingo stopped the caravan and surveyed the area, realizing they were very close to the spot where he'd met Santos and Diego. He explained to his companions that he'd run into outlaws on the way and killed them.

Vicente and Pedro looked at each other with shocked expressions. Then Vicente asked, "Where are they?"

"They're laying over that way…somewhere," said Domingo as he pointed. "I'd like to bury them."

"Let them be. If they were outlaws, they aren't worth our time," said Pedro. "Let's keep moving."

Domingo walked over to the oxcart and pulled out the shovel he'd gotten in Tucson. "You guys can keep moving. I'll catch up."

"Really, brother, just leave 'em," said Vicente.

Domingo looked up at his brother, still on horseback. "I know they were bad men, and I had no choice but to kill 'em, but sometimes even good men do bad things." He took a long swig from his canteen. "I'm gonna bury 'em. You guys keep moving."

"All right, Domingo," said Vicente, raising his hands slightly.

Domingo handed the leader to Vicente and watched as the men went on their way. He walked to the spot where he'd placed Santos and Diego. Their bodies had been dragged and partially eaten, probably by a cougar. He had seen dead and decomposed bodies before, but it took all he had to roll the bodies into the hole he dug.

"Damn," Domingo said as he turned away and spat.

He placed a few tree limbs over the grave, washed his face and hands with water from his canteen, then said a small prayer over the grave.

In all, it took him an hour to bury the men, mainly because of the hard ground and hot sun. Now he wanted to hurry and catch Vicente just in case they ran into trouble themselves. Even though they had rifles, they would probably not use them until it was too late. He climbed up on his horse and set off at a quick pace to catch them. After about thirty minutes of fast riding, Domingo saw the cart and someone lying on the ground beside it. His heart sank as he charged toward the scene, jumping from his horse before coming to a full stop. He rushed toward his brother, sprawled out on the ground.

"Vicente!" he shouted.

Vicente's head popped up, and he gazed at his brother through sleepy eyes.

"You asshole!" said Domingo.

"Shoot, man. I'm tired," Vicente explained.

Domingo began laughing and looking around. "Where's Pedro?"

"He rode off after a deer up by those trees over there."

Domingo kicked Vicente's boot. "C'mon, get your ass moving. He'll have to catch up."

Vicente got to his feet and headed to his horse. "How much are you paying me again?" he asked sarcastically.

Domingo and Vicente set off. After a good twenty minutes went by with no gunshot and no Pedro approaching from behind, Domingo wondered what Pedro was up to. He and Vicente rode another half hour and then decided to wait for Pedro for a few minutes. As the two scanned the horizon behind them, it suddenly occurred to Domingo that Pedro may have gone on without them to surprise Arabella, which made him instantly angry. As the thought sunk in, he knew in his heart that Pedro was already at his ranch.

Domingo

Climbing on his horse, Domingo barked at his brother, "Let's go, goddamnit."

"What's wrong with you?" asked Vicente.

"You know what's wrong. Now c'mon!" said Domingo.

Arabella stared across the terrain, hoping to see Domingo who should be arriving home anytime. She finished hanging the washed towels and rags she'd been using for the injured soldiers that had poured into the homestead a few days earlier. The man she had given bread and beans to that fateful morning was dead, and of the many men who had camped the night before, laughing and singing, only a few remained. Yorba and Cota had taken General Sanchez to the mining town of Lordsburg about eighteen miles west, where they have a medical facility. She feared for the general's life but was more than certain he would lose his leg.

After healing for a couple days, the remaining soldiers—Santoyo, Munoz, Loupe, and Lanza—headed south to their nearest fort in Janos, taking with them the body of Sergeant Balas, who had died at the hands of the Apache chief.

Arabella knew Domingo would be coming soon and dreaded having to tell him what had happened. Her focus now was to get the place cleaned up and make it appear as normal as possible. She kept a constant watch, hoping to see her beloved Domingo ride into view safe and smiling.

As she hung the last towel up on the clothesline, she noticed a man she did not recognize approaching on a horse. She quickly gathered the kids from playing on the porch, rushed inside, and locked the door. Peeking through the edge of a curtain, she watched the man stop his horse at the fence line beyond the yard and wipe his face. Then he got off his horse and headed toward the house. Losing sight of him because of the clothesline, she grabbed one of Domingo's pistols and waited by the door.

At first, the man tried to open the door. Then he knocked on it and said in a slow, sarcastic voice, "Arabella."

"Who is it?" she replied, pointing the pistol toward the door.

"Open and see," the man said.

"Say your name or go away!" she barked through the door, pistol at the ready.

"It's Pedro!"

Recognizing his voice the moment he said his name, she dropped the pistol to her side and jerked the door open. There stood Pedro, dirty, long-haired, bearded, and wearing a bandolier across his chest.

When she only stood there gaping at him, Pedro quipped, "Well, aren't you going to say something?"

She remained frozen, staring at Pedro for some time.

He smiled and took a step into the doorway. "Arabella… it's Pedro."

"I'm sorry," she replied. "I'm so surprised. I don't know what to say."

"Don't say nothing. Just give me a hug," Pedro said as he held his arms wide to invite her in.

The two embraced, then she quickly pulled away.

"What brings you here? Where's Domingo?" she said in a concerned tone.

"Domingo and Vicente are coming." Pedro took off his sombrero and shook the dust from it. "We got separated a few miles back, and I just continued on. I was quite lucky to find the place." He looked back outside toward his horse and scratched his head. "I'm surprised they're not here yet."

Arabella stepped back from the doorway and said, "Come in, and I'll get you something to drink."

Pedro followed her inside the house after kicking dirt from his boots. "Arabella, you are as beautiful as ever," he said.

"Thank you, Pedro. Just remember that I'm a married woman," she replied, offering him a seat at the dining table.

Pedro smiled. "I know that. Just making sure you did."

Arabella rolled her eyes a bit, not surprised that he would say something like that, and poured a glass of tea for him.

"*Gracias*," said Pedro.

"I must say I'm surprised you are riding with Domingo. You're not one of his favorite people," said Arabella.

"I don't know why. I mean, he stole you from me!" replied Pedro.

"I was hardly yours," replied Arabella. "And we need to change the conversation before they arrive, and not talk of it again."

Pedro took a drink from his glass and put his feet up on a chair. "Very well, but I still love you," he replied.

Catching Arabella's eye, Marcello peeked too far around the corner while eavesdropping on the conversation.

"Outside!" she barked at the boy. After he rushed out to play, she looked at Pedro. "And you can go too." She picked up the empty tea glass and knocked his feet off the chair. "I don't want you inside when Domingo arrives."

Pedro stood and put on his sombrero. "Well, all right then. Thanks for the tea." He smiled and strolled out the door.

Arabella followed several paces behind as Pedro exited her house. Reaching the porch, she checked that Marcello was busy nearby and then looked out toward the horizon. Domingo and Vicente were just coming into sight. She watched Pedro walk casually over to Marcello and put his hand on the boy's head, then she smiled with pride as Marcello pulled away to show his displeasure with the conversation he'd overheard between this stranger and his mother.

"Don't worry, son. I won't bite," said Pedro as he lit a cigar. "Name's Marcello, right?"

Marcello glared up at him. "That's right," he answered.

Pedro looked him over for a second. "Son, I've known your mama for a long time, and your papá too."

Marcello took a few steps to distance himself from the stranger. "Stay away from my mama," he said, dashing back into the house.

"Boy, you are a lot like your papá," said a smiling Pedro.

Arabella turned her focus back toward Domingo and Vicente, now riding faster toward the house. Knowing better than to interfere with her husband's need to protect his family, she could only watch as Domingo jumped from his horse and let go of the ox leader. He stomped quickly toward Pedro, who stood at the bottom of the steps, between her and her husband.

"What happened to ya?" asked Pedro with a smile.

Domingo's face grew redder with each step, causing Pedro to take a few steps backward nervously.

Vicente arrived at the hitching post and dismounted, calling over Domingo's shoulder, "You rode off. That's what happened!"

"No, I came back and you were gone, so I just rode on in," Pedro replied in an innocent tone of voice.

Domingo stopped in front of Pedro, glaring down at him with fists clenched at his sides.

Domingo

"I didn't take the trail. Just having the one horse, it was quicker to keep to the hills," said Pedro.

Domingo demanded through gritted teeth, "Are you gonna move? Or am I gonna move ya?"

Pedro quickly stepped aside.

Domingo reached the top step and embraced Arabella as she stood there, smiling. "Am I so glad to see you," he said, kissing her several times.

After a few moments, Arabella leaned back from Domingo. "How was your trip?" she asked.

"It was fine," replied Domingo with a smile. "How did you and the children get along?"

Arabella quickly answered, "We were fine." Then she shook her head, eyes tearing up a bit, and said, "Let's talk later." She released Domingo and went to Vicente.

"There she is!" said Vicente with arms wide open.

Arabella hugged Vicente, her eyes tearing up even more. "I am so happy to see you, Vicente!"

Vicente pulled away from her and kissed her cheek, then looked at Pedro standing nearby. "I reckon you already saw Pedro?"

She glanced over at him, then back to Vicente. "Yes, I have," she replied. "Let's go inside and have something to drink. You men must be exhausted." She grabbed Domingo's hand and led him to the door of the house.

As Domingo entered, Arabella looked back at Pedro and Vicente eavesdropping on their conversation.

"Nice job, padre. You will be sleeping outside tonight, I'm sure," said Vicente through his teeth.

Pedro glared back at Vicente. "Don't think I'll be staying at all. I'll be riding home shortly."

Vicente shook his head and gave Pedro a disapproving look. "Don't be a fool. C'mon." He gave a quick tug on Pedro's sleeve, then went up the steps to the porch.

Head hung down, Pedro wiped some dust from his pants and followed along.

After Arabella, Vicente, and Pedro entered the home, Arabella and Domingo quickly embraced yet again before turning arm in arm to face their guests.

"C'mon and grab a seat," said Arabella, smiling and pointing at the table.

Domingo followed closely behind his wife, into the kitchen, and helped her pour four glasses of tequila. The couple returned to the dining table, where Pedro and Vicente had settled, and passed out the glasses.

"To our safe trip and our families," said Vicente, raising his glass.

"Indeed," said Domingo. He touched his brother's and wife's glasses before drinking it down.

Arabella was not much of a drinker, but after the few horrific days she'd had, she slammed her drink back and relaxed into her chair.

Domingo sat his glass down on the table and smiled at Arabella, then he looked around the room. "And where are my children?" he called out loudly.

Marcello and Camille rushed from the back room and charged their papá, embracing him for some time. Domingo kissed them on the foreheads and pulled out some candy he had gotten in Tucson. Arabella told them not to spoil their dinner and winked at Domingo.

Domingo looked over at his son. "Say hello to your uncle, then put the steers in the fence and tend to the horses."

Domingo

The children's smiles dropped, disappointed at not getting to stay inside with the excitement of having company.

"Run along now, and take Camille with you," added Arabella.

With the children out of earshot, Arabella began telling Domingo of what had happened to General Sanchez and his men.

Domingo stared at her in complete disbelief as the story kept getting worse. His family had been in harm's way during his absence, and he now felt indebted to his new friend, General Sanchez, for protecting them. From what Arabella said, it sounded like they were safe for the time being.

"We have to take shifts sleeping tonight so we can watch over the steers, sheep, and horses," said Domingo to Vicente and Pedro.

His brows creased, Vicente looked down at his glass, rolling it around on its bottom edge in deep thought.

Domingo took note of his brother's demeanor. "Vicente," he said, looking directly at him from across the table.

"Yes, brother, that's a good idea," said Vicente while nodding. Then he and Pedro stood up to head outside.

Domingo also stood from the table. "I'm gonna wash this dust off and lay down for a bit."

"We'll help Marcello and then take first watch," said Vicente.

"It's so good to see you, Vicente," said Arabella, giving him another hug. "I'll prepare some food for you boys shortly."

When Pedro and Vicente exited the home, Domingo grabbed Arabella, pulled her close, and kissed her passionately.

"I'm so glad you are safe. It terrifies me to know you could have been hurt," he said.

Arabella smiled and kissed him again. "I'm glad you are safe too, but we must pray for General Sanchez."

"I owe him so much. I look forward to seeing him again," said Domingo.

Arabella smiled and said, "Get cleaned up. I'll have dinner ready soon." Then she went to the kitchen and began lighting the cook stove.

Domingo took off his shirt and walked into their bedroom. "I have something for you, honey. I will get it in just a bit," he called out to her from the back room.

She replied, "I hope it's nicer than your new boots!"

Domingo laughed and walked back into the kitchen. "God, I missed you." He reached her and tried to raise the front of her dress.

"Stop it!" said Arabella. "There will be none of that until after I see what you got me, and if it's not good… Well, you can do the math."

Domingo stared at Arabella as she started gathering items in the kitchen for dinner. She glanced up at him a couple times and smiled, but he couldn't relax and smile back as much as he wanted to.

"What is it?" she asked.

"You know," replied Domingo.

She quickly answered, "Was I surprised to see Pedro? Yes, I was. Very surprised."

Domingo stood. He looked down at the floor, scratching his cheek. "You still have feelings for him?" he asked, finally looking up at Arabella again.

Arabella stopped what she was doing and turned toward Domingo with an expressionless glare and hands on her hips. "That was a long time ago. Now let's change the topic before I get angry."

Domingo nodded and sucked his teeth. "Well, it's obvious he still has feelings for you."

"He can have all the feelings he wants toward me. I chose you fifteen years ago, and I would still choose you today."

"I don't trust him. I should send him home."

"You trust me, don't you?" Arabella replied. "Besides, that would be awful rude after he just traveled here to help you."

Domingo smiled, then walked over to her and kissed her forehead. "Of course I trust you. Just let me know if he does or says anything inappropriate. I don't believe he came to help me as much as he came to see you, and I'll beat his ass like I did before if he misbehaves."

"Are you done?" asked Arabella, leaning away from Domingo.

"Yeah, I'm done," replied Domingo.

"Good! Now go change your clothes, and change your attitude while you're at it."

Domingo smiled and quickly kissed Arabella, then embraced her for several moments. "I love you," he said, heading for the back room to finish cleaning up.

Vicente and Pedro stayed at the ranch helping Domingo for two days before returning home. Arabella could hardly contain her anticipation and excitement that Vicente would be returning a month later with his entire family to stay the summer. Domingo was equally excited to see Pedro finally leave.

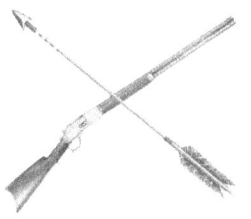

CHAPTER 10
WINCHESTER RIFLE

Luis and Jose had returned shortly before Vicente and his family arrived at Domingo's ranch for the summer, and with their help, the four men added much-needed fencing. They managed to grow the ranch substantially, reaching two hundred head of sheep. It was so hot that they worked in the early morning, cooled off inside during the middle of the day, and got back to work in the late afternoon until sundown.

Domingo also purchased a wagon—called a schooner—to make his trips to Tucson and other nearby towns much easier. With the new wagon, he could load twice as much cargo and travel twice as fast. He not only sold wool and mutton to Mexican merchants but to American merchants as well. There had been no sign of the Apache or any contact with General Sanchez since the two clashed at the river. Domingo was confident the Apache had left the area, and he even felt safe enough to start making trips to the Gila again.

Arabella's life also became much easier after the newest addition to the family; a healthy baby girl they named Laila, in honor of Arabella's aunt. With the success of the ranch, Arabella's days of food gathering were over. She would still make clothes and blankets, but more for a hobby than anything else. The children seemed to play from morning until night, and when the time came for Vicente, Maria, and their children to return home to Tucson, it was hard on everyone to say goodbye.

Marcello continued becoming more of a great help to Domingo. He was highly skilled for a young man of his age, mainly because Domingo took the time to show his son how things were done. Life was good, food was plentiful, and Domingo and his family were finally living happily and comfortably.

It was another hot morning in late summer when Marcello exited the barn with a bag of cracked corn to feed the chickens. He scattered some on the ground, watching as the chickens raced toward him. He glanced up and shouted, "Papá!"

On the roof repairing some leaky spots, Domingo kept beating nails with his hammer after checking that Marcello was feeding the chickens.

"Papá, look!" Marcello shouted again.

Domingo looked up this time, wiping his brow and squinting from the glaring sun. Seeing three riders approaching in the distance, he rushed down from the roof and headed inside to get his rifle. As he came back outside, Marcello was on the front steps of the porch, waiting for him.

"Go inside, son," said Domingo. He headed toward the riders steadily approaching his ranch. "Tell your mama I said everyone needs to stay inside!"

Marcello dashed into the house.

Domingo walked fifty feet toward the men, then saw one of the riders raise his hand in a kindly manner. He stared into the sun, unable to see who they were until he finally heard a familiar voice.

"Don't shoot me!" shouted General Sanchez, playfully putting his hands in the air.

Domingo smiled in great surprise and relief to see his old friend alive. "You can't die anyway, can ya?" he asked with a chuckle.

"Well, no, but I only have one leg left and don't want to lose it," replied Sanchez, pulling his horse to a stop in front of Domingo. "You know how hard it is to ride with one leg?"

Domingo stared at the space where the general's missing leg should have been. "Well, you seem to be doing fine," he replied, looking up at the man.

Sanchez removed his sombrero and wiped his forehead. "Well, I fell off twice on the way here and damn near broke my ass!"

Domingo grinned as he reached up to shake hands.

"It's good to see you, my old friend," said Sanchez, grasping Domingo's hand.

"Damn good to see you," replied Domingo.

Sanchez then looked over at his soldiers. "Help me down, men. Get me off this filthy beast!"

Domingo stood back and watched as the two soldiers helped Sanchez down from his horse. When the general was on the ground, they fastened a wooden leg to him. He then reached for his cane and quickly pushed the men away, wanting no further help.

"If I'd known you were coming, I could have sent my oxcart for you," said Domingo with a chuckle.

At first, Sanchez stared blankly at Domingo, then he laughed. "Don't let it fool you. I'm still keen as a hawk and deadly as a rattlesnake!"

Domingo smiled. "Well, your mouth rattles, that's for sure."

Sanchez laughed and hobbled forward.

Domingo kept a hand on his arm to help stabilize the man as they ambled toward the front porch.

"Geez, want me to carry you?" said Domingo as he shook his head and laughed.

"You couldn't carry shit. Don't think I didn't notice those little arms," said Sanchez. "Life's been too easy for you, and you're getting soft!"

Arabella and the kids appeared on the porch as the men reached the first step.

"Arabella!" said a cheerful Sanchez. "Come over here. You are much quicker than I am!"

Arabella smiled with great delight at the general as he kept one hand on his cane and opened his other, awaiting her embrace. She rushed to him—Marcello close on her heels—and said, "General, it's so good to see you again!"

"Yeah, what's left of me," answered the general jokingly.

Arabella looked down and then back at the general. "You're still alive, General, and that's what makes me happy." She kissed the general's cheek. "Come on in. I'll get you and your men something to drink," she said, waving them inside.

"Thank you kindly," replied Sanchez.

Sanchez looked at Marcello standing close by, pulled

a coin from his pocket, and held it out to him. "Go tend to those horses, boy."

Marcello dashed off as Sanchez watched the young man gather the horses and start leading them to the barn.

"Boy sure has grown since I saw him last," he said, looking at Domingo. "How old is he now?"

"Thirteen, and twice the worker I was at that age," replied Domingo. "Don't know what I'd do without him."

Sanchez asked, "You ever tell him that?"

Domingo stared at Sanchez for a second, then he looked back at Marcello. "Don't have too. I'm sure he knows that."

Arabella came back outside and put her hands to her hips. "Will you boys come inside? I want to visit too!"

Sanchez and Domingo looked at each other, then continued up the steps. Domingo placed his hands on the general's elbow and bicep to help him up and into the house. Inside, they joined the two soldiers already sitting at the table and drinking tea. Domingo pulled up another chair for Arabella as she returned with two more drinks.

"Thanks for the help, fuckheads," Sanchez said to his soldiers while finding his seat.

The soldiers quickly stood to assist him.

"Sit the hell down! I'm already in the goddamn chair," barked the general. He looked at Domingo, and they both laughed.

General Sanchez took a long drink of the tea Arabella had placed in front of him. "That tastes mighty fine, Arabella," he said.

Arabella sat at the table beside Domingo. "You men must be thirsty after riding in this heat," she said.

"Yes, ma'am," said one of the soldiers as he was about to take another drink.

The general gave the soldier a look that clearly said he should shut up.

"It's good to see you well, General," said Domingo. "When I returned from Tucson and Arabella told me what happened, I'll tell ya, I didn't think you were going to make it from the sound of it."

Sanchez nodded. "It was a dark, horrible day," he replied, offering Domingo a cigar.

Domingo took the cigar, and Sanchez lit it for him.

"There's no doubt in my mind that they were heading here," added Sanchez.

"I can't tell you enough how much I appreciate you and your men for stopping them," replied Domingo, his voice cracking with emotion.

Sanchez nodded as he took a big puff off the cigar he was lighting. "Well, they surprised us by their tenacity, but we held them off."

Arabella cast a sympathetic look at the general. She'd seen firsthand the horror that returned that afternoon between the severely injured men and how many didn't return at all.

"I lost a lot of men that day, and I couldn't even give them a proper burial," said Sanchez as he shook his head. "Had to leave them lying out there on the ground for the coyotes and buzzards. It was a week later when some men returned for their bodies. I guess you could imagine what condition they were in." Sanchez shook his head. "Arabella probably told you, but one of our dead was takin' by wolves."

Domingo nodded, looking down at the table, then put his

hand on Sanchez's shoulder. "Friend, I am in eternal debt to you. Anything you need of me."

Sanchez smiled. "Well, it sure is funny how things happen. When we first arrived, you wanted me gone." He laughed. "Now, we are like brothers!"

Domingo laughed and nodded. "Yes, brothers!" he replied as he patted the general's shoulder and raised his glass to him. After taking a drink, he asked, "So, what brings you back through this time?"

"Well, the Mexican army has recently put me in command of a post not too far from here," explained Sanchez.

Arabella and Domingo both looked at each other, smiles growing on their faces.

"About twenty miles east," added Sanchez.

"That is great," said an enthusiastic Domingo.

"Yeah, over a thousand men," said Sanchez with a tinge of pride in his voice. "With artillery and cavalry…the whole deal. The Mexican war department believes the Americans might be coming down through here, and we must stop 'em if they try."

Domingo's and Arabella's smiles disappeared simultaneously.

"Americans coming down here?" said Domingo, his brow heavily creased.

"Well, you know about that deal in Texas, right?" asked Sanchez.

Domingo nodded.

"It is looking like Texas is to become an American state, and that's gonna be a problem."

Domingo looked at Arabella for a second, taking in the worry on her face.

"Think we should be heading south?" she asked.

"Not sure," said Sanchez, shaking his head. "Still too early to say what's exactly going to happen."

Domingo and Arabella looked at each other, both frowning at the prospect of the Americans taking their land. Domingo stared down at the table as he began thinking of what to do about this news, his mind racing.

Sanchez leaned forward and tried to sound reassuring. "The Americans' fight is not with you, and they shouldn't do more than pass through, but the gringos and Apache are working together on this one. We already know you must certainly worry about the Apache," he added, wagging his finger at Domingo.

"The Apache working with Americans?" asked Domingo with a confused look.

"Oh, yeah. You bet. We been driving them north for years, and this is their chance to come back down," explained Sanchez.

Domingo sat and looked out the window in deep thought as the general continued.

"We plan to patrol north of the Gila for the coming months. If we come across the Americans, we should be able to get word to ya soon enough," said Sanchez.

"Would the Americans really come this far down?" asked Domingo.

Sanchez shook his head in uncertainty. "It's bound to be an American invasion. I don't know how far they will come or how much they will try to take, but I will fight them all the way." He took a drink from his glass and lightened the conversation by adding playfully, "They might not come through here at all, and we have one hell of a force waiting for them if they do!"

Domingo

Domingo nodded, still reeling from the conversation. He took a hit off his cigar, then looked at the general. "Is there anything I can do for you or your men?"

Sanchez tilted his head to the side. "Well, actually there is. We've been working day and night on the outpost. You know—fences, defenses, and barracks. And we haven't had time to head south for much-needed supplies."

Domingo nodded. "Well, I have over two hundred head out there and an extra oxcart for you," he said with a grin.

"I knew I could count on you, Domingo," said Sanchez as he reached into his pocket and pulled out some money.

"The army gives me enough to buy the supplies we need. I'll take whatever mutton and blankets you can spare, and here is plenty of money for it." Sanchez placed the money on the table.

Domingo smiled as he counted the money. "More than fair."

"Well, take the money while I have it. I am sure they will be less generous if the war drags on too long." Sanchez picked his cigar back up and put it in his mouth, biting it with his teeth. "I will send some men back in a couple days to round it up. Go ahead and fill the cart with whatever you think would be useful."

"I'll have it here ready for you," replied Domingo.

"We will be heading north and up that way for some time. It's good to know we have you down here to fall back on if food supplies run low," said the general.

Domingo nodded. "Glad to be of help."

Marcello walked through the front door and over to his father.

"How are the horses, son?" asked Domingo.

"All set, Papá," replied Marcello.

"That's a fine job," said Sanchez as he took his last drink of tea and stood from the table, almost falling.

Marcello quickly came to the general's aid, steadying him with a kind smile.

"Damn it!" Sanchez said, catching himself with the edge of the table and Marcello alike. Then he looked at the soldiers still sitting at the table. "Why don't you boys bring me that bottle of tequila from my saddlebag, then go up there and give Domingo a hand on that roof."

"Yes, sir," replied his men.

"I'm gonna go have a drink in the shade and a little siesta," he added with a grin, then he hobbled his way to the door with Marcello by his side.

Arabella got up from the table and looked at Domingo with concern still written all over her face.

Domingo stood and faced her, then kissed her forehead. "It's all right. Everything will be fine," he said softly.

Arabella squeezed Domingo's hand, then made her way to the kitchen to prepare some breakfast for their visitors.

With Sanchez and his army in the area scouting for American troops and keeping the Apache north, things remained quiet for Domingo and his family as the months went by. He made a couple trips to Tucson and other nearby towns, trading mutton and wool. He purchased more livestock from another ranch twenty miles southwest of him. As Domingo's herd of sheep and steers grew, he purchased an ox-drawn plow, planting wheat and about a half-acre of corn. Although he worried about there being enough water, the plants grew and provided a successful harvest.

Sanchez and his men bought a cart full of mutton, blankets, and eggs every month, and the general even had a few men help with the enormous task of butchering the livestock and smoking the meat. Luis and Jose spent most of their time rustling the large herd of sheep, protecting them from wolves and thieves. However, no one was more help to Domingo than his son. Marcello, now fourteen years old, was Domingo's right hand. Even when he made trips to Tucson, he felt safe leaving Marcello behind to watch over their family.

Late one afternoon, Domingo returned from a trip to Tucson with two more steers and supplies. He asked Marcello to take them to the barn and then come right back.

Marcello did as he was asked and ran back to help his dad unload the wagon. But Domingo was waiting with a surprise for his son. He watched his son's face transform as the boy saw the shiny rifle he held out for him.

"Oh, thank you, Papá!" he said several times before Domingo stopped him.

"Son, you have more than earned it," replied Domingo with a large grin.

Marcello looked down at the shiny barrel and dark cherry stock in awe. "Can I go shoot it?" he asked with overwhelming excitement.

"Well, I don't know. Can you?" Domingo smiled and handed Marcello a box of bullets.

Marcello spun on his heels and dashed across the landscape, away from their home.

While Domingo was in Tucson, he had come across this beautiful Winchester repeating rifle. It was a new type of rifle and a little expensive, but he traded some wool to counter the cost and also bought three hundred rounds of ammunition.

As he watched the boy head off, Arabella appeared beside him.

"What did you do?" she said sarcastically.

"The boy deserves something nice," said Domingo.

"Couldn't just give him one of yours?" asked Arabella.

"Nah, that one is a lot better than mine, and that one is his. It will always be his," replied Domingo. Then he turned to Arabella and embraced her. "How's my beautiful wife doing?"

Arabella smiled and lifted her lips to his for a kiss, then they held hands as they walked toward the house.

"Well, I'm fine, but Laila is a little sick," replied Arabella, gazing up at her husband's face.

Domingo's smile disappeared, and he hung his head with worry over the news. He had always been strong and could handle about anything, but he struggled when his kids were sick.

"Will you stop! She will be fine. She has a little cough and a slight fever," said Arabella.

Domingo let go of Arabella's hand, opened the door, and went inside, finding his youngest lying on the sofa in the living room with a blanket wrapped around her.

Just days from her first birthday, Laila looked up at her father with a small smile.

Domingo knelt beside her and placed his hand on her head. "How are you feeling, sweetie?" He kissed her forehead. "I'll get you some water." He stood, then felt a little tug on his pant leg. He looked at his daughter and reassured, "I'll be right back, sweetie. I promise."

Domingo

Laila smiled and closed her eyes, quickly drifting back to sleep.

Camille emerged from her bedroom, and upon seeing her father standing in the living room, rushed to him. "Papá!" she squealed.

Domingo scooped her up in his arms, gave her a big hug, and kissed her cheek. "How's my princess?" he asked.

"I'm fine," she said.

Arabella sat on the couch and cuddled Laila, smiling up at her husband.

Domingo sat Camille down and said, "I swear every time I leave for a few days, you look so much older when I get back."

"Well, I *am* older, Papá," said Camille.

A shot rang out, making Camille jump back into her father's arms. "Papá!" she said with a startled look.

"It's okay, Camille. I got Marcello a new rifle."

Camille smiled up at Domingo, tilting her head to the side. "Papá! Did you get me something?"

"Why do you always think I can afford to buy you things?"

"Well, did you?" asked Camille. "Did you, Papá?"

Domingo shook his head no, then said, "Yes! C'mon and help me empty the wagon, and I'll give it to you." He returned Camille to her feet and headed out the door.

Upon reaching the wagon with Camille at his heels, Domingo reached inside one of the boxes containing a set of bowls. He pulled one of the bowls from the box and held it out to his daughter.

Camille looked at the bowl, creasing her brow and frowning. "You got me a bowl?"

"Here, take it," said her father with a smile.

She took the bowl and peered inside, then pulled out a

little silver chain with a topaz stone. Her little eyes lit up as she held it in her hand. "Thank you, Papá." She jumped up, dropping the bowl to the ground as Domingo caught her. She kissed his cheek and quickly ran to show her mama.

Domingo watched her run toward the house, then looked at the cracked bowl lying on the ground beside him. He shook his head, then began to smile

Shots rang out in the distance from Marcello firing at a fast pace.

"Easy, boy," yelled Domingo. "Take your time and work on being accurate." Marcello was already a great shot, but Domingo didn't want him running out of bullets too quickly. He reached in the wagon and then turned back toward Marcello. "Actually, come on in, son. Your mama is making dinner for us."

Marcello ran toward Domingo with a big grin on his face. "Let's go hunting after dinner, Papá!"

Domingo shook his head. "Boy, I just got back."

Marcello dropped the barrel toward the dirt, lowering his head.

Seeing the boy's disappointment, Domingo put a hand on his shoulder and said, "Let's get up early, take care of the animals, and then we'll go out for a bit." He reached in the wagon with his free hand and grabbed out a sack of flour. "Now help me carry this stuff inside."

Marcello grinned up at his father, then laid the rifle in the wagon and grabbed a box. The two walked side by side toward the house, up the porch steps, and went inside.

"Dinner is almost ready, so clean up and come sit down," said Arabella.

"Mama, I have to clean my rifle!" replied Marcello.

Arabella looked at Marcello, making a face that said there was no room for discussion.

"All right," said Marcello in a disappointed tone.

Domingo sat the flour on the floor in the kitchen and the box on the table, then he reached down into the box again and pulled out a white and brown teddy bear. He made his way into the living room to Laila and rubbed his hand over her forehead. She looked up for a second, then closed her eyes and drifted off to sleep. He smiled and placed the teddy bear by her side, then watched his little girl for a moment as she slept.

Arabella came up behind him and whispered in his ear, "C'mon, you sweet man. Dinner is ready."

The four sat at the table, happy to be together again as they filled their plates and waited for Domingo to start telling stories of his latest journey. He obliged his family, starting with the rifle he'd seen for sale in the window while riding through Tucson.

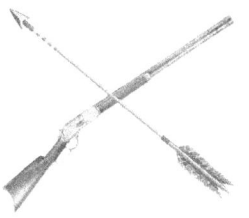

CHAPTER II
WHITE MAN'S WOMAN

General Ezra Johnson had been active in the local militia before enlisting in the army, then spent several years stationed at Fort Monroe in Hampton, Virginia. As more settlers moved west, he'd asked to be transferred to the Oregon Territory. Shortly thereafter, his request was granted, and he was appointed to the 1st Regiment Infantry. Johnson had always wanted to see the western frontier that seemed to spur endless stories of outlaws, Indians, and beauty. His wife, Clara, had not been happy with his decision. Not only would she have to move away from her family, but she was afraid to move her children to such hostile territory. So, in the end, he had made the trip west to Fort Walla Walla alone.

General Justus Hood of the 1st Infantry had been in command of five companies, A through E. When the general added five more, Johnson was promoted to Officer in Charge of H Company. This had been an exciting time for Johnson, even though he often missed his family. The landscape was beautiful, like none he had ever seen. He'd enjoyed writing to Clara and his children about the mountains, valleys, and huge redwood trees, though he'd found searching for the right words to describe such a magical place frustrating.

Johnson's company had one main task—protecting the settlers coming west from the hostile Snake River Indians, assisted by the friendly Nez Perce Tribe that was also a common enemy of the Snake River Indians. When gold was discovered in the Nez Perce territory, Johnson had been confronted with yet another task—keeping the peace between miners and the Nez Perce. He had the trust of both sides and managed the situation pretty well, considering the tension between them.

In early 1846, Johnson was promoted to general and transferred to the Nuevo Mexico province. He had not been excited about leaving Oregon, but the war between the US and Mexico had begun, and his men and services were needed there. Johnson and his men had secured the southwestern border by taking three Mexican forts and stopping several Mexican regiments in their tracks. He'd had several things working in his favor. Among them, the treaty with the Apache and Lieutenant Wells, who was Johnson's field commander.

Lieutenant Wells was a slender man with a long mustache. He always wore a cowboy hat and kept his uniform surprisingly clean, taking great care in polishing every brass button. He was ruthless, and Johnson sometimes did not condone his war methods.

The Mexican-American War began over an area that is now western Texas. Lieutenant Wells was promoted to Lieutenant General and dispatched to the southern part of Nuevo Province to oversee the 1st Dragoon brigade, which was under the command of General Johnson. Trained to fight on the ground, this infantry brigade rode horseback to cover distances more quickly.

One thing that had been a bone of contention between General Johnson and Lieutenant Wells was the treatment of captured Mexican soldiers. As the fight extended across the southwest, Wells could not have been happier about it. He was stern and direct, having little reserve for killing, and his hatred of Indians was notorious. But this was a war against Mexico, and the recent treaty with the United States and Apache guaranteed safe passage through Apache land for US troops. Though Wells would have preferred to take out Apaches on his way down into Mexico, General Johnson had made it clear that he was not to do anything that would disrupt their treaty. His orders were simple: terminate all Mexican forces and their outposts in the southern part of the Nuevo Province—which today is known as Arizona and New Mexico.

Lieutenant Wells had not always been that way. He'd had a wife, a son, and a home just outside New Orleans. When his family died of yellow fever, Wells had left the army only to return soon after, but he was not the same man. Even his long-time friends and comrades pulled away from him. He was cold, withdrawn and callous, cruel even. The only thing he knew in his heart was pain, and it was the only thing left he could give. He rarely took prisoners even when they surrendered. He did not have any sympathy for the sick, wounded, or dying. His own soldiers rarely informed him of their injuries, fearing Wells might send them on patrols or have them lead an attack. However, as brutal as Wells's tactics seemed, they were quite effective in war. As he'd made his way through the ranks, he had quickly become Johnson's right-hand man.

Wells and his men moved south, heading into Apache territory. His dragoon army totaled over three thousand men and included a large artillery division, fourteen wagons, twenty-eight medics, and six engineers, plus a bilingual Blackfoot scout named Hani Yu—who Wells called Hugh. Although Apache was not Hugh's best language, he could communicate, and that's all Wells needed. The first battle Wells had fought in Canoncito—which sits northeast of Santa Fe—against General Armijo, when the war first began, sent many Mexican soldiers retreating in fear of the enormous army. To the lieutenant's dismay, many Mexican soldiers had successfully escaped. In his second battle, Wells had divided his men and caught the fleeing Mexican army in a crossfire that left very few survivors. This quickly became the tactic he preferred; to not only win the battle but also cause heavy casualties.

Lieutenant Wells set his sights on General Sanchez, the Mexican general who commanded a sizable force in the territory and had been wreaking havoc against the Apache for several years. The Apache eagerly provided very useful intel to the American commander about General Sanchez's whereabouts and specifics of his army.

Red Sleeves, like many Apache in the area, patrolled day and night to learn of the hated Mexican general's position so he could keep his tribe a safe distance away. Even as many Apache and Navajo tribes worked together, they were running out of places to hide, desperate for food, and low on warriors to offset the general's continuous attacks. The bounty Mexico placed on Apache scalps continued taking its toll, as the Indians found themselves unable to safely partake in fairs and rendezvous. Lieutenant Wells's army brought hope to many Indians that their life would return to the way it was before the Mexican Republic—and its evil general—arrived.

Domingo

By fall, Red Sleeves had moved up to the most northern point of his territory, the northern plains of Nuevo. His tribe stayed close behind, exposed on the open plain, while he and a small hunting party took down several buffalo and set about the work of butchering them. Red Sleeves took a bite of raw buffalo meat, blood dripping through his fingers, in celebration of the hunt, as he always did. But this hunt was more special because it was the first time his son, now twelve years old, was with him. After taking his bite, he handed the bloody meat to his son, who also took a bite. With pride, Red Sleeves watched his brave son, who shared his name and would be chief of the Apache someday.

A flash of light in the distance caught Red Sleeves's eye, and he scanned the horizon until his gaze fell on a large group of soldiers coming over a hill in the distance, heading straight toward their hunting party. He knew he would have to confront the soldiers with his hunting party while the tribe's women and children headed for safety.

Turning to his son, Red Sleeves said, "Head back to the tribe and alert the warriors. Have the others hide in the trees along the plains."

The boy jumped on his horse and sped off toward the tribe with a look of determination that made his father proud.

Red Sleeves looked back at the approaching army, knowing very well if it was Mexican soldiers, this could be his final battle. Just five years ago, the Apache tribe had several hundred warriors, but now just under fifty men remained.

He climbed up on Whom'tu, then rubbed the horse's neck. "Let us have one final charge together, my old friend, and let our spirits rise to the clouds." He then turned his horse, making several circles and raising his rifle while belting a war cry as his men quickly climbed on their horses and raced toward him.

Red Sleeves set out at a fast pace toward the oncoming soldiers. As he approached, he noticed the soldiers were mostly dressed in blue instead of the usual red and white the Mexican army wore, then he saw the American flag. He was more than relieved, even though he was always willing to fight. Now was not the time with his whole tribe nearby on the open plain. Pulling back on the reins, he brought Whom'tu to a halt and then jumped down. He grabbed a handful of dirt, looked toward the sun, and chanted a small prayer as he released the dirt into the wind.

Lieutenant Wells led about eighty of his men over the hill and brought them to a stop about one hundred yards from the small group of Indians. The rest of the army and wagons were in the valley behind him, out of sight. He ordered Sergeant Warden and the Blackfoot scout, Hugh, to accompany him onward toward the Apache chief. When the three men reached the small group of Apache, Hugh raised his hand in a friendly gesture toward the chief.

The chief replied by raising his hand as well, then looked at Lieutenant Wells and waited for a greeting from him.

Wells didn't care about the Apache treaty, so he did not return the gesture. He figured this was American land now, and the Apache had no say about what happens in it. "Tell him we are here to drive the Mexican army from these lands," he said to Hugh.

As Hugh translated, Wells added, "Our horses are tired. We plan to camp here for the night."

Hugh continued translating as Red Sleeves looked at Wells.

"You cannot stay here. We have already set up here and now have buffalo to cut and cook," replied the Apache chief.

Wells looked out across the plain, took off his hat, and wiped his brow. Then he shouted down at the chief, "I don't think you understand. The American army does not care about Apache affairs. Now move your tribe along!"

The chief stared at Wells a moment longer, then turned to Hugh for the translation.

Hugh looked at Red Sleeves with a smirk on his face, discrediting Red Sleeves and his objections, then told Red Sleeves what the lieutenant had said.

Red Sleeves looked at Hugh for several moments with his eyes squinted in anger before he looked back at Wells. "This treaty did not come from me. Not from the Apache people, not from the Apache land. This treaty came from the hair faces." He turned his head to the left and spat.

Wells turned toward Hugh, eagerly awaiting the chief's words.

Hugh began nervously translating to his commander.

Wells leaned back in his saddle with his eyes locked on the Apache chief.

The chief stared right back at Wells, unmoved. "The only voice the Apache hears is the land's. Tonight, the land tells us to stay." He moved his hand from left to right. "I do not care which way you pass, but pass you will," he added, then Hugh translated.

Now furious, which made him unreasonable and dangerous, Wells wanted nothing more than to pull his pistol and put a hole through the chief's head. And he was about to do just that when Sergeant Warden stepped in.

"Sir, we have to keep the treaty intact," said Warden.

Wells continued staring at the Apache chief, then slowly

moved his hand from his pistol. "Hugh, tell him when this war is over, I will be riding back through here and expect a much warmer welcome, or we might mistake these Apache savages for Mexican rebels."

Lieutenant Wells turned and rode back to his army as Hugh finished translating.

Red Sleeves reached down and grabbed a handful of dirt, said a few words, and threw the dirt down with disgust.

Hugh smiled at him.

Now even more angry, Red Sleeves stated to Hugh, "You are a white man's woman!"

Hugh's smile quickly disappeared, and he stared angrily at Red Sleeves.

"I should cut out your tongue so you can no longer say your poisonous words," added Red Sleeves.

Hugh spat on Red Sleeves, then turned his horse.

Red Sleeves quickly slammed the Indian scout to the dirt before his horse made the full turn, then pulled his knife and put it into Hugh's mouth. Blood trickled out the side of Hugh's mouth, and the fear in his eyes was matched by that of the calm, determined eyes of Red Sleeves glaring down into them.

Wells heard the commotion and looked back, then turned his horse and pulled out his pistol. He shot it at the dirt next to the Indian chief. The chief looked up at Wells, then pulled his knife away from Hugh's mouth, wiped the blood on Hugh's shirt, and got to his feet.

"Move back, goddamnit," said Wells, pointing his pistol at

the Indian. "Help him to his horse, Sergeant!" he barked to the soldier at his left.

Sergeant Warden climbed down from his horse and helped Hugh to his feet while keeping a close eye on the Apache still wielding the knife only ten feet away. Hugh made his way to his horse, wiping the blood from his mouth and feeling his tongue to make sure it was still there. Sergeant Warden then returned to his horse, climbed up, and looked toward his commander, awaiting orders.

"Goddamn savages," Wells muttered. "Oh, yeah, we'll be coming back through here all right!"

The three men trotted their horses back toward the awaiting army. When they reached the soldiers, they came to a stop as Wells pulled out his field glasses and surveyed the area.

"What's the orders, sir?" asked Sergeant Warden.

Wells continued looking around at the surrounding landscape for a few more moments, then said, "Let's move out following that creek, and we'll camp on the other side of that ridge." He pointed toward the ridge in the distance about a quarter-mile away.

"Yes, sir," said the sergeant.

Sergeant Warden rode to the top of the hill and signaled the convoy to come along.

Red Sleeves and his warriors watched in disbelief as the soldiers came over the hill and onto the plain. They looked like ants. There were so many, and they never seemed to stop coming. He now realized the danger he'd put his tribe into but figured he would rather die than be ordered about by a white man.

He returned to the tribe, letting them know the danger had passed.

The tribe moved into the open plains and cut up the buffalo while watching the American army disappear into the distance. Later that evening, after all the American soldiers had moved away from the area, the tribe enjoyed a much-needed feast around a large fire, honoring Chief Red Sleeves in celebration of the day he alone turned away such a massive army with just his knife.

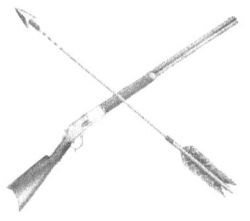

CHAPTER 12
BLOOD FROM THE SKY

SANCHEZ AND HIS MEN CONTINUED north, seeing little of the Apache in the areas they marched through. Just a few minor squabbles, but nothing that could even come close to matching the strength of the army he now commanded. They traveled at a quick pace and sent scouts in all directions but found no trace of the once-mighty Apache warriors who had fought him so bravely just two years ago. Hardened by the battle that had cost him his leg, and more than a little offended that the Apache chief had continued gaining popularity in the southwest among Apache, Americans, and Mexicans alike after stopping him at the river, Sanchez dreamed of facing Red Sleeves again.

After two more days of hard marching and coming up empty, Sanchez grew tired of the search and ready to head back to his outpost. He raised his hand, bringing his men to a halt. "Heading back, men!" he shouted. "Our job is done here."

Domingo

The men displayed their desire to return to the fort by cheering and raising their fists.

Sanchez wiped his brow and pulled a cigar from his saddlebag. He lit the cigar and watched as the horses and wagons slowly began turning around. Through the smoke he blew from his mouth, he caught a glimpse of a rider on a ridge to the south, looking right at Sanchez and his army through field glasses. Sanchez quickly reached for his field glasses and put them to his eyes. He could see it was a scout for the American army by his blue uniform. Sanchez frantically searched the surrounding hills, relieved he didn't see anyone else. The scout rode off, disappearing over the ridge in a southerly direction. Clearly, he had been riding behind them to see where they were going. Now the scout knew they were coming back the same way they had traveled, and that was a dangerous thing for Sanchez and his men.

"Hold them up, Major, and keep them quiet," barked Sanchez.

The major turned to the men and conveyed the general's message.

The soldiers looked around in all directions, awaiting orders.

Sanchez watched the ridge and surrounding hills, listening for several moments, but there was nothing. The general realized if he and his men continued the way they'd come, not too far ahead of them was a high ridge that would be a perfect spot for the enemy to launch an attack using the higher ground.

"They know we're here, and we have to prepare for a fight," explained the general.

"Sir, who knows we're here?" asked the major.

"Americans," replied Sanchez. "Didn't think they were this far west, but I certainly could be wrong."

The soldiers quickly dismounted and began digging in while some prepared the cannons and emptied the wagons.

"You two men scout that area," said Sanchez to his scouts, pointing to the ridge in the distance.

As the men got up on their saddles, a shot rang out in the distance.

Boom!

Sanchez whipped around toward the source of the noise but could only see a puff of smoke rising into the air. "What the hell? They can't hit us from there," he said, raising his field glasses, confused as to why they gave their position away.

The shell harmlessly landed about eighty yards away from Sanchez and his men, turning up the ground and throwing dirt in all directions.

"Load the cannons, men! Move those damn wagons out of here! It's the Americans." Sanchez rode around his men, watching over them as they scrambled to meet his demands. "Americans. Damn Americans!" he shouted. "On *our* land, men! Let's make them pay for this aggression!"

Sanchez looked back at the area the shell came from and saw well over one hundred American soldiers coming over the hill toward them. The American army was a dragoon division, and many of them had already dismounted. American soldiers moved their cannons into position to fire, and Sanchez turned toward his artillery to see if they were ready.

"Here they come, men. Get ready to fire the cannons!" General Sanchez shouted.

Then he watched as the American soldiers continued flooding over the hillside, now just four hundred yards from his men. Unsure how many American soldiers raced down the hill toward them, he believed it was approaching a thousand.

Knowing he might be outnumbered, he turned to his artillery. "Fire!"

The ground shook as six cannons rang out in the open terrain. The ground turned up as huge chunks flew in the air, and massive clouds of smoke began filling the valley.

American soldiers fell to the ground while others took cover.

"Reload!" barked Sanchez.

The American army seemed confused, as only one of their cannons fired in response and still came up short of the Mexican soldiers, while their other cannons struggled to get into position.

General Sanchez ordered two of his cannons to target the American artillery on the hill while the others continued targeting the troops. He circled behind his cannons and raised his sword. "Fire!" he shouted again.

All six cannons rang out simultaneously, and the Americans took cover again. Several of the American soldiers were hit as the cannonballs bounced through their ranks, taking limbs and lives with them. One American cannon was also hit, blowing a wheel off as the artillerymen around it fled up the hill.

"C'mon, boys. Reload those cannons! They're running. Let's lay into them!" Seeing the upper hand was his, Sanchez felt pretty good about his chances. The Americans were badly prepared for a fight against such a seasoned general as himself. "Reload!" he yelled as his men scurried to refill the chambers.

About to order a full charge after the next round of cannon fire, Sanchez happened to look over at the ridge behind him to the northwest. His heart quickly sank in his chest at the sight of more American soldiers placing cannons and preparing their firing lines. He had been trapped into a crossfire and now had the enemy on both flanks. Even worse, the second part of the army was larger than the first. Eighteen cannons bore down on his men.

"Ready to fire, sir!" shouted one of Sanchez's artillery commanders.

Sanchez looked back and forth at the two American armies on either side.

"General, sir, we are ready to fire, sir," said the commander.

"Fire when ready," said Sanchez. The enthusiasm in his voice disappeared, and he scrambled for his field glasses.

Boom!

The Mexican cannons rang southeast, out across the plains, completely stopping the American charge as their soldiers scrambled back up the hill.

Sanchez turned back toward the artillery behind him, unsure of what to do.

"Reload, sir?" asked the commander as he looked over at his general.

Sanchez pulled the glasses from his eyes and looked at his commander. "No, son, we need to take cover," he replied in a disheartened tone.

Ground-shaking artillery fire came from behind the Mexican Army, and the valley, hills, and ridges became a haze of smoke. The ground rumbled like a hundred thunderstorms.

General Sanchez's men looked behind them and froze at the sight of smoke from the enemy's cannons rising into the air.

"Take cover!" yelled Sanchez. "Take cover, men!"

Sanchez's army dropped to the ground and covered their heads.

The shells slammed into the ground all around them, blowing body parts, dirt, and metal in all directions. All six Mexican cannons exploded in a ball of fire and smoke, consuming the artillerymen along with them. At least fifty horses and twelve wagons collapsed to the ground. The fires spread from wagon to wagon as some soldiers desperately tried to put them out before it reached the ammunition boxes, but they finally had to give up and run away to seek cover.

The battle went silent for Sanchez, his eardrums ringing from a cannonball exploding nearby. He sat helpless to do anything as dirt and the blood of his men and horses poured from the sky like rain.

Within a few moments, the ground shook again as his ammunition and gun powder charges began detonating around him, further injuring and killing several more of his men. Then just a few moments later, the ground rumbled yet again as the American army he'd first encountered fired a round from their cannons.

Sanchez could only watch as more of his men were blown to pieces. After somewhat regaining his composure, he realized their only chance of escape was to charge the American force they'd initially engaged before they reloaded again.

"On your horses, men!" he shouted.

Sanchez looked down at a young soldier next to him lying on the ground, covering his head and frozen with fear. "Get up, boy…on your horse. It's okay, son," he said to the soldier.

The soldier slowly got to his feet and quickly made his way to his horse.

"Break through and ride southwest to the fort!" shouted

Sanchez. Unable to locate his officers, he pointed to two soldiers nearby. "You two men ride with me."

The general and his few hundred remaining men—some on horseback and some on foot—charged the smaller army, taking shots from their enemy's cannons and rifles. He watched in horror as over half his men were dead before even reaching the enemy. The last to arrive, he could clearly see that his men were sorely outnumbered in the hand-to-hand battle that ensued. Looking behind him and seeing the second and larger force moving toward them, he resolved to rally his men for a full retreat.

"Move, men! Retreat!" he shouted while galloping along the rear of his fighting line to avoid the American soldiers and their fire the best he could.

Sanchez and the two soldiers beside him rode south before turning slightly west, in the direction of the fort. Although smoke from the cannons and rifles made visibility difficult, Sanchez turned and looked behind him. The cavalry division of Wells's brigade had reached the retreating Mexican soldiers, who were on foot, and begun cutting them down. Of his great army, only about sixty of his men remained, all on horseback and riding hard to evade the cavalry. He could hardly listen to the cracks of gunfire and screams of dying men from the battlefield behind him.

As the moments passed, gunfire all but stopped, signaling that most of his men were dead and the battle was over. Continuing their fast-paced ride for about an hour and several looks behind them, Sanchez and his men finally stopped on a high ridge so he could look in the distance using his field glasses. His soldiers used the time to survey their injuries and bandage each other up using their shirts. Several men and horses alike were covered in blood from the spray of bullets they'd faced when charging the American Army. Sanchez looked in the distance and didn't see any American forces heading their way. The smoke in the far distance from the battle made his heart sink in his chest and tears fill his eyes. He hastily unhooked the straps keeping him secured in the saddle, falling from his horse in a rage.

"Damn Americans!" he yelled as his men scurried to help their general sit up. Sitting among what remained of his soldiers, he shouted again and again, "Goddamn Americans!"

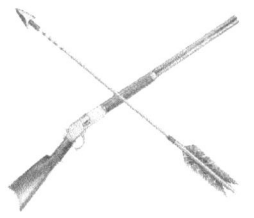

CHAPTER 13
RETREAT

A FEW DAYS LATER AND A few miles northwest of Santa Fe, a scout returned with news for General Johnson of Wells's decisive victory over the main Mexican force in the southern area of Nuevo. With General Sanchez in retreat, Mexican soldiers began fleeing the neighboring towns as American forces swiftly moved in, taking the towns they deserted. Johnson, with the bulk of his army, would take Santa Fe by the day's end and set about building a fort just outside of town. He also planned on building a prisoner camp in Santa Fe for the hundreds of captured Mexican soldiers soon to be arriving. The war was off to a bad start for the Mexican Republic, who had greatly underestimated the strength of its northern enemies.

The American's treaty with the Apache was another obstacle for the Mexican soldiers fleeing the territory. They faced not only the American forces in the towns and main fairways but Apache forces in the plains, valleys, and hills as well. The

Mexican soldiers could hardly move without their positions being revealed to the Apache, who then reported the movements to American scouts.

To the south, Lieutenant Wells and his brigade continued leaving a path of destruction where once had been forts, homes, barns, and businesses of Mexican sympathizers he felt had supplied food and munitions to the Mexican army. Once Wells finished his sweep southwest, his orders were to march north and take several towns still fortified by Mexican troops, then make his way back to Santa Fe and prepare for a march deep into Mexico.

After taking Santa Fe, General Johnson divided his division, sending brigades in several directions. In less than six months since the war started, Santa Fe, Albuquerque, Tucson, and Phoenix were held by Johnson's men. With the major cities falling to the Americans on the west coast and in the southwest, the Mexican provinces of Alta California and Nuevo Mexico were almost completely under American control. The whole Mexican Republic was close to collapsing as the Americans set their sights on the Mexican capital.

With the Mexican forces retreating from the territory, the Apache tribes began making their way south again. It was cause for great celebration as they entered their homeland after many years of forced migration north. However, the celebration was short-lived when they found that numerous mining camps and ranchers had settled the area in their absence. Within weeks of their return, Red Sleeves and his Apache warriors began attacking the intruders to fully reclaim their rightful land. The war with the Mexicans was over for the Apache, but the war to protect their land would continue for several more decades.

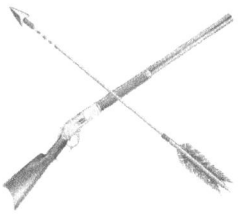

CHAPTER 14
A LITTLE WOODEN CROSS

Outside repairing a fence, Domingo looked over at Marcello a short distance away, shooting at a can with his rifle. It was another hot spring day, and Luis and Jose were out driving the woolies to more bountiful grassland along the creek bed. Arabella and the girls were inside working on a blanket together.

Domingo took a hard swing with his hammer, breaking the handle in two. Still holding the piece of fencing in place, he turned toward his son and shouted, "Marcello!"

"Yes, Papá," replied Marcello.

"Run in the barn and grab me another hammer, will you," said Domingo. "Should be one on the shelf in there."

"Yes, Papá," replied Marcello.

Rifle still in hand, Marcello ran over to the barn, then raced back out to his father carrying the hammer he'd gone after instead of the rifle. With a smile, he looked up at Domingo and said, "Here ya go, Papá."

"Hold this for a second, son," said Domingo as he reached in his pocket for more nails.

Marcello held the board in position and waited for his father to hammer the nails in place.

Domingo started driving in the nails but stopped when he noticed Marcello looking out at something in the distance. "What you are looking at, son?" he asked after a few moments.

Marcello stared in the distance, blocking the sun with his hand. "Looks like soldiers, Papá."

Domingo could now see the dust rising in the distance from the soldiers' horses. "Yeah, it sure does," he said. "Probably Sanchez's men."

Marcello's eyes were much keener than Domingo's, and he quickly replied, "No, Papá. They are wearing different outfits than the general's men."

Domingo knelt back down to finish nailing the fencing to the post but kept an eye on the approaching soldiers. When they were a few hundred feet away, he could clearly see they were American troops. It was hard to say how many, but it was well over a hundred cavalry.

"Go inside, son, and tell your mama and sisters to stay inside as well," Domingo said without taking his eyes off the soldiers.

Marcello dashed across the yard and into the house, shutting the door behind him.

Domingo got back to his feet and gave a friendly wave.

The soldiers abruptly came to a stop just a few yards away, and their Indian scout raised his hand to acknowledge him. "English?" asked the scout.

"Español," replied Domingo.

Domingo

The man next to the scout said, "The name is Lieutenant Wells. Is this your ranch?"

The Indian translated.

"It is," replied Domingo.

"Who all lives here?" asked Wells.

"Me, my family, and two ranchos," replied Domingo.

"How many head of sheep do you have?" asked Wells as he looked around.

"Maybe two hundred," replied Domingo.

Wells looked at the steers, barn, and the pile of blankets by the door of the house. "That's an awful lot of livestock for just one family and a couple of ranch hands," he replied.

"It's not just for us," replied Domingo. "I sell meat and wool to Mexican and American merchants."

Wells pulled a cigar from his pocket and lit it as he looked down at Domingo from the saddle of his horse. "What do you know of General Sanchez?" he asked.

"I know *of* him, but I haven't seen him for some time," replied Domingo.

Wells smiled and replied, "Well, that seems hard to believe, especially with his fort just up the way from here."

All heads turned at the sound of horses approaching. Returning from the fields for lunch, Luis and Jose trotted toward Domingo and their visitors.

"These your men coming?" asked Wells.

Nodding, Domingo replied, "Yes, they are."

"Well, I guess you already know America and Mexico are at war, and we just sent General Sanchez and his men running. I thought for sure they would have come this way," said Wells. "So, you sure you haven't seen him or his soldiers? There's a heap of tracks between here and that Mexican fort."

Domingo shook his head as Luis and Jose dismounted and came to stand beside him. He gave them a nod and held up his hand as if saying, "Just a minute." Then he glanced at Arabella standing on the porch, shooing the girls back inside, and turned back toward Wells. "No, I have not seen him or his soldiers. I am only a simple farmer. Sanchez has only been through here a couple times in the last few years."

Lieutenant Wells leaned down from his horse toward Domingo and said, "Just a simple mutton puncher, huh? Why don't you tell me what exactly Sanchez took with him as he passed through here those couple times? Food and supplies, maybe?"

"No, he only passed through," replied Domingo.

Wells took off his hat and knocked the dust from it, then looked around the ranch for several moments. "Well, greaser, I am not sure I believe all that."

Sensing danger in the way the man was talking to him, Domingo began to fear for his family and his ranch. He was not sure what to do, but he also knew there was very little he could do.

"You know this is American land, right?" asked Wells.

Domingo began shaking his head no, then quickly nodded. "Yes," he replied.

"If you are supplying the Mexican army with food, then you are aiding the enemy, therefore making yourself the enemy. Do you understand that, sir?" said Wells, glaring down at them.

"No, sir. As I mentioned, I only seen him a couple times, and we been here for many years," explained Domingo, stepping closer to the lieutenant while removing his hat to plead his case.

Domingo

Luis and Jose stood still, keeping a close eye on the lieutenant.

The lieutenant raised his hand, signaling for Domingo to stop his approach. "Well, see, that's where I don't believe you," Wells quipped with a shrug of his shoulders. "I am sorry, but I just don't." He folded his hands in front of him on the saddle horn. "Those horse tracks from here to the fort tell me you are supplying the enemy forces."

Domingo's mind raced with anger and fear, as he could clearly see where this was going. He turned to Luis and Jose. "When is the last time Mexican troops been through here?"

Luis shook his head and shrugged his shoulders while Jose quickly said, "A long time."

Lieutenant Wells turned to Sergeant Warden. "I'm done talking. Burn it!" he said, pointing at the barn and fences. "Knock those damn fences down, and let's take what we can. Grab those blankets too."

Warden turned to his men. "You heard him, boys. Light it up, and let's move out!"

Several soldiers climbed down from their horses and headed toward the structures, lighting torches and tossing them into the barn first. Other soldiers tied ropes to the fencing and pulled it down with their horses while others collected blankets, wool, mutton, and anything else they could pack in Domingo's wagon.

Domingo's eyes blazed as he started yelling at the soldiers. When he moved toward the lieutenant, Wells quickly put his hand on his pistol. Luis and Jose grabbed Domingo and led him back toward the house.

Arabella rushed from the porch, frantically yelling at the soldiers.

Domingo broke free of Luis and Jose and rushed to console her, directing her back to the porch. As smoke poured out of the barn, Scratchy came running out and went to the porch to stand near Domingo's feet, then barked at the soldiers. Marcello also emerged from the house, freezing just outside the door in shock from what he was witnessing.

"Sir, what about the home?" asked Sergeant Warden.

Wells looked at the barking dog and family standing on the porch. "Leave it," he replied.

As billowing smoke darkened the sky above, Marcello took off running straight for the barn.

"Marcello! No! Come back!" shouted Luis.

Domingo let go of Arabella and raced toward the barn as Marcello entered the engulfed building. Before he could make it thirty feet, his son came running back out with his rifle in his hands. Domingo looked over at the American army just as Lieutenant Wells reached for his pistol and raised it at Marcello. Domingo started to shout, but Wells pulled the trigger. The sound of the gunshot and Arabella's scream were almost simultaneous. Time seemed to stop as everything moved in slow motion.

Marcello dropped his rifle, reached for his chest, then dropped to the ground.

Domingo, Arabella, and the ranch hands ran at full speed to Marcello. Dropping to their knees, the couple lifted their son's head from the dirt, calling his name. All they heard in response was the boy's weak efforts to breathe and gurgling as blood trickled from his mouth.

Marcello opened his eyes and looked up at his mother and father, then died in their arms.

Domingo

Lieutenant Wells returned his pistol to his holster and led his horse away from the ranch.

"C'mon, boys," said the sergeant. "Mora is waiting."

The soldiers returned to their horses, a few stopping on the way to stare with remorseful expressions at the dying boy on the ground, his family gathered around him.

"On your horses, dammit!" barked Sergeant Warden. "Let's move out…now!"

The line of cavalry slowly made their way down the trail, away from Domingo's home.

Domingo grabbed Marcello's rifle and jumped up but was quickly subdued by Luis and Jose.

"No, Domingo," said Luis quietly. "They will kill you!"

Domingo let go of the rifle and fell to the dirt, punching the ground and crying uncontrollably next to Arabella, who hunched over holding their son and moaning as if she had been shot herself.

After just a few minutes, the American soldiers had disappeared from sight.

The next morning, Luis and Jose dug a hole and helped Domingo lower Marcello into it. They placed a cross made of two branches tied together by a leather strap above the grave. The family mourned together at the grave for several hours. Domingo showed no emotion, frozen by his grief and anger.

Later that night, Domingo pulled Luis and Jose aside and asked them to take Arabella and the girls to Vicente's home in Tucson. He instructed them to return to the ranch and sell off the sheep, then stay at the house and await his return. It was clear he was going after the man who had killed his son.

Luis and Jose made every effort to convince Domingo not to leave, but the grief-stricken father would have none of it. Arabella furiously fought with Domingo about his decision to ride out after the American soldiers, begging and pleading for him to stay. She told him if he died, she and their daughters would be left alone—the girls without a father—yet Domingo's mind was made up. He figured if that murdering US officer was left alive, he and his family would never have peace again, nor any other ranchero in the area. He knew he was not the only ranchero to come across that murderer and felt he was doing a favor for all those who had suffered at the hands of Lieutenant Wells. He explained that he would then go to Tucson and get Arabella and the girls, and they would head south into Mexico and start over.

After several hours of discussion, Arabella was too emotionally and physically exhausted to keep arguing. The couple eventually lay in bed and held each other tightly until the morning sun rose from the eastern sky, bringing with it shining rays of hope or signaling the end of their beguiling dream.

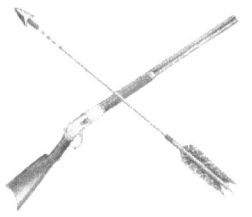

CHAPTER 15

FOOL'S GOLD

As the early sun cast its rays over the Santa Fe trail, three prospectors and their two guides packed up their gear. It was the second morning of their expedition, and they expected to reach their destination by midafternoon. They'd hired the Navajo guides in the nearby coal-mining town of Madrid. They referred to one of the guides as Half Breed, and he spoke English quite well. The other guide was Tahwa, but they simply called him Tower because of his tremendous height.

Bill Sheridan made his way to the seat of the wagon, pulled out his field glasses, and stared in the distance. After a few minutes, he said, "Hey, Carson, come up here for a second."

Joe Carson finished kicking dirt over the coals of their morning fire, picked up his gear, and headed toward the wagon. "Whatcha got, Bill?" he asked.

"Come up here for a second and take a look at this," replied Bill.

Domingo

Joe tossed his gear in the back of the wagon and climbed on board with his rifle in hand.

Bill handed the field glasses to Joe and said, "Take a look out there at that group of trees and that hill out yonder. I see four horses on the hill and what looks like Indians hiding in the brush below it."

Joe placed the glasses to his eyes, and after a good minute went by, he realized there was something up there. He pulled the field glasses away, wiped the lenses, and looked through them again. "Fuck," he said after just a few more seconds, quietly so as not to alert the guides. "It's a goddamn ambush. Those bushwhacking bastards set us up for a goddamn ambush." He handed the field glasses back to Bill, checked his rifle, then turned to see if Half Breed and Tower were still about forty yards away by the little creek, watering their horses and filling their canteens. Their fellow prospector, Henry Hood, was also there, filling his canteen.

"You really think they're in cahoots with Half Breed?" asked Bill.

"Goddamn right I do," replied Joe. "I sensed that something was weird, especially with that tall son of a bitch. Have your pistol handy, and don't act queerly until we can alert Henry."

"Then what?" asked Bill. "We gonna kill those Navajo sons a bitches?"

Bill pulled the field glasses back out.

"Put them fucking things away," said Joe hastily, looking back at their companions. "We don't wanna alert these savage fucks."

Half Breed and Henry started back from the creek while Tower finished cleaning his riding blanket.

"This is perfect," said Joe as he turned toward Bill. "Listen, I will distract Half Breed with the map, and you let Henry know what's going on." He climbed down from the wagon to get his map from his saddle. "Listen now, when I am talking to Half Breed, you come up from behind and knock his head off with the butt of your rifle. Keep hitting him until he stops moving. Do you got it?"

"Got it!" answered Bill. "But what about Tower?"

"Tell Henry to have his rifle on him, but remember, no shots," explained Joe.

"If those savages up that trail hear a goddamn gunshot, they will be on us before we can get the wagon turned around," said Joe, looking in the distance toward the ambush. "And don't let that Navajo get on his horse, got it? If he gets away, we are as good as dead!"

"Got it," replied Bill.

"All right, Billy, let's fix these fuckers," said Joe as he made his way to his saddle.

Bill climbed down from the wagon and walked toward Henry, who was almost back at their camp with Half Breed. Standing near his horse looking at a map, Joe signaled for Half Breed to come over to him. Half Breed walked toward Joe, then Bill reached Henry and filled him in on the situation. Bill walked his horse out of view of Tower, now returning from the creek, and pulled his rifle from the sling. Now just feet from Henry, Tower adjusted his riding blanket on his white horse. Bill came up behind Half Breed and hit him so hard with the butt of the rifle that he fell unconscious into Joe's horse, then was stepped on several times by the horse's hooves before Joe could grab the reins.

The horse's whinnying and stomping made Tower look

over to see what the commotion was. As he turned around, he came face to face with Henry pointing his pistol right at him. Tower turned to jump on his horse, and Henry swung his pistol into the back of the Indian's head. Tower fell to the ground, and Henry hurried to put his weight on him and hold him there. Henry held the pistol against Tower's back, but the big Indian twisted quickly and knocked Henry off him, then grabbed for Henry's pistol with one hand while punching the prospector in the nose with the other. Henry continued taking the punches while holding onto the pistol for dear life.

Billy saw his companion struggling and ran to his aid, and the three men wrestled across the ground, throwing punches, kicking, and cussing. Tower hit Henry with a right hand that knocked him out while Billy quickly reached for the gun just before Tower could fire, and the two men struggled for the gun.

"Joe!" yelled Billy. "Help!"

Joe ran over as fast he could and just in time. Bill was all but licked by the Navajo scout. Joe hit Tower in the side of the head with his rifle, knocking him out, then kicked the Indian several times as he lay motionless in the dirt. Bill got to his feet and joined in on the beating until both men were completely exhausted.

"What the fuck, Bill!" said Joe. "Two of you fuckers couldn't lick him?"

"That's a tough son of a bitch," replied Bill as he struggled to catch his breath.

Joe walked over to Henry and knelt beside him.

"He okay?" asked Bill.

"Yeah, I think so. He'll come around in a few." Joe returned to his feet. "Let's tie these two up and throw them in the wagon."

Joe and Bill tied Tower's hands and feet and carried him to the wagon. Bill's face was bleeding pretty heavily, and he had to keep wiping blood from his eyes, which made carrying Tower even more difficult.

"Man, this is one big heavy ass Indian!" said Bill as he struggled to lift him into the wagon.

The two men made their way over to Half Breed, still lying motionless by Joe's horse.

"Here," said Joe as he handed Bill some rope while putting his knee on Half Breed's back. "You tie his feet."

As Bill started tying his feet, Joe examined Half Breed a little closer. "Man, I think he's dead," he soon said in a somewhat surprised tone, looking over at Bill.

Bill let go of Half Breed's feet and knelt next to Joe. "Let me see," he said, reaching for Half Breeds neck to feel for a pulse. "I don't feel nothing," he said as he put his head to Half Breed's chest to listen for a heartbeat.

"Anything?" asked Joe.

"Nothing," replied Bill.

"Well, fuck him then. Leave him there," said Joe as he stood and turned to go help Henry.

Bill searched Half Breed for the money they'd paid him. Only finding $12 dollars and a few bits of turquoise, he turned to Joe and said, "What did this fucker do with the money we gave him?"

"Probably spent it on tequila. I swore that bastard drank a whole bottle last night," answered Joe. He knelt next to Henry and lightly tapped him on the cheek. "Wake up, Henry," he said. "We got to move, boy."

Domingo

Henry rousted, looking around in complete confusion about what had just happened. Half delirious, he mumbled, "Where is he?"

"We ain't got time to dilly dally. We have to hightail it out of here, and I mean now!" answered Joe, helping Henry to his feet and toward the wagon. "Bill, tie the horses off to the wagon!" he shouted. "I'll tie your horse to mine just in case we have to make a run for it." Helping Henry to the seat of the wagon, Joe asked him, "You all right to steer this wagon?"

"I think so," answered an unsure Henry, rubbing his head.

Bill finished tying the horses and climbed onto the wagon, then reached for his field glasses to see if they'd been spotted by the war party ahead.

"See anything, Billy?" asked Joe as he climbed in his saddle and tied Bill's horse off to the saddle horn.

"No, nothing," replied Bill.

"Now listen, men. We need to turn this wagon around real slow and move at a normal pace toward Santa Fe, and if we're lucky, we will be there in four or five hours," said Joe. "Billy, I need you on those field glasses the whole time. Don't move it away from your eyes for one damn second. You hear me?"

"I hear and see just fine. It's the rest of me that I am unsure of," answered Bill.

"If you see them moving this way, you put a bullet through that Navajo's head and ditch the wagon." Joe looked at Bill and then over at Henry. "You hear me, boys? There ain't nothing, and I mean nothing, on that wagon worth dying for."

Henry and Bill nodded to acknowledge Joe. Henry snapped the reins to get the wagon moving. As the three men and their Navajo prisoner headed toward Santa Fe, Joe asked every few minutes if Bill had seen any movement.

Eventually fed up with Joe asking, Bill exclaimed, "Joe, will you just leave this to me? I will tell you if I see something."

"You damn sure better," replied Joe.

Joe rode a little ahead of the wagon as Bill faced toward their rear, looking out of the field glasses.

"How ya feeling, Henry?" asked Bill.

"Like shit. Fucking head and neck are killing me," answered Henry.

"Well, when we get to town, we'll turn this piece of shit over to the sheriff and see the doc," said Bill as he looked down at Tower, who was starting to move around a little. "Looks like our friend is starting to wake up," he said.

"Well, keep your gun on that fucker," answered Henry with an angry face.

"I say we just choke his ass and leave the savage fuck right here in the dirt," said Henry, still rubbing his head and neck.

"Well, that would be grand, but so would seeing him hang," answered Bill.

CHAPTER 16
NO MORA

IN THE COMMAND TENT, LIEUTENANT Wells briefed his officers for the next day's march toward Santa Rosa. Once reaching Santa Rosa, Wells would send most of his brigade northeast to Santa Fe to meet up with General Johnson while he and approximately eighty cavalry—and a small number of artillery—would continue to Mora. During their march north, Wells and his army were to engage any Mexican soldiers retreating south. Many of the Mexican soldiers they'd been confronting were poorly armed and unprepared for a fight, usually electing not to fight at all and just surrender.

Having received news that to his southeast, General Scott was driving fast toward Mexico City, Lieutenant Wells was frustrated. He wanted nothing more than to be part of the capture of Mexico City. He figured the last of any real fighting would be to the south, if there was any at all. But to his disappointment, his orders were to head north for now and regroup with Johnson. He was sure his missions would soon not be of war, but more to keep the peace.

Wells stood from the table and gathered up his map as the officers stood and saluted him. He turned out of the command tent, followed by Private Jenkins, the lieutenant's orderly—or "dog robber" as he was often called—who had been standing guard at the tent's entrance. As Wells approached his own tent, he stopped, and Jenkins came to attention.

Wells pointed toward a soldier's horse tied off near his tent and gave the private a stern look.

"Sir," said the private.

"That damn horse," said Wells. "If it makes a ruckus, move it. I need to get some sleep."

"Yes, sir," said Jenkins.

The two men made their way into Wells's tent, just a brief walk from the horse.

"Can I help you with your coat, sir?" asked Jenkins.

Wells handed Jenkins his hat, then turned around as the private began removing his coat. Jenkins then hung the lieutenant's coat and hat from the hook near the entrance.

"Help with your boots, sir?"

"That's all, Private," said Wells.

"Yes, sir," replied Jenkins. On his way to exit the tent, he turned and asked, "Would you like some water or something, sir?"

"No, Jenkins. I am going straight to sleep."

Jenkins nodded and left the tent to take up his guard duty just outside again.

Reaching a small table by his bed, Wells turned up the lantern and removed his boots. He carried the lamp to an area where he had several maps laid out and spent a half hour looking over the maps before he finished undressing. He climbed into his cot and said a quick prayer, then turned down the oil lantern, stretched out on his back with his hands behind his head, and fell asleep.

Click.

Wells slowly opened his eyes.

A man standing over him had a pistol pointed at his face.

A startled Wells blurted out, "What—!"

The man crammed a rag into Wells's mouth, then gestured for him to be quiet with his finger in front of his lips. He slowly reached over and turned up the lantern.

Wells's eyes widened at the sight of Domingo glaring down at him.

Domingo leaned down close to the lieutenant's face and whispered, "You remember me, don't you? You killed my son."

Though Wells could speak very little Spanish, he was sure he knew what Domingo was saying. He tried to speak but couldn't with the rag in his mouth.

The two men stared at each other in silence for several moments, then Domingo placed his finger in front of his lips to remind the lieutenant to be quiet, and he removed the rag.

Through clenched teeth, Wells said, "It was an accident."

Domingo replied, "My son, you killed him."

Getting mad as a hornet, Wells said, "If you fire that weapon, fifty soldiers will be in here before you can pull that hammer back again."

Domingo stared down at Wells as he pulled a piece of rope from his pocket, then he placed it in front of Wells's hands. "Put your hands through here," he said.

Wells slowly put his hands through the rope, and Domingo pulled it tight.

"We are at war with Mexico, and you were aiding their troops," said Wells.

Domingo picked a rope up from the floor and put it around the lieutenant's neck. Wells tried to shift away from the rope and was about to yell, so Domingo stuffed the rag back in his mouth. Domingo then placed the barrel of the pistol under the lieutenant's chin until the man became calm again.

"You have taken all I have," said Domingo. "I was no harm to the Americans. The war was not with me." He pointed at Wells. "*You* brought it to me."

The soldier stationed out front peeked inside to check on the noise.

Domingo whipped around and looked at the soldier upon hearing the sound of the flap opening. Their eyes locked, but before the soldier could come to grips with what was happening, Domingo slipped out the rear of the tent.

Wells sat straight up in his bed, and after a few tries, spit the rag from his mouth. "Jenkins! Come here quickly!" he shouted.

"Yah!" came a voice from behind the tent, followed by the sound of a horse's hooves thundering away.

Jenkins quickly rushed across the tent to assist his commander, finding Wells sitting on the bed with his hands tied and trying to reach the back of his neck.

The sound of rope brushing rapidly against fabric caught both men's attention, then Wells was yanked by the neck right through the back of the tent and disappeared into the darkness.

Jenkins stood frozen in shock through the commotion of several soldiers piling into the lieutenant's tent.

"Oh, my God," said Captain Taylor as he ran to the hole in the back of the tent.

Soldiers with lanterns on the other side of the hole gathered around their commander's lifeless body.

Domingo had tied the rope around Wells's neck to the horse. By the time the slack drew tight, the horse was at full speed. The rope had broken, but not before snapping Wells's neck and killing him instantly.

Major Bolan looked through the hole in the tent, then ripped it open farther. Stepping through, he moved to stand over Wells, then quickly looked back at the captain. "Captain Taylor, find Sergeant Warden and have him ready the cavalry," barked Bolan.

"Yes, sir!" replied Taylor, then he raced for the sergeant's tent.

"You men help me carry the lieutenant inside and get a medic," he added.

The men carried Lieutenant Wells inside his tent as blood poured from his neck and head. The medic tried to revive Wells, but it was hopeless.

Major Bolan walked out of the tent, shaking his head in disbelief and anger.

Captain Taylor and Sergeant Warden approached the tent on horseback with several cavalry soldiers in tow.

"Find him, men. Bring him back dead or alive!" shouted Major Bolan.

"Yes, sir!" said Sergeant Warden, then he quickly led the cavalry out of the camp, after Domingo.

The major walked back into the lieutenant's tent and past the soldiers still gathering around to see their fallen commander. He removed his hat and swatted it against his leg while walking back and forth, then turned to his men. "Secure the camp, men. I want two guards at every officer's tent. Understand?"

"Yes, sir!" replied the men in unison.

He then pointed to three soldiers. "You men follow me."

Major Bolan grabbed a piece of paper and a pen from Wells's table and began writing. After a few short minutes, he fastened the letter with a wax seal and handed it to the soldiers. "You men grab some rations and horses, get up to Santa Fe, and give this to General Johnson."

"Yes, sir."

"Move quickly, men," added the major.

"Yes, sir," replied the soldiers.

He then walked over to Lieutenant Wells's side, placing his hand on the dead man's arm and bowing his head. Then he covered him up with a blanket.

CHAPTER 17
COZY CAVE

Domingo had left his horse tied to a tree a couple of miles from the American camp to avoid detection. As he fled the camp on one of their horses, he realized he was turned around and unsure of where exactly he had left his horse. He searched the area frantically, but to no prevail. Hoping his horse was somewhere close by, he stopped for a second to listen. At first, he heard nothing. Then he heard horses. A lot of horses. And he knew they were searching for him.

He had packed his horse with plenty of food and water so he could travel a long distance. Also, in the sling on the saddle was Marcello's rifle, so Domingo was very determined to find it. He also knew that without his well-supplied horse, his plan of escape would have to be altered considerably. He looked all around for a few more minutes, then kicked the soldier's horse repeatedly and charged out of the area. He rode as fast as he could without knowing the terrain or direction he was heading. It was dark, hilly, and very confusing. At one point, he had to turn back because he came to the edge of a cliff. He soon found himself in such rough terrain that he had to get down and lead the horse. After several hours, hard riding had left him and his horse completely exhausted. Domingo came across a small cave at the foot of a rocky cliff. He tied off the horse and scanned his surroundings under the light of a full moon, then stared at the dark, creepy cave for a minute.

"Well, if there's a cougar in there, it's going to have to share," he said, steeling himself to enter.

Domingo only went in a couple feet and then listened. Not hearing anything, he went a bit farther. Resigned that he was alone, he made himself as comfortable as he could. He leaned back against the rocky cave with his pistol resting on his lap. He hadn't made it as far as he'd hoped from the army camp, but he was sure he'd gone a lot farther than he thought. With so much adrenaline running through him, it felt like it had only been twenty minutes ago that he'd tied the rope to Wells's neck. He smiled at the thought of what had just happened. Revenge was his, though it had come at a high price. He already found himself missing Arabella terribly.

His eyes filled with tears as his thoughts switched from the officer he'd killed to his wife and family. The overwhelming feeling of being utterly alone overcame him, and tears streamed down his face.

"I'm sorry, my love," he whispered, thinking of Arabella's repeated attempts to sway him from pursuing the man who had killed their son.

Now that it was done, Domingo realized he hadn't gotten much comfort from killing his son's murderer after all. He'd expected a big weight to be lifted from his shoulders, but he felt no lessening of his burdens. He only wanted to get home to his wife and kids who, he now realized, he'd only hurt even more by leaving.

"My God," he cried. "What have I done?"

He shook his head and wiped the tears away from his cheek, desperately wanting to get back on his horse and head for Tucson, but he knew he had to wait until first light. He drew some deep breaths and leaned his head back. How badly he wanted to sleep, but his mind raced, and he had to fight off his thoughts.

Domingo started thinking of the Indian he'd run into on the way home from the Gila. He was sure the Indian had informed Wells of the Mexican soldiers visiting his ranch, and the thought of it made his blood boil. As another hour rolled by, Domingo kept hearing noises, but he knew it was just critters stirring around outside the cave. After a while, he didn't react to the noises, his mind settled down, and the exhausted Domingo finally fell asleep.

CHAPTER 18
THE NAME'S DOMINGO

THE SOUND OF HORSES AND men talking woke Domingo as the morning sun began creeping into the cave. His heart raced as he grabbed up his pistol and listened.

"He's down there, Lewis," said one man.

Americans, Domingo thought, angry at himself for not waking before sunrise.

He listened to the men up the hill above him, making their way down. He was certain it wasn't soldiers because there only seemed to be a few men, but whoever it was sure seemed interested in him.

"Damn, I should have kept going last night," Domingo whispered.

"Hold up!" one of the men said, followed by some quiet talking between the men.

Domingo crouched, pistol at the ready, and aimed toward the cave entrance.

A voice much closer than before said, "You there! Come out with your hands up where we can see 'em!"

Domingo answered in Spanish, "Just resting here. Keep moving."

"Damn Mexican," said one of the men.

"Yeah, riding a US military horse," replied another man. "Come on out, boy!"

Domingo knew they were not leaving. They didn't sound unfriendly, and maybe he was on their land and they wanted to know who was riding through it, or maybe they were outlaws looking to rob him. Nevertheless, he figured it was not going to be good and decided he wasn't going to voluntarily leave the cave. Then he heard loose rocks rolling down the hill and small brush cracking under feet. He sat quietly, watching and listening. The men moved around just outside the cave, probably trying to see in. Domingo caught a glimpse of one of them, but they could not see a thing inside the cave.

"Come out, señor," said one of the men.

Growing angrier by the moment, Domingo yelled, "Go away!"

"Jim, I bet there's a reward for this one," said one of the men.

"He's hiding from something," replied Jim. "Let's go get the sheriff."

"Ain't no sheriff. Just Mitchell," replied the man.

"Well, let's fire a couple into that cave. Maybe then he'll come out," said another man.

"Go ahead," replied the first man.

Someone climbed over some rocky terrain, and Domingo spotted him hiding behind brush cover and looking around for a better vantage point. He lifted his pistol until the gunsight was on the man's chest as the man raised his pistol to fire into the cave.

Bang!

The man dropped his pistol and fell to the ground, moaning in pain.

"Holy shit, he shot Lewis!" yelled Jim.

Then bullets pounded the dirt and rock all around the entrance of the cave. Domingo retreated farther inside and crouched down. After a minute, the shooting stopped.

"Lewis? Can you hear me?" asked a man's voice.

"Yeah, I hear you, goddamnit!" replied Lewis.

"Where did he get you?"

"In the arm!" Lewis yelled back.

"Shoot his horse," yelled one of the men. "That Mexican ain't going anywhere now."

A few more shots rang out, and Domingo heard the horse yelping in pain and then hit the ground.

"Damn gringos," said Domingo, shaking his head as he caught a glimpse of the horse's rear legs frantically kicking outside the cave. He wanted to just kill these guys and get moving, but he was trapped. Although they couldn't get him, he could not escape either.

"Doug, run back up there and go get the sheriff," said one of the men.

"I told you there ain't no sheriff. Just Mitchell," replied Doug.

"Well, go get somebody, goddamnit!" replied the man.

"I'll keep fire on him, so he doesn't pop out and get you," explained one of the men.

Shots fired into the cave, but Domingo heard the man moving away from the cave in between. There were just two men left, and the one they'd called Lewis was already hit and not much use. Domingo sat in the cave another fifteen minutes, wondering what to do. Every few minutes, another shot rang out, but he couldn't see anyone. He knew the guy he'd shot was still on the ground in that general area, but he could no longer see him. After a few more minutes of nothing, he heard them talking again.

"How are you doing, Lewis?".

"I'm okay, Jim, but if I move, he'll shoot me," replied Lewis.

"Yeah, you just stay tight. Won't be long now," said Jim.

Domingo figured if he ran out and made for the hill, he would be an easy target. Especially since the hill was steep and rocky. Now without a horse, he would certainly have to beat them up the hill and reach their horses first.

"I gotta kill 'em," whispered Domingo. "That's the only way out of this."

He checked his pistol to make sure it was fully loaded, then drew a few deep breaths and stood up. He walked quietly toward the cave opening, peered out, and could see the man he'd shot lying on the ground. He couldn't see the other one, so he listened for a minute to see if he would give away his position.

Bang!

The shot sent Domingo retreating into the cave.

"He's coming out, Doug!" the man said in an obvious attempt to make Domingo think all three men were still there.

Domingo saw where the shot came from and where Jim was hiding. He raised his pistol, then stormed out of the cave and fired heavily toward Jim. Jim quickly took cover, and Lewis sat up and started firing at Domingo. Domingo

Domingo

turned and shot at Lewis, just missing him. Lewis fell back to the ground and dropped his pistol as the bullets whizzed past him. With both men ducking for cover, Domingo turned and started up the rocky slope. He was amazed at how fast he was making it up the hill, placing his feet carefully so as not to lose his balance.

The men began firing up at him, but Domingo was too far from them, and they didn't have a clear shot at the moving target.

"C'mon, Jim! He's gonna get the horses," yelled Lewis as they started after Domingo.

Domingo was over three-quarters of the way up the hill when a shot fired in the air from above him.

"Hold it there, boy!" a man said from atop the hill.

Domingo stopped and looked up at several men looking down at him with their pistols drawn.

"Drop that pistol and raise those hands above your head," the man added.

Then another man said in Spanish, "Hold it right there, put your pistol down, hands up."

Domingo was more than ready to die at this point. He realized he wasn't going to see Arabella anytime soon and had no reason to live. He looked at the men again, ready to point his pistol.

Seeing Domingo's desperation plain as day on his face, the man in a tan leather cowboy hat said, "Hold up now, boy. Don't be foolish! We just wanna talk to you."

Domingo stared at the man, then nodded and put his pistol down.

"Now put your hands in the air and walk toward us real slow," the man ordered.

As Domingo put his hands up and began to walk toward them and away from the pistol, four of the men started down the hill toward him. Jim and Lewis continued climbing up from behind him.

"Get down on your knees," said the man on top of the hill as Domingo got closer.

Domingo got down on his knees, placing his hands behind his head.

Jim was the first to reach him and kicked him in the back. Domingo went face-first into the rocky slope, then Jim kicked him again.

"Knock it off!" said the man in the tan hat.

The men gathered around Domingo, securing his hands behind his back with some rope, then walked him the short distance to the top of the hill. When Jim reached the other men, he looked at the one who seemed to be in charge.

"You the sheriff?" asked Jim as the men ordered Domingo back to his knees.

"I'm Mitchell, the town constable. The sheriff was killed two months ago."

"I told you that already. There ain't no sheriff anymore," said Doug.

Ben Mitchell was a tall, thinner man with a deep voice and a scar that ran from his cheekbone to his chin. He wore a light tan leather cowboy hat and black vest. Now in his early forties, he'd lived in Taos for quite some time and was a friend of Kit Carson, who had moved to Taos in 1843. Carson had recently become somewhat famous by a series of novels about his life as a mountain man. Mitchell liked Carson well enough, but he believed the stories were farfetched with very little truth to them. Mitchell, on the other hand, most certainly had seen his share of fighting and was approached for the sheriff position, but he turned it down because his wife had been seriously ill at the time. Town resident Steven Lee had taken the position only to be killed shortly thereafter.

The men gathered around, staring down at the Mexican.

"We got a man hurt over here. Needs to get to town," said Jim.

Mitchell looked over at Lewis and asked, "Can you ride?"

In obvious pain, Lewis nodded. "Yeah, believe I can."

Mitchell looked at a couple of the men with him. "You fellows head out, get him to the doc, and I'll be along shortly to chat with him."

The men headed toward their horses.

"What's your name, sir," asked Mitchell, looking down at their prisoner.

"Montoya," replied Domingo, looking up at the tall man in front of him while squinting his eyes from the sun.

"Boy, we've had enough Montoya's around here lately, haven't we, Pete?" replied Mitchell, looking at one of the men standing next to him and shaking his head.

"We sure have," the man replied with a chuckle.

Mitchell turned back toward the Mexican on the ground. "What's your given name?" asked Mitchell.

"Domingo."

"Well, Domingo, looks like a fine mess we have here," said Mitchell, adjusting his hat. He looked at the men around him. "Put him up on a horse and tie it off to mine," he said.

The men lifted Domingo onto the horse and laid him across the back, on his stomach.

"What do you want with me?" grunted Domingo.

"Just hang tight. We'll figure out what's going on here soon enough," said Mitchell.

"Those men attacked me for no reason," said Domingo.

"They said you fired first," replied Mitchell.

Domingo shook his head as he shifted his weight, trying to get more comfortable in his awkward position.

"Name is Mitchell, right, señor?" Domingo asked.

"That's right, and I'm the only authority left around here," replied Mitchell, putting a steamer in his mouth and taking a few quick puffs. "When we get back to Taos, I'll hear what you have to say." Then he went to his horse and climbed on. "Set him up in that saddle. No need to have him riding like that. His hands are tied." He waited as the men returned Domingo to an upright position in the saddle. "All right, men, let's move!" Mitchell ordered.

The group started on their way with Jim riding alongside Domingo with a sour look on his face. "Heard you come past our camp last night. You were running from something, señor," said Jim as he looked over at Domingo.

Domingo turned his head and looked at him.

"Better turn your head, boy. I'll knock you off that damn horse!" said Jim.

"Knock it off!" shouted Mitchell. "And get your ass back in line."

Jim made an angry face at Domingo, then rode up by Mitchell.

"He was riding an American soldier's horse, probably a Mexican scout or running from the American army," Jim said. "He must have killed a US soldier and took that horse."

Mitchell looked at Jim. "Why do you boys always go looking for trouble?"

Jim gave Mitchell a surprised look. "Shoot, we heard him come flying by last night and set out after him this morning. We didn't know who or what it was," he replied. Jim took off his hat and wiped his brow. "We thought it could be someone in trouble with the Indians or something."

Mitchell smiled. "So you figured firing pistols at him would help him out?"

Jim's eyebrows drew close, and his forehead creased. "That man is a murderer. Anyone can see that!"

"I'll send a messenger to Santa Fe, see if General Johnson is still there, and tell him what we got here," explained Mitchell. "Now get back in line!" he said, squinting his eyes and pointing toward the rear of the group.

Jim slowed his horse, making a face of displeasure at Mitchell. "What's that fucker mean 'you boys?' He don't even know me," he muttered to himself.

The men rode into Taos about fifteen minutes later. The townsfolk looked at the group and their prisoner with great interest, some probably thinking the man being brought in had something to do with the recent revolt and killing of their sheriff.

"Get another one of 'em, Mitchell?" said one of the bystanders.

"Not sure what we got here yet," Mitchell replied, tipping his hat. "But I'll find out."

"Where did they take Lewis?" asked Jim.

"Just up yonder to Doc Martins," said Mitchell, pointing up ahead.

Jim started off to check on his friend, and Doug followed him.

"You stay with me," said Mitchell to Doug. "They will meet up with ya soon enough," he added.

"What? Are we in trouble?" asked Doug.

Mitchell turned his horse and stopped at the hitching post in front of the jailhouse, then paused and looked over at Doug. "I don't know. Should you be?" he asked, climbing down from his horse and tying him off to the rail.

Doug climbed down from his horse while shaking his head at Mitchell's comment.

Mitchell walked to Domingo's horse and led it to the rail. Two other men climbed down from their horses and started helping Domingo down from his.

"Untie his hands," said Mitchell to his men. "He ain't going nowhere."

Mitchell looked at the Mexican and asked, "What's the name again?"

"Domingo," he replied while Pete cut the rope holding his wrists.

"That's right…Domingo," replied Mitchell, nodding his head.

Mitchell then stopped at one of his men standing close by and put his hand on his shoulder. "Grab Frank and head over to Santa Fe, find General Johnson or Sheriff Ricks, and tell 'em what we got here. See if they know anything about a Domingo Montoya."

Pete began to turn away, and Mitchell grabbed his arm. "Let 'em know he was riding a military horse," added Mitchell.

"Sure thing. We'll head out right quick," replied Pete.

Domingo

Pete headed back to his horse as Mitchell, two of his men, Domingo, and Doug went inside the jailhouse.

Domingo and Mitchell sat at a table as Mitchell's men stood by the door.

"Have a seat," said Mitchell to Doug.

"Just the same, I'd rather stand," said Doug as he glared at Domingo.

"No, I think I'd rather have you sit." Mitchell kicked a chair out from under the table with his foot.

A reluctant Doug found the seat and slid it away from Domingo as he made a disgusted face.

Mitchell opened his tobacco pouch and filled his steamer while glancing up at Domingo, then back down as he struck a match and lit his pipe. "So…Domingo," he said, putting his feet up on a stool and leaning back in the chair. "Whatcha running from?"

Domingo shook his head. "Not running. Just trying to get home."

Mitchell drew a couple puffs from the pipe, then began nodding. He put his feet back on the floor and reached for a bottle of whiskey sitting on the table, poured a little into a glass, and drank it down, then refilled it again. "Where did you get that horse?" he asked, sitting the bottle on the table and looking at Domingo.

Domingo looked Mitchell straight in the eye. "I came across it during the war, wandering near my ranch. I've had it for some time."

Mitchell picked up his second glass of whiskey and drank it down. "So, you have a ranch?"

"*Si*," replied Domingo.

"Where?" Mitchell asked.

"Below the Gila, near the Camino Real," replied Domingo.

"What do you have…steers?"

"Sheep mostly," replied Domingo.

"Oh, so you're a scab herder?" said Mitchell with a small grin.

Doug shifted in his chair, growing impatient. "Can't you see this guy is feeding us a bunch of coral dust?" he snapped. "Now, I want you to arrest him."

Mitchell looked at Doug, putting his pipe back in his mouth for another puff. "Are you through?" he asked as he pulled the steamer away from his mouth. "May I continue?"

Doug sat back in his chair and crossed his arms, staring at Mitchell.

Mitchell looked back at Domingo. "What happened this morning with these men?"

Domingo looked over at Doug and said, "I had just found a nice cool place to relax and get some sleep when they came along, hollering and shooting."

"Whatever he's saying, he's lying," said Doug with an angry face.

"You know this is a US territory now and no longer Mexico?" asked Mitchell, pouring another shot of whiskey and sliding it in front of Domingo.

Domingo gazed at the whiskey for a brief second, then reached for the glass and nodded. "*Gracias*."

Doug lowered his head then quickly looked at Mitched with his eyes squinted.

"You *are* the law around here, ain't you? Not just some highfalutin cowpuncher, right?" asked Doug, glaring at Mitchell.

Domingo

Mitchell's eyes quickly fixed on Doug as Domingo downed the whiskey.

"I mean damn, you speak that Mexican shit, give him whiskey, not listening to a damn thing I say an…an…meanwhile, I have a partner down the way with his arm nearly blown off!" Doug took his hat off. "Now, I want that man arrested and hung!" he added, hammering his index finger on the table.

Mitchell chuckled before he leaned over to refill his glass. "Now surely, Doug, you understand this man may be arrested and may be hung, but it won't be for defending himself against you." He stood from the table with the glass of whiskey. "No, sir, it won't be from that at all." He then walked over to the window. "I don't know what happened this morning and don't really care." He turned from the window and looked at Doug. "I know it's not illegal to ride by a camp, then take a nap in a cave," Mitchell said with a grin. "However illegal that may seem to you, that don't give you any right to start shooting. Now maybe he woke you from a deep slumber. And yes, that can be annoying but not against the law."

Doug shook his head in disagreement, then reached for a glass on the table.

"Your story is just not interesting to me," added Mitchell, looking over at Doug. "What is interesting to me is that military horse lying dead back there at the cave. So for that, I'm gonna hold him here for a day or two…and wait to hear something back from Johnson."

Then Mitchell made his way back to the table, where Doug was just finishing pouring a glass of whiskey for himself, and grabbed the glass of whiskey before Doug could lift it. "Thank you kindly," he said, then he lifted the glass and drank the whiskey down. Mitchell then returned to his chair and looked at Domingo. "In a couple days, if it checks out, I'll have my men escort you to the border, and when you reach it, you keep riding and don't come back through here."

Domingo nodded.

Mitchell then looked at Doug. "As for you, Doug, you and your boys are free to go," he said calmly. "And quit stirring up trouble for yourselves, and most importantly, me," he insisted, hammering his finger on the table.

Doug looked at Mitchell, then at Domingo, and without saying a word, stood from his chair, grabbed his hat, and walked out of the jailhouse.

"Lock him up, boys," said Mitchell to the two men that had been waiting nearby.

They grabbed Domingo by the arms, and Mitchell watched as they led him into the cell.

Domingo staggered into the cell and made his way to a chair inside as the men locked the gate behind him. He listened to the men talk for a few moments, then began thinking about all that had happened. He could only hope they didn't find out about Wells. He was already planning his trip back to Tucson after his escort to the border.

Señor Mitchell…not too bad, Domingo thought as leaned his head back, and a small smile came across his face.

CHAPTER 19

BUSHWHACKIN' BASTARD

The three outlaws crouched in the brush, looking down from the steep ridge at the Apache Indians grouped around a bunch of trees along the Santa Fe Trail. The Apache seemed focused in the other direction.

"What you think they're doing down there?" asked Red.

"Looks like they're waiting for someone to come along so they can ambush 'em," replied Quinn.

"What do you wanna do?"

"I wanna kill 'em," replied Quinn. He took the field glasses away from his eyes and put them in his pouch. "Eddie, you make your way down from here to get a clear shot at 'em, and be careful on those loose rocks, so they don't hear ya moving around."

"Oh, hell, let's just move on. They ain't got nothing on them worth taking." exclaimed Juan.

Quinn looked over his shoulder at Juan, who sat on his

horse a few yards back. "You can go. We can do it without you," explained Quinn.

Juan looked at Red for a second and shrugged his shoulders. "Well, all right," said a seemingly pleased Juan. "I guess I'll be seeing you fellers." He started to turn his horse.

Quinn jumped to his feet, then raised his pistol and said in an angry tone, "You go…the horse stays."

Juan stared at Quinn with a scowl on his face, shaking his head. "You ain't taking my horse, Quinn."

Quinn walked over to Juan and pointed the gun at his chest. "Get down or die," he said, staring directly at Juan with determined eyes.

Juan's eyes opened widely, then quickly turned toward Red. "Red? You just gonna stand there?"

Red looked away briefly, then stood and walked a few steps toward him. He reached for his holster and pulled his pistol, pointing it at Juan. "Get off the horse, Juan."

"You're all fucked in the head!" said an angry Juan, shaking his head in disbelief.

As Juan sat there for a few moments thinking about what to do, Quinn's patience ran out. He reached up and pulled Juan down from the saddle, then pistol-whipped him. Juan struggled for a minute, but after a few good blows to the head, he fell, motionless.

"Fucking cowardly bastard! I been sick of hearing his shit since we left Lordsburg," said Quinn. He spit on Juan as he wiped his pistol and put it back in the holster. "Tie his ass up good, and gag him just in case he wakes up," he said.

Red started tying up Juan as Eddie made his way slowly down the ridge to get a good vantage point.

Domingo

"When I put my hat on, you start shooting," ordered Quinn.

"Will do, boss," replied Eddie.

Red got on his horse and rode about fifteen feet, stopping next to Quinn, who was already in his saddle.

"All right, we're gonna ride down yonder, then turn and come right up the trail straight at 'em," explained Quinn.

Red looked around for a second, scratching his head. "Don't you think they'll either start shooting or skedaddle as soon as they see us?"

"It don't matter. Run, stay, or fight, we'll kill 'em. Now c'mon, let's go," replied Quinn.

The men rode down the back side of the ridge to avoid detection. Reaching the Santa Fe Trail, they rode right toward the Apache ambush. The Indians were focusing in the other direction, and by the time they noticed Quinn and Red, they were within fifty yards of them. The Apaches rose to their feet, and Quinn took a quick survey of them. There were four total and just two horses. The Apaches moved toward the horses tied off behind them, seeming confused by the approaching men. Quinn raised his hand in a friendly gesture, hoping to buy a few more seconds. Two Apaches climbed on their horses, and Quinn lifted his hat and placed it on his head.

Bang! A shot came from the hillside, knocking one Indian to the ground.

As the other Indians turned to look, Quinn pulled his pistol and shot another off his horse.

Red pulled his rifle and shot one of the Indians horses. When the horse reared up and tossed the Apache to the ground, he pulled his pistol and fired at the Indian several times, finally hitting him. The Indian fell to the ground, motionless.

The last Apache dashed behind a tree while shooting back at Red and Quinn, all the while looking for the other gunman on the hill. Another shot rang out from Eddie's rifle, knocking the Indian to his knees.

After a moment of silence, Quinn went over to the Apache.

He was crumpled against the tree with a bullet in his back. Blood trickled from his mouth as he gasped for air.

Quinn put his pistol to the Apache's head. "Bushwhackin' bastard!" he spat, then pulled the trigger.

The Indian collapsed to the ground, blood and brain matter splattering the tree behind him.

Quinn put his pistol in the holster and wiped the blood from his face with his bandana. He then looked up at Eddie, who stood on the hillside, and waved him down. "Grab your horse, Eddie, and come on down!" he shouted.

The horse Red had shot grunted and groaned, unable to put weight on its front leg. Red lifted his pistol and shot the horse in the head. The horse staggered for a few seconds, then fell to the ground.

"All right, Red, let's search 'em," said Quinn.

Juan had been right—there wasn't much to take. One horse and some scalps were the only things of any value.

"Bark 'em," said Quinn as he pulled his knife and started to scalp what was left of the Apache he'd shot in the head.

Red walked the few yards over to the Apache he'd shot and kicked the body over on its back. "Holy shit!"

"What is it?" asked Quinn as he turned toward Red.

"This one's a woman," replied Red, shaking his head in disappointment. "Goddamnit. I wish we knew that before we started shooting."

Domingo

"Drag her over here by my horse," shouted Quinn.

After dragging the Apache woman over by Quinn's horse, Red tied the remaining pony to his saddle horn. He then stood, watching Eddie coming down the trail toward them.

By the time Eddie reached his partners, they were about ready to leave.

Quinn reached for his field glasses.

"Where to, boss?" Eddie asked.

"Well, I don't know who these savages were waiting for, but I don't see nothing coming," said Quinn, looking in both directions. He removed the rope from the side of his saddle and walked toward the Apache woman lying on the ground. "Whoever is coming, let's leave them something to look at," he said.

Quinn got down on one knee and cut the clothing off the Apache woman. Once he had her completely naked, he tossed the rope over a tree limb hanging nearby about fifteen feet off the ground, tied the rope to her ankle, then tied the other end to his horse. The other men exchanged confused and somewhat disturbed glances, although they didn't dare say anything. As Quinn's horse pulled forward, the Apache lifted feet first in a gruesomely awkward way that made the other men turn their heads.

"Come grab this rope, boys," said Quinn.

Eddie climbed down from his mount and joined Red as they walked over to Quinn's horse, took the rope end, and tied it off to a tree while struggling to keep the Apache woman off the ground. As the two exhausted men quickly sat to catch their breath, Quinn walked over to the woman hanging from her ankle. He took his knife and cut her from waist to chest, letting her intestines spill out.

"Oh, my God," said Red, turning away again.

Quinn laughed as he turned back to his men, but his smile disappeared at the sight of Red looking the other way and not enjoying the moment. "Get up, you fuckin' chicken shits," he said angrily. Then he wiped his blade on his leg and headed for his horse.

Red and Eddie stared at each other for a second, wanting to discuss what they'd just witnessed.

"Move, goddamnit!" shouted Quinn.

The men jumped to their feet and mounted their horses.

Quinn pulled tobacco from his pouch and put it between his cheek and gum. He looked at the Apache woman hanging from the tree with blood dripping to the ground below. "Ain't she pretty, boys?" he said with a smile, then he turned his horse and rode up the trail.

Red and Eddie caught up to Quinn.

"What about Juan?" asked Red.

"Fuck him," replied Quinn.

Eddie glared at the back of Quinn's head. "You just gonna leave him up there to starve? That could take days."

Quinn smiled and looked back at Eddie. "Nah, either wolves or Apaches will get him before he starves. If it's the wolves, he'll die quickly, and if it's the Apache…" He smiled and turned his attention back to the trail ahead. "They'll probably hang him in the tree next to their squaw."

CHAPTER 20

THUNDER FROM THE SOUTH

On the second evening of his incarceration, Domingo sat across from Mitchell at a table opposite the cells, eating beans and cornbread. With still no word from Pete or General Johnson, Domingo became more relaxed and started enjoying Mitchell's company, feeling lucky to be held by what seemed to be a fair man.

Domingo scraped a few beans on his fork, then looked over at Mitchell, who was refilling his glass of tea. "When we first met at the cave, you asked me my name," said Domingo.

Mitchell looked over at him while setting down the pitcher of tea. "Yeah, I remember."

"Then you turned to another man nearby and mentioned my name, but I couldn't understand what you were discussing. It almost seemed like you recognized my name?"

Mitchell started nodding as he remembered what he and the other man were talking about. "It wasn't your first name we were discussing, but your last name," he said, lifting a piece of cornbread toward his mouth.

"What about it?" asked Domingo.

Mitchell chuckled a little as he finished chewing his cornbread and swallowed it down, then reached for his tea. "Well, a few months ago, we elected our first sheriff, and I was pretty much set to take the position, but instead, my wife came down with pneumonia. I decided to step out of the running to take care of her. So a young man named Steven, who also desired the position, got it."

Domingo nodded. "So his last name's Montoya?"

Mitchell smiled. "No, his last name was Lee. Now, the man who killed him—his last name was Montoya. Pablo Montoya." Mitchell shook his head. "Let me tell you, it's been a rough few months around here. I guess lucky for me, my wife was sick." He smiled and then began eating again. Placing an elbow on the table and pointing his fork toward Domingo, he said, "See, after General Johnson and his men took Santa Fe, it sent Mexicans running here. They decided to sack the town."

Domingo listened and nodded, looking around the room. His heart was with the Mexicans.

"Pablo led the Mexicans and some Indian savages into town, killing and scalping not only the sheriff but several officials, including my friend, Charlie, who was governor." Mitchell's brow creased, and his eyes squinted as his expression turned to anger. "Those savages scalped him right in front of his wife and kids!"

Domingo realized that while Mitchell seemed like an easygoing man, he didn't want to get on his bad side. After a few moments had passed, and Mitchell began eating, Domingo put his fork down, grabbed his glass, and took a quick drink, still riveted by the conversation. "So, what happened to them?"

Mitchell looked up at Domingo. "To the Mexicans and the savages?"

Domingo nodded.

"Well, they continued their killing streak for a couple days, eventually killing a group of miners. I'd say that was more the Indians' doing than the Mexicans, though." Mitchell tossed his fork on the plate, finished with his meal. "Until General Johnson sent a company of soldiers and some volunteers to send them running again after killing a couple hundred of them."

Domingo nodded. "And Pablo?"

"Captured him and several others of his party who had coordinated the attack," replied Mitchell.

"What did they do with them," asked Domingo, sitting his fork down beside his plate.

"The soldiers marched them right through town with drums a'beating, straight to the gallows." Mitchell smiled. "Fifteen men hanging by the neck right in the middle of town." He stood up and took his plate and Domingo's to the counter a short distance away.

Domingo ran his hand across his chin, thinking about what Mitchell had just told him and how he wished the Mexicans had won.

A few moments later, Mitchell returned to the table, carrying a bottle of whiskey and two small glasses. He then sat back in his chair, placing the glasses down in front of him. "The rest of the Mexicans and Indians fortified themselves in Mora, a town just southeast of here, and they're still there today." He poured a glass for each of them.

Domingo started thinking that if he'd known that, he would have gone there.

"It won't be long before the general sends another force to root them out, I imagine," explained Mitchell as he slid a glass of whiskey over to Domingo.

"*Gracias*, Señor Mitchell," said Domingo, lifting his glass.

"Yeah, the whole thing really started over the land Mexico gave rancheros, and they were afraid they were gonna lose it."

Domingo nodded, thinking about his own ranch.

"Well, you're a rancher, and I am sure you might have that same fear," added Mitchell.

Domingo nodded as he replied, "Yes, I do have that same fear."

Mitchell slammed his whiskey, wiping his mouth while not taking his eyes off Domingo. "See, I can understand that. But what business do those Navajo and Apache savages have coming in here?" He sat his glass back on the table, shaking his head. "Just a bunch of murderers and thieves."

"Now that I can drink too," said a smiling Domingo as he raised his glass of whiskey. Then tilting his head back, he slammed the entire glass.

Mitchell smiled back, nodding, then picked up his pipe. "Well, señor, I have to step out and hit the shit house," he said, standing up from his chair.

Domingo stood as well, knowing he had to return to his cell. He walked inside as Mitchell shut the gate, locked it, and then started for the door.

"You don't have to lock it, señor. I won't go anywhere," said Domingo with a grin.

Mitchell turned toward Domingo and smiled. "You know,

I almost believe you," he said, wagging his finger at Domingo before walking out the door.

Domingo sat in his chair, feeling pretty good. He had a little buzz from the whiskey and a full belly. After a good thirty minutes had passed and Mitchell still hadn't returned, Domingo figured he went to get more whiskey or pipe tobacco. A short time later, he laid on his bedroll and started to drift asleep until he heard the jailhouse door open. He rose to his feet and approached the gate.

First, a man Domingo didn't recognize entered, then Mitchell came in. Mitchell looked at Domingo with an expression of disappointment, and he started shaking his head while walking past the gate. Domingo turned his attention to the still wide-open front door as the two men sat down at the table. The two men began talking, but Domingo could not make out what they were saying. Then his heart sank as two soldiers entered the jailhouse. They peered at Domingo through the bars, then joined the other two men at the table. Leaning his head against the cell gate, Domingo knew he was caught. He continued listening until he heard a name he recognized— Lieutenant Wells—then he turned away from the men and leaned his back against the gate. He had spent the last two days with Mitchell and thinking of seeing Arabella soon that he'd almost forgotten he was a wanted man. He walked over to his chair and sat down, staring at the men talking about him.

The men continued talking for about another ten minutes, then stood and shook hands. The man Domingo hadn't seen before left while the two soldiers followed Mitchell toward the cell. The soldiers stopped about ten feet from the door as Mitchell approached the gate. He shook his head and looked at the floor, then back at Domingo.

"I reckon you know why they're here?"

"*Si*," replied Domingo, nodding. He stood from the chair and approached the gate.

"I guess I can't blame you for lying. I mean, what choice did you have?" said Mitchell.

With his gaze fixed on the floor, Domingo nodded and said quietly, "I wanted to tell you the truth." He smiled as he looked up at Mitchell. "But I also wanted to make that trip to the border."

Mitchell grinned a little as if agreeing with Domingo. "Well, Johnson is a fair man. Tell him exactly what happened, and who knows? Maybe you will make that trip," he replied with a nod, then reached through the gate and shook Domingo's hand. "Tell him what happened," he said again quietly.

Domingo began to wonder while shaking Mitchell's hand if he knew more than Domingo realized.

Mitchell released Domingo's hand and pulled the gate key from his pocket. As he put the key into the lock, Domingo stood back from the door. One of the soldiers pulled his pistol, and the other stepped forward to help Mitchell with the prisoner. The door opened, and Domingo extended his hands out in front of him. The soldier put iron clasps around Domingo's wrists and led him out of the cell, Mitchell slowly following, as all four men went outside to three waiting horses. Mitchell helped Domingo onto a horse tied off to one of the soldier's horses, then waited as the soldiers climbed up on their mounts. The soldiers looked back at Mitchell, who stood alongside the horse carrying his new Mexican friend.

"Thanks for your help in catching this scoundrel," one of the soldiers said.

"No problem. Give my best to the general," replied Mitchell, raising his hand.

The soldier nodded and then turned to the soldier alongside him. "C'mon, Private. The general is waiting."

The soldiers' horses began to move as Mitchell stared up at Domingo and reached up to pat him on the shoulder. The line drew tight as Domingo's horse lunged forward.

Domingo turned around several times, looking back at the man he got to know so well over the last couple of days. Mitchell stood and watched them ride away, his tan leather hat in his hand at his side. Then a stagecoach blocked Domingo's view for just a few seconds, and the man was gone.

The two soldiers led their Mexican prisoner southwest about twenty miles, following the Rio Grande River. It was smooth, easy traveling until they reached a point where the river continued west, and they needed to go straight south toward Santa Fe. The ground quickly became rocky and hilly, with several steep drops the men had to navigate around. There was a lot more brush and low trees as the men ducked their way south, and the sun dipped low in the west. Having ridden for over seven hours, the soldiers were plenty tired. They decided to make camp by the Pecos River, about fifteen miles from Santa Fe, figuring they'd have no trouble reaching Santa Fe early the next morning. Following the smooth ground along the river for a short while before reaching the Santa Fe Trail, it would make for a nice, easy ride come daybreak.

As the river came into view, Corporal Stevens found a nice spot to set up for the night. The area he chose had a nice open area with plenty of trees and loose brush to start a fire. With the river nearby, they could wash off the trail dust and water the horses. Also, there was a nice patch of healthy grass the horses could graze on. Stevens climbed down from his horse and led it to the water's edge. He tied his horse off to a nearby pine tree and made his way back to Private Maydew, now just a short distance away.

"We'll camp here tonight," he said as he grabbed gear from Maydew's horse.

Looking around in every direction, Maydew asked, "Any chance we'll see Indians through here?"

Stevens shook his head and replied, "No, not through here. Most of them have gone south."

"I don't know…maybe we should just keep on riding?" added Maydew while still looking around.

"Never make it in the dark. Besides, that would be another five hours, and the horses need to rest. C'mon, help set up camp."

Maydew climbed down from his horse, then tied the horse off to the pine tree and went to the prisoner's horse. "Guess we're camping here tonight," he said, sounding disappointed.

Stevens glared over at Domingo, still sitting in his saddle. "Get down from that horse!" he said, drawing his pistol.

Domingo turned in the saddle, lifted one leg over the horse's neck, and jumped down. He lost his balance as he hit the ground—since his wrists were still clamped with the irons—and stumbled, then fell to his knees.

Stevens laughed at him, and Maydew followed his lead. As the men snickered, Stevens put his pistol back in the holster.

Domingo grabbed some dirt up in his hands, turned, and threw it into Stevens's face.

Domingo

"Bastard!" yelled Stevens between spitting out dirt and wiping his eyes.

Domingo jumped to his feet and charged Maydew. Taken off guard, the private looked down to get his pistol out as the prisoner raised his iron-clad hands and came down on the back of his neck. Maydew dropped to the ground, and Domingo went for the soldier's gun. Although Maydew was dazed and in pain, he held on tight to the pistol as Domingo tried to wrestle it away.

"Shoot 'im!" yelled Maydew.

Domingo let go of the pistol and made a dash for the river, but at the bank, he lost his footing and fell into the water. As he tried to stand and continue fleeing, Stevens caught up to him. Domingo looked back for a quick second as Stevens's pistol came down hard on his temple. Dazed, he still tried to escape into the river, but Stevens came down on his head again, this time bringing him to a stop.

Maydew waded into the shallow water, where the prisoner's body lay half in and half out, as Stevens struck Domingo again and again with his pistol. He had no intention of stopping until the Mexican was dead. Both soldiers kicked and punched Domingo over and over until Maydew stepped back and stood silent while Stevens continued.

Maydew finally grabbed Stevens and pulled him back just enough that his kicks subsided.

"Let me go!" yelled Stevens as he pulled his arm out of Maydew's grasp.

"No, wait!" said Maydew, grabbing Stevens again.

"Let me go!" Stevens elbowed Maydew in the face.

The private let go and grabbed his nose. "The general!" he shouted.

Stevens grabbed Domingo by the back of the shirt, ready to land yet another blow to his head, then looked up at Maydew.

"General Johnson, sir. He wants this prisoner alive, remember?" said Maydew, wiping blood from his nose.

Stevens knew if he killed the Mexican, he would be in a world of trouble. With his pistol ready to come down on Domingo's head, he let go of the shirt, and Domingo's face fell into the water. Blood poured from his face and head. Stevens stood up straight, then walked out of the water. As he passed by Maydew, he stopped for a second as if he had something to say, but then he just continued toward his horse and gear.

Maydew rushed to Domingo's aid, raising his head from the water so he wouldn't drown, then dragged him ashore.

"Is he dead?" asked Stevens.

Maydew placed his ear by Domingo's mouth, then replied, "He's still breathing, thank God." He looked back at Stevens, who was clearing dirt from his eyes.

"Just drag him by that tree there and tie him up," said Stevens as he poured water onto his face from the canteen. "He ain't going nowhere now unless a bear takes him."

Maydew grabbed Domingo by his bloodied shirt and dragged him to the tree, then went to his horse and grabbed a rope and his canteen. After tying Domingo securely to the tree, he poured water onto Domingo's face to rinse some of the blood and dirt away. Domingo didn't respond. Maydew then laid his canteen by Domingo's side and went to help Stevens set up camp.

Stevens tossed Maydew a rag for his bloody nose and stood, glaring at the prisoner.

Maydew glared at Stevens as he wiped his face.

Domingo

Sensing Maydew's disapproval, Stevens said, "Mexican son of a bitch could have killed us." He pointed a stern finger at the private. "And don't think for a second he wouldn't have if he'd gotten that gun away from you!"

Maydew nodded his agreement, flinching and then moving his head back and forth in pain.

Stevens removed his saddle and set it down on the ground, then gestured for Maydew to sit as he said, "Sit here and rest a sec, and let me take a look."

Maydew sat on the ground with his back against the saddle and let Stevens examine his neck.

"Aw, hell, it ain't nothing. Just rest up. I'll go round up some wood for a fire," said Stevens, then he walked toward some nearby trees.

Within a couple hours, the soldiers laid out their bedrolls near the campfire and lay down, gazing up at all the stars on the clear, cool night. In the distance, they saw a flash of lightning followed by a low rumble of thunder from the south.

Domingo woke several times from the rumbling thunder and rain that came down quite heavily at times during the night. His head pounded from the blows he'd taken from the soldier's pistol. He tried looking up at the sky, but his eyes were completely swollen shut. He did his best to wiggle free from the ropes holding him to the tree, but with no luck. He hoped Indians or Mexican bandits would come by and kill the soldiers while they were sleeping. Even if they didn't free him, he would just be happy to hear the soldiers scream in pain while fighting for their lives.

In the early morning hours, just as the sun began to break,

Corporal Stevens nudged Maydew awake. The men packed up their gear, then approached Domingo. Stevens tied a long leather strap to the irons on Domingo's wrists and tied it to the back of his horse, then Private Maydew untied Domingo from the tree as the prisoner climbed to his feet.

"Hope you got a good night's sleep, asshole, 'cause you're gonna ride the shank's mare the rest of the way," Stevens said with a grin.

"That's a long walk to Santa Fe," said Maydew. He raised an eyebrow, then shook his head.

"What do you mean? It's a beautiful day for a walk," said Stevens, looking up at the sky. "Clear skies. I bet it don't get one degree over ninety," he said with a chuckle.

The two soldiers climbed on their horses and moseyed along the bank of the river with Domingo in tow. After a good half hour, they reached the Santa Fe Trail, which would take them straight into town. As the two men rode along, Domingo tried his best to keep up with them so the strap didn't pull on his wrists, which were beginning to bleed from the constant stress of the shackles. Making it even more difficult to keep up, his eyes were mostly swollen shut, which made it hard for him to see the ground in front of him. Most of his vision was blurry as he tilted his head around several ways, trying to see around him.

About another twenty minutes into their trip, they came across an Apache woman. She hung naked and gutted from a tree above a few dead Apache men and a horse lying on the ground. The soldiers' horses came to a halt.

"What the fuck happened here?" asked Stevens.

Stevens and Maydew looked all around to make sure whoever had done this wasn't close by.

"Fuck this. Let's keep moving," added Stevens.

Maydew replied, "Yeah, let's keep moving." Pulling his bandana up over his nose.

Domingo began wishing whoever had done this would return and do the same to the soldiers. The strap to his wrists pulled tight, and he fell to the ground. He was dragged about ten feet before he recovered his stance. He grimaced in pain as another round of fresh blood began to creep out around his shackles.

Stevens looked back and grinned at Domingo, then lifted his canteen and took a quick drink. He poured some around his neck. "Ah, that's good," he said with a smile, then he turned back around toward the trail ahead.

CHAPTER 21

PERSEVERANCE

Just a half-mile from Santa Fe by midafternoon, the three prospectors noticed several US soldiers riding toward them. Joe rode out to meet them. After a short time, he rode back to his comrades, who had been caring for their wounds and drinking from their canteens while they waited.

"Looks like they want us to head that way into Santa Fe," said Joe, pointing toward the east side of town. "I guess there is a new fort up ahead there, and they don't want us riding through."

"Did you tell them about the war party out there ambushing people? Maybe they could do something about it?" asked Henry.

"Yeah, I mentioned it, but they didn't seem to give a fuck. Said we didn't look like we been ambushed and laughed," answered Joe. "I reckon they only care about the Mexican army right now." He looked back at the soldiers trotting away in the distance. "Assholes," he mumbled, then turned toward Henry. "C'mon, let's get moving."

Henry shook his head, then snapped the reins.

The men continued toward town, and within thirty minutes, they arrived in front of the jailhouse.

Joe rode alongside the wagon and took notice of their prisoner awake and sitting up. Tower's face and head had covered the wagon floor with blood. Although in bad condition with hands and feet already tied, Joe wasn't taking any chances. He instructed Bill and Henry to tie him to the rail in the wagon so he couldn't escape. After watching them secure the prisoner, he removed his hat and turned toward Henry. "How you feelin', ol' boy?"

"Like hell. I think my collar bone is broken, and I still can't close my mouth all the way without it hurtin'," replied Henry.

Joe nodded and looked over at Bill. "Bill, you take Henry to see the doc, and I'll go have a word with the sheriff."

"Sounds good," replied Bill.

Bill and Henry climbed down from the wagon and made their way down the dusty street. Patrons passing by couldn't help but stare at the battered men as they passed.

Joe dismounted and tied his horse to the hitching post at the jailhouse, then walked up on the porch and went inside, finding the sheriff sitting at a table and talking to a gentleman. When he entered, the men stopped talking and looked at him. The sheriff was a bearded, overweight, squinty-eyed man with a distinguished look about him.

"And how can I help you, sir?" asked the sheriff, looking around the man dressed in fine clothes and smoking a pipe seated in front of him.

"The name is Joe Carson. I have a couple men with me,

and we were ambushed by Indians about fifteen miles from here."

"The name is Ricks," said the sheriff, taking a moment to look Jim over from head to toe. "Well, you seem fine now." He smiled, lifting his hands and shrugging his shoulders.

Joe bit down on his lip, then shook his head. It was the second time someone had made light of his near-death experience, and he was getting irritated. "We weren't actually ambushed, but real close to it," he said, widening his eyes and nodding. "About that close!" he added, raising his hand and putting a little space between his thumb and index finger.

The sheriff made a puzzled face, then looked at the man seated in front of him.

The man quickly shrugged his shoulders.

The sheriff scratched his cheek, then leaned back in his chair. "Sir, I guess I'll have to ask again…how may I help you?"

"One of my men was badly hurt, and I have one of the Indian bushwhackers in the back of my wagon right outside this door," said Joe pointing behind him.

The sheriff made a disappointed face and started to get up from his chair.

The other man grabbed his things off the desk and said, "I will catch up with you later, Sheriff." He quickly headed toward the door.

"Sounds good, George," replied the sheriff.

George shuffled toward Joe, still standing by the entrance, and said, "Good day, sir."

Joe simply nodded while holding the door open for the gentlemen.

"Okay, let's see what you got out there," said Sheriff Ricks as he adjusted his gun belt.

The two men walked outside and to the wagon, and the sheriff stopped abruptly when he saw the Indian. "Whoa now! You know who you have there?"

"His name is Tawah, a Navajo scout," answered Joe.

"Not hardly," said Ricks as he examined the Indian closer.

Joe looked at the Indian and then back at the sheriff with a puzzled expression. "Well, who is he then?"

"That's no Navajo, boy. That's an Apache," said Ricks, smiling and shaking his head in disbelief.

"Well, whatever. It's the same thing, isn't it?" answered Joe.

"Maybe to some, but this ain't no ordinary Apache," said Ricks, looking back at Joe.

"That's Mangas Coloradas, but you might know him better as Red Sleeves," said Ricks.

Joe looked at the Indian in the wagon and shook his head, trying to grasp what the sheriff told him. "Mother fucker," he whispered. Then almost instantly, he became excited. "Holy hot damn! Are you sure?"

"Damn sure! He's famous through these parts. I'm surprised you dip shits didn't know him when you saw him. Even more surprised you're still alive," said Sheriff Ricks, still wide-eyed. After a few more moments of gazing at the Apache in the wagon, Ricks turned back to Joe with his head tilted and eyes squinting. "So, tell me how you ended up with ol' Red Sleeves?"

"Well, we met this half-breed Navajo in Madrid, near Cedar Mountain mine, and hired him as a scout. Half Breed told us of a secret spot where there's gold, so we paid him to take us there. Then when we got close to leaving, he said he wanted to bring this one along," explained Joe, pointing at Red Sleeves.

"How many in your party again?" asked Ricks.

"There's three of us."

Ricks scratched his head, looking confused. "You and two other men fought off Red Sleeves and some of his warriors?"

"No. See, we spotted the ambush before we reached it, so we attempted to take him and Half Breed prisoner before they could alert their friends. Well, that was the plan anyway, but Half Breed didn't make it," said Joe, shrugging his shoulders.

"Where is the half-breed now?" asked Ricks.

"Out on the plains, I suppose, unless the ambush party took him."

"Well, you may not of hit gold, but Silver City Mining Company is offering a $2500 reward for Red Sleeves," said Ricks with a nod to Joe. "And General West will be damn happy to hear we got Red Sleeves, for sure. He is one Apache-hating bastard." He chuckled. "Can't blame him, though. They are dreadful. Now help me bring him inside and then get this damn wagon out of here."

Joe Carson was more than happy to hear about the reward. He helped the sheriff drag the badly injured Red Sleeves inside and throw him to the cell floor.

"Good enough," said Ricks. "Now, I want you boys to stay close the next couple days until I can get this reward worked out. I got some piece of shit Mexican coming this way and like to have this wrapped up as soon as I can."

"Another prisoner?" asked Joe.

"Yeah, I guess he killed a US officer, and the general at the fort outside of town wants him," said Ricks, shaking his head in disgust. "All I need now is a couple chinks and a nigger, and I would be completely miserable."

"What do you plan to do about the Apache war party we ran into?" asked Joe.

"Not shit!" answered Ricks. "You got the only important one."

"What if they come looking for him?" asked Joe.

Sheriff Ricks thought about it for a few moments, then started to get worried about his own ranch just outside Santa Fe. In addition to the large ranch, he had plenty of money from the general store he owned in town as well as a hefty inheritance left by his family. This was the main reason he held the position of sheriff in Santa Fe. The position may have been easy to buy, but it was not as easy to keep. Santa Fe had recently been placed under American control, and many residents were not happy with the new change of order. In the nearby town of Taos, the sheriff and governor had been killed in a recent uprising. Sheriff Ricks feared the same could happen in his town if not for the presence of Johnson and his men.

Ricks was not the type of man to put himself in harm's way. When there was a little fuss, say at the saloon, he would ask the bartender to stop serving, and soon enough, things would cool down. He had pulled his pistol recently to arrest a horse thief, but only after he'd had the bartender give the thief several drinks on the house until the man nearly passed out. When Ricks had gone to cuff him, the thief had perked up, grabbed a stool, and knocked the hell out of Ricks. Fortunately, a couple of bystanders had grabbed the thief to defend their sheriff. Ricks had been so angry and humiliated that he'd pulled his gun from the holster and put the barrel to the thief's cheek.

Domingo

"You li'l bastard! I'll kill you right now!" a red-faced Ricks had yelled.

Within a few seconds, he'd regained his composure and finished cuffing the thief, but the townsfolk still talked about that night while making fun of ol' Ricks. At the saloon every now and then, someone would mock Ricks by saying, "You li'l bastard! I'll kill you right now." Then the saloon patrons would break out laughing. However, there was no laughing today. With the fear of a revolt, the military presence, and the outlaws to be hung, the people were on edge.

Ricks said, "Hey, where you boys gonna stay the next couple days?"

"Hotel, I suppose," answered Joe.

"Nah, come out to my place. You boys can stay there," said Ricks. "I have plenty o' room for ya."

"That's awfully kind, Sheriff," answered Joe.

"You boys being such good Apache hunters, it would be nice to have you around until this blows over. Besides, I could use a little help around the place," said Ricks with a grin.

"Well, if being an Apache hunter gets us a free bed, food, and money, then that's what we are," said Joe, holding back a laugh.

"Red sleeves." Ricks shook his head. "Goddamn, you're one lucky bastard."

"I reckon so," replied Joe with a chuckle.

"Okay, go find your boys and come back here around five, and we'll head out," said Ricks.

"Sounds good, Sheriff. I appreciate your help," said Joe as he walked to the door.

The sheriff sauntered over to his desk, pulled off his boots, poured a small glass of whiskey, and sat back in his chair. He looked over at Red Sleeves when the Indian said something to him in Apache while moaning in pain.

"Shut the hell up!" shouted Ricks as he threw one of his dirty boots at the cell door.

Arriving late in Tucson with Jose and Luis, an emotionally and physically exhausted Arabella all but collapsed into Maria and Vicente's arms when they answered the door. They helped her inside as Jose took their horses around to the barn, and Luis guided the two girls inside behind their mother. They placed Arabella on the couch, and she curled up on her side with her hands over her face. Vicente and Maria both sat by her as Maria drew her close, placing her hands on Arabella's back and shoulder, trying to console the grief-stricken woman. Vicente looked back and forth at Arabella and Luis, his eyes wide and mouth hanging open, awaiting an explanation.

Arabella struggled through telling them the horrific story. Luis pulled a chair close to them and helped when she could not continue. Maria and Vicente wept about Marcello and tried their best to comfort Arabella. After a lengthy discussion and plenty of tears, Maria led Arabella and the girls to the back room for some much-needed rest.

Vicente accompanied Luis and Jose over to Pedro's home next door. After explaining to Pedro what had happened, he arranged for the ranch hands to stay in Pedro's extra bedroom. The plan was for Luis and Jose to head back to the ranch after breakfast the next morning to sell the sheep, and then they would return to meet up with Domingo before he took his family deeper into Mexico.

Vicente stayed up alone that night, worrying about his brother and hoping he would see Domingo walk through the door at any moment. As the hours ticked by, he eventually fell asleep in a chair by the front door.

"Papá?" said Raul, placing his hand on his father's arm.

Vicente opened his eyes and drew his son close to him. After embracing for a few moments, he told his son what had happened. A visually shaken Raul pulled up a chair beside his father, and the two eventually fell back asleep in their chairs, side by side.

As the sun announced a new day, Arabella stood and stared out the window behind the couch. She soon spotted Luis and Jose getting their horses ready for the ride home. She went outside and approached them as they were filling their saddlebags.

"You can stop packing. We're staying here one more night," she said.

Jose and Luis gave her a puzzled look.

"We really should be getting back to the herd, Arabella," replied Luis.

"And we will, tomorrow morning," said Arabella with a smile.

"We?" asked Luis as his brows drew together.

"Yes," replied Arabella. "I have lost enough, and I refuse to lose anymore. If you will return with me and help me rebuild the barn and repair the fences, I will make you partners. You have been there for me and Domingo through the years, and we owe you that much."

"Domingo might likely be there when we return. How will he feel about this partnership?" asked Jose.

Arabella thought about it briefly, then looked at the men with even more determination. "When my husband returns, it won't change a thing," she replied. "From now on, the success of the ranch will be shared equally."

Luis and Jose smiled and hugged Arabella, thanking her for her kindness.

About that time, Pedro came walking out of his house. "You boys about to head out?" he asked from his porch while stretching his arms and back.

Luis turned and answered, "No, it looks like we're gonna stay another night."

Pedro trotted down the steps toward Arabella. "That sounds like a fine idea," he said, stopping in front of her and placing his hand on her shoulder. "How you holding up?"

"Better today," she answered, tears welling in her eyes.

Camille emerged from Vicente's house and announced breakfast was ready.

Pedro followed alongside Arabella toward the house.

"We'll be there in just a few," said Jose as he and Luis picked up some of their belongings and headed toward Pedro's porch.

As Arabella and Pedro reached the door still held open by Camille, Pedro placed his hand on top of the young girl's head and smiled at her.

Camille gave an awkward smile and swiftly moved away

from the strange man while looking back at him from a distance.

"Camille, this is Pedro. You remember him, don't you? He helped your father on the fences last summer," said Arabella.

Camille shook her head and rushed off to the kitchen.

"Sorry. She is upset and misses her father," said Arabella. "Like we all do," she added while staring aimlessly off into the distance.

"No apology needed, Arabella. I know all of you are hurting, and my heart aches for you," said Pedro as he and Arabella continued toward the dining room.

While everyone gathered around the table, Arabella made her decision known to Vicente and Maria. At first, Maria tried to convince Arabella to stay, but Arabella made it clear that her mind was made up. Vicente and Pedro offered to return with her and help rebuild the ranch. She quickly said that was not necessary, explaining that they would be fine with Luis and Jose, and Domingo would be returning soon.

Vicente smiled and reached for Arabella's hand and kissed it. "You are an amazing woman, Arabella," he said.

Pedro looked down at his plate, moving the fork in different directions with no interest in eating. He then looked over at Arabella and said with a smile, "It's really no trouble, Arabella. You could use the extra hands."

Arabella turned toward Pedro, placing her hand on his arm. "We will be fine," she said with a smile, then she turned to Maria and began discussing the day's plans.

Pedro's smile disappeared. He set his fork down, leaned back in his chair, and folded his arms.

After breakfast, Jose and Luis purchased a two-horse wagon in town with money Arabella had given them and filled it with supplies. Arabella spent most of the day with Maria and all the kids, visiting shops in town and walking along the river.

Later that evening, back at Vicente's home, Arabella and her two girls packed up their belongings and placed them in a pile by the front door. The whole family gathered in the living room, talking as the younger children played together around the house. Still visibly upset about his cousin Marcello and his uncle Dom, Raul sat closely by his mother, and she held his hand.

After saying goodnight to Vicente, Maria, and the children, Arabella went to the kitchen and got a glass of water for herself and milk for the girls, bustling them off to the bedroom. She tucked Laila in and then sat on the bed to change Camille into her nightdress, but Camille climbed up next to her and asked about her papá. Arabella tried to hold back tears as she explained her father had to leave but would return as soon as he could. Camille talked about how Papá would throw her high in the air and catch her. Arabella lay back on the bed, and Camille cuddled up next to her.

"Mama, are we going to have animals again?" asked Camille.

"Of course," answered Arabella as she ran her fingers through the young girl's hair. "Sweetie, we still have our sheep, horses, and chickens, and let's not forget about Scratchy."

Camille smiled wide. "We should have brought him with us."

Arabella quickly answered, "He will be just fine for a couple days." She turned toward her daughter. "Besides, he is protecting the sheep."

Camille chuckled. "Not hardly."

Arabella smiled.

"Mama, can I get my own horse?"

Arabella smiled at Camille. "Someday, honey. I promise."

Arabella rose from the bed, pulling the blanket from under her daughter. Camille smiled as her mother tucked her under the covers.

"Now get some sleep. We have a long day ahead of us tomorrow," said Arabella.

"Goodnight, Mama. I love you."

Arabella kissed Camille's forehead. "I love you too," she said. Then she leaned over and kissed the already sleeping Laila goodnight and whispered, "Goodnight, sweetie. I love you."

Arabella lay in her bed across from the girls, thinking of what else she may need to bring with them, when she heard a light tap on the door. She slowly climbed out of bed, careful not to disturb the girls, then walked quietly to the door and opened it slightly.

"Hey, did I wake you?" asked Pedro.

Arabella fussed with her hair and covered herself the best she could with the robe Maria had loaned her. "No, Pedro. I wasn't asleep yet," she whispered.

Pedro stood, searching for the correct words for a second.

"Anything else?" whispered Arabella, shaking her head, her eyes wide.

Pedro smiled. "Want to have a drink and talk for a bit?"

Arabella looked back into the room to make sure the kids were still sleeping. "Well, I…um… Hang on. Let me change, and I'll be right out," she said, quietly closing the door.

A couple minutes later, Arabella moved quietly through the house, looking for Pedro. Finding him on the back porch with two drinks poured and a lit cigar hanging from his mouth, she sat down on the wooden bench next to him.

Handing Arabella a glass, Pedro said, "Are you really heading back down there?"

Arabella nodded, then smiled up at him. "I reckon I am." She cocked her head. "If it doesn't work there, I'll probably return to Guadalajara. It would be nice to see my family again. It's been so long now." She raised the glass for a sip.

Pedro smiled. "It's been a while since I've been there too. I doubt much has changed, though."

Arabella nodded, then looked at Pedro.

Pedro looked back at her with longing in his eyes.

Arabella stared back until she sensed he was going to kiss her. Holding her hand up, she said, "Pedro, you must understand."

Pedro nodded, then tilted his head and said, "Arabella, Domingo is a great man. Strong and smart, and I truly hope he does return because I know you love him dearly."

A tear fell from Arabella's eye. "Yes, I do," she replied as she wiped her cheek.

"But I don't want you to be alone down there," said Pedro.

Arabella took another drink. "I won't be alone. I have Jose, Luis, and the girls. Besides, I fear nothing or no one, and I'm quite handy with a pistol."

Pedro giggled.

Taking offense, Arabella said with authority, "I am!"

Pedro put his hands up and giggled some more.

"Now listen, Pedro. I'm going inside if you don't stop it."

Pedro tried to cover his smile and be serious. "I'm sorry, Arabella. I've just never seen you shoot a pistol before." Still grinning, he lifted his glass to his lips.

Arabella quipped, "Well, you haven't exactly been around me a lot in the last fifteen years."

Pedro raised his glass and touched it to hers. "I'll drink to that. Fifteen years? That's nothing!"

Arabella took a quick drink and replied, "You will drink to anything."

They both laughed for a moment, then things got quiet again.

"Arabella," said Pedro, "I would like to go with you tomorrow. I will work hard and earn my keep."

Arabella sat quietly, thinking for a few moments, then said, "I don't know…"

"I just want to make sure you are safe. I will help you take care of the animals, rebuild the barn; help with the girls," added Pedro.

Arabella shook her head. "And what happens when Domingo shows up?"

"I will leave," replied Pedro. "Besides, Domingo would be glad I was there to help his family."

Arabella gave Pedro a funny look and started to say something but stopped. She looked out across the backyard for a moment, then said, "Okay, fine. You can come, but you have to sleep in the dice house with Luis and Jose. There is no way you're sleeping inside the house."

"That's fine with me, and when the barn is finished, I'll sleep in there," replied Pedro.

Though she didn't want Pedro in the house in case Domingo returned, part of her had wanted Pedro to come with her. At the very minimum, he would be great company, and they could talk about the old times, which she'd always enjoyed.

"Okay, it's a deal. I will pay you for your help," said Arabella.

"I'm an American now. You can't afford me," said Pedro with a smile.

"You are less an American as you are a human," replied Arabella.

Pedro nodded his head, smiling. "Just consider it a friend helping a friend."

"Fine," replied Arabella.

"It's settled then," said Pedro, turning toward her as he raised his glass and smiled from ear to ear.

Arabella smiled back. "I guess you'll drink to that as well, huh?"

Camille came out the back door and whined, "Mama? What are you doing?"

Arabella put her glass down and walked over to her. "Coming to bed right now, honey. Goodnight, Pedro," she said with a smile as she walked inside.

Pedro raised his glass and replied, "Goodnight." He then

Domingo

poured what remained in Arabella's glass into his and relit his cigar. Leaning back in his chair, he looked up at the stars and grinned. "What a pretty night," he whispered. Still looking up, he began wondering where Domingo was under all those stars. Then he saw a flash of light across the sky, followed by a low roar of thunder from the south. By the time he finished his cigar, the rain had started coming down heavily, and he quickly made his way back to his house.

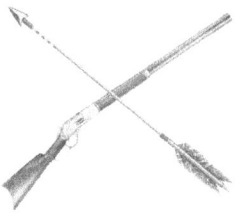

CHAPTER 22
WELCOME TO SANTA FE

As the soldiers' horses dragged Domingo by the irons clamped around his wrists, he struggled to stay on his feet. He often fell to the dirt only to be dragged until he could regain his stance. His wrists dripped blood on the ground in front of him, and his arms were bleeding so badly it looked like he was wearing a red-sleeved shirt. His clothes were ragged, and his face was covered in dirt. The outlaw cussed at the men dragging him while keeping a smile on his face to get under their skin.

The townsfolk stared at them as they made their way through town, and the soldiers smiled and tipped their hats.

When they reached the jailhouse, the horses stopped. Domingo collapsed to the ground, then unsuccessfully tried to get back up.

A young boy across the street rushed to his aid.

"Get back! That man is dangerous! A murderer!" shouted one of the soldiers.

Ignoring the soldier, the young boy pulled a hankie from his pocket and handed it to the outlaw.

The Mexican squinted as he lifted his head to see who was helping him, but he couldn't make out anything more than a silhouette. "*Gracias*," said the outlaw as the boy ran off.

With little strength left in him, Domingo lay on the ground, exhausted, dirty, and bleeding.

On the front porch of the jailhouse sat General Ezra Johnson, the commander at Fort Marcy in Santa Fe. Johnson was a tall drink of water with a tapered beard that came to a point at his chin. His hair was neatly kept and matched his striking facial features. Dark blue, his suit was decorated with many gold buttons to show his well-earned military status.

With the war coming to an end, Johnson had been looking forward to returning to Oregon until a few days ago, when he'd received news that Lieutenant Wells was dead and the Mexican lying on the ground in front of him was responsible. Although the details were unclear, the soldiers claimed a Mexican man had attacked Wells while he was asleep. When Domingo was spotted just days later with a military horse, it appeared they'd caught their man. Even though Johnson hadn't always seen eye to eye with Wells, he still found himself struggling with his death. He knew if the Mexican lying on the ground in front of him had killed Wells, he would surely have to hang. The majority of Wells's brigade would be arriving in the next couple days, so Johnson had decided to keep Domingo at the jail in Santa Fe until the soldier who witnessed the attack could identify him as the killer.

Domingo

The general stood from his rocking chair and walked out to the soldiers.

Corporal Stevens and Private Maydew saluted Johnson, then turned toward Domingo as he finally managed to get to his knees, head hanging down.

"Here he is, sir, the filthy, murdering scoundrel," said Stevens.

General Johnson looked angrily at the corporal. "Mr. Stevens, get down from that damn horse and hand him your canteen!"

Stevens looked puzzled. "Sir? This man killed—"

"On the double, Corporal!" barked the general.

Stevens jumped down from his horse and walked his canteen over to Domingo.

"I hope you didn't drag him all the way here from Taos," said the general.

"Um…no, sir," said a nervous Maydew. "He tried to escape last night and hit me right on the back of my neck, sir."

Maydew tried to show the general his neck, but Johnson showed very little interest. Instead, he watched Corporal Stevens as he tossed his canteen down in front of Domingo and started back toward his horse.

"Help him drink, Corporal," said Johnson.

"Sir?" quipped Stevens. Now angry, he kept his gaze focused on the ground for fear Johnson would see the animosity on his face.

"Mr. Stevens, when you were asked to deliver him here, he was to be *on* a horse, not *dragged* by one."

Stevens was now standing at attention.

"Now you help this man drink, or I'll have you brought

up on charges!" General Johnson stared hard at the corporal, then said sternly, "Do you understand?"

More than willing now, Stevens replied, "Yes, sir!"

"Then move!" barked Johnson. Well aware of Stevens's service under Wells in Texas and here in New Mexico, he could understand the corporal's anger toward the man accused of killing Wells, but he was the type of man who played by the book, even though it was not always the most popular way.

Domingo was not sure why the general came down on his own men for his sake. He guessed maybe the man felt sorry for him or perhaps knew of what Lieutenant Wells and his men had done to his family. Whatever the reason, it felt good to be treated like a human, even if only for a few moments. He helped the soldier place the canteen to his mouth and took large gulps as if the water was air, paying little attention to the sand and blood he washed down his throat as he guzzled the canteen dry. Wiping his mouth with his hand, he slowly made his way to his feet. When he could not walk on his own, General Johnson ordered the soldiers to help him up the stairs.

Sheriff Ricks looked up from his newspaper, taking a long draw from his cigar as General Johnson walked through the front door. Taking his feet from the desk, he nodded to the general and closed his newspaper while glancing beyond the general, at the prisoner.

"That's him, huh?" asked Ricks while removing his spectacles and placing them beside the newspaper. "That's one dirty bastard. Damn, he's gonna dirty up my cell."

Domingo

"Hello again, Sheriff," said General Johnson as he reached across the desk to shake hands.

"Nice to see you again, General," said Ricks, accepting the general's hand.

"I appreciate you holding him here," said Johnson, nodding toward the prisoner being held up under each of his arms while his head hung limp.

Sheriff Ricks nodded, trying to hide his disappointment with the situation. "No problem, General. I'm just glad ya'll are here. Those goddamn Mexicans and Indian savages are causing me a heap of grief around here! Just the other day, had some damn Apache bushwhackers a few miles out of town waiting for innocent folks to ride by."

Johnson looked down at the cigars sitting on the desk. "May I?" he asked with a glance up at the sheriff.

"Help yourself," replied Ricks.

Johnson picked up a cigar and sat down in a nearby chair. The soldiers waited just inside the door, still holding up Domingo, as the general lit the cigar and took a large puff. Pulling the cigar from his mouth, Johnson looked at it and then nodded to Ricks, signaling he liked the flavor.

"Sheriff, I have a favor to ask of you," said Johnson.

"What can I do for you, General?"

"Will you make sure this man is given food and water?" asked Johnson.

"Sure will," replied Ricks.

"Also, some clean towels, bandages, and a shirt, if possible?"

Ricks thought for a moment while adjusting his hat, then answered, "I'll see what I can do."

Johnson signaled his men to bring Domingo to the cell behind the sheriff's desk.

The sheriff shifted around in his chair, making what seemed to be a great effort to get out of it, then walked to the gate and unlocked it. The soldiers drug Domingo into the cell and laid him onto a small cot inside.

Johnson followed the men into the cell. "Stevens, Maydew, remove his cuffs and his boots," he said, pointing at Domingo's hands and feet.

Maydew pulled the prisoner's boots off gently while Stevens jerked the prisoner's forearms up and roughly removed the cuffs from his wrists. Stevens then stood back from the prisoner, carefully looking away from the general to hide his angry red face.

Johnson stepped closer to the Indian sitting knees up and head down in the corner of the cell, looking him over. "You, sir," he said.

The Indian sat still.

"That's Chief Red Sleeves. Colonel West wants him to hang," said Sheriff Ricks.

"I know who he is, and Colonel West would have them all hang if he could. Why is he injured so badly and not been cleaned up?" replied Johnson.

The Apache prisoner slowly lifted his head and looked at the men talking about him.

"They said ol' Red Sleeves here came in their camp, guns a-blazing. Killed two miners and seriously wounded a few more." Ricks pointed at the chief and made a gun sound, jerking his hand simultaneously for effect, then smiled. "And with no reason at all. Oh, except to kill more white folks, of course." He shook his head, then looked at Domingo and snickered. "Funny thing is, one of those men was a Mexican half-breed. At least that's how the miners explained it to me."

General Johnson knelt down to get a better look at the Indian's injuries, then shook his head in disbelief. The prisoner's nose was clearly broken, his eyes swollen, and his front teeth broken clean off at the gum line. Johnson glanced at the large puddle of blood on the floor directly below the Indian's face, then noticed he was holding his left hand over his right. He gestured for the Indian to move his hands apart, seeing that the bones of his knuckles were exposed.

The general shook his head. "Apaches helped us fight the Mexicans. It appears they helped the wrong side."

Ricks rolled his eyes and began shaking his head before he caught Maydew staring at his reaction to the general's statement. The sheriff quickly looked away from Maydew and started rubbing the back of his neck while searching for something to say. "I swear he came in like this, General. We didn't touch him." He looked back at Maydew. "See, those miners around here don't like Apache. Especially ones that come in their camp shooting at them. So, when they captured ol' Red Sleeves, they beat him within an inch of his life. It's a good thing I had room in my cell, you know…to protect him."

Still kneeling and looking over the Indian's injuries, Johnson said in a sarcastic tone, "Oh, yes, real lucky."

Corporal Stevens cleared his throat. "General, sir, we came across some Apache dead along the Santa Fe trail on the way here." He shook his head. "It was a real gruesome sight, sir."

Johnson quickly stood and turned toward Ricks. "Where are the miners who brought Red Sleeves here?"

"Well, they're over at my ranch, I suppose," replied Ricks.

"Well then, I suppose you have some questions for those boys when you get home?"

"Well, I suppose I do," replied Ricks, lifting his hat and scratching his head.

General Johnson looked back at Red Sleeves before exiting the cell as the Apache chief put his head back down. "Do me another favor, will you, Sheriff? Give him the same as the Mexican and get him a bedroll, if you have one handy."

Ricks scratched his beard and looked around for a second, then back at Red Sleeves. He had the appearance of being in great thought as Johnson patiently waited for his response. Finally, he turned back toward Johnson and said, "Sir, you know I'm a fair man, but—"

"Then there should be no problem," insisted the general as he made his way out of the cell. He headed straight over to Ricks's desk and picked up his still smoldering cigar from the ashtray, watching as the two soldiers walked out of the cell and stood on guard by the front door.

Sheriff Ricks struggled to understand why he should do that when Red Sleeves was going to die anyway, but he knew Johnson, and there was no use in arguing. "Okay, General, I'll personally see to it," he said.

"Perfect. It's settled then," said Johnson as he shook his head. He then placed his cigar in his mouth, taking a deep draw while glancing at the newspaper lying on Rick's desk. It was folded around an article about the recent revolt in Taos.

Sheriff Ricks kicked one of Domingo's boots as he glared at the Apache prisoner. Although he fancied himself a fair man, he really wasn't. He didn't like strangers or kids, and that was if you were white. Any other race, and he just didn't like you. So, having a Mexican and an Indian in his cell was bad enough, but the idea of having to feed and cater to them made

Domingo

his blood boil. He locked the gate and ambled back to his desk, placing the keys in the drawer.

"Thanks again," said General Johnson as he nodded to Ricks. Heading toward the front door, he stopped directly in front of Maydew and Stevens and stared at them both for a moment. Then he said, "You men wait here and guard this front door. No one in or out except the sheriff. Understand?"

"Yes, sir," answered Stevens and Maydew.

"And stay away from the prisoners," said Johnson as he reached for the door handle.

"Yes, sir," they replied, saluting the general as he exited the jailhouse.

Just before noon, Ricks returned with the store clerk, helping him carry the bundle of clothes, towels, bandages, and a basket of bacon rolls.

"Sorry, sir. Only the sheriff is allowed to enter," said Stevens as they approached the cell.

The clerk looked at Ricks.

"Aw, damn. Just sit the stuff down, Bob," said Ricks, sounding a little irritated, but being out of a chair for very long always made him a little moody. "I don't know what General Johnson was thinking, but I ain't staying here all day and night!" He stomped over and dropped the basket onto his desk. "That's what I have Deputy Collins for."

Stevens nodded his head and said, "One of your deputies will be fine."

"I don't know why we need so much protection over a half-dead Indian and a Mexican anyway," growled Ricks. "I mean half the damn tribe is dead. There ain't no one coming for 'em." Glaring back at Stevens and Maydew, he added, "They're your all's problem! Why don't *you* keep 'em? I mean, this jailhouse is brand new—we just finished it a few weeks ago. It was so nice, and now we have those two bleeding all over it."

Ricks stepped up toe to toe with Stevens since he seemed to be listening to his complaining the most. "See, the way we do it around here is just chain them to a tree. That way, we don't have to see or smell them." He crossed his arms and waited for a reply.

"Sorry, Sheriff. I would love to see that Mexican chained to a tree, but I have my orders."

Ricks shook his head. "Yeah, I heard what he did down there, killing that man in such a cruel way."

"Well, the sorry bastard will be dead soon enough," answered Stevens.

Ricks drew a deep breath and forcefully exhaled, while reaching for the keys from his desk drawer. He unlocked the gate as the soldiers followed him to the cell. "Here," he said to Domingo, then kicked a bacon roll across the cell floor. He sat two large bottles of water on the floor by the cot where Domingo was still lying. "Now, here's some water to drink, and this here is for cleaning." He tossed Domingo some rags, then went over to the Apache still crouched in the corner, looking at the floor. "And the same for you, savage," he said, tossing the food and rags at his feet.

The Apache looked up at Ricks for a quick second, then he looked toward the food at his feet and put his head back down.

"I reckon you're not used to my wife's cooking?" said a smiling Ricks. "Well, you better eat! It's all you're getting!

You all don't even know what the hell I'm saying, do you?" He glared at each of the prisoners, then said, "Here's a fuckin' blanket." He tossed it to the floor. "I couldn't find any damn hen skins! We don't just keep bedrolls laying around the jailhouse, ya know."

Stevens and Maydew resumed standing on either side of the cell as Ricks made his way out, then locked the door behind him. Upon returning to his chair, Ricks placed his feet back up on the desk and glared at the prisoners for a few moments before grabbing up his spectacles and newspaper. Stevens and Maydew moved to the chairs near the front door and sat down.

Domingo reached for a bottle of water and poured some into his hand, then rubbed his face. After washing the dried blood off his hands and arms with the rags and water, he used small handfuls of water to clear out the dirt from his eyes. He moved the pile of rags and towels now filthy with blood and dirt over to the cell door and then reached for the bacon roll still lying on the floor.

Although Domingo's vision was still blurry, he glanced over toward the Indian, who still hadn't moved. "Eat, señor. You need your strength if you want to get out of here," he said softly to his cellmate.

The Apache looked over at Domingo and then reached for his bacon roll.

"Congratulations, we are that much closer, my friend." Domingo finished eating his bacon roll, then lay back down on the cot. He soon noticed the Apache pulling the blanket over his legs while still crouched on the floor.

Stevens wandered over to the cell door and glared at both prisoners.

Domingo moaned in pain, trying to look as weak as possible.

"Quiet down! No one wants to hear your bellyaching," said Stevens.

Domingo made up his mind that if someone had to die, he would make sure it was Stevens. "You will feel all the pain, my friend, once I get a hold of you," he said in a quiet voice as he lay down.

"Sheriff! Open the cell!" barked Stevens.

Domingo lifted his head as the sheriff moaned his frustration at having to wiggle out of his chair.

Stevens glared at Domingo through the bars of the cell door, fists clenched and face growing redder by the moment.

When the sheriff reached the gate, he looked at Domingo and then at Stevens with a puzzled expression. "What is it?"

"I need to teach this piece of Mexican shit to keep his mouth shut!"

Ricks looked back at Domingo, then to Stevens. "But the general said to stay away from them."

Stevens turned and glared at Ricks, then walked away.

"Well?" said Ricks, clearly irritated.

"Forget it," Stevens said as he returned to his post by the front door.

"Well, don't that beat all?" said Ricks. "Deputy Collins should be arriving directly, and I can't wait!" he shouted toward Stevens.

Domingo put his head back down with a small smile on his face.

Domingo

Red Sleeves spoke to him in broken Spanish. "Hobble you lip if you want to get out of here."

Domingo's smile grew a little. As he drifted closer and closer toward sleep, he thought of his wife Arabella, son Marcello, and daughters Camille and Laila, and wondered if he would ever see any of them again.

A few hours later, someone jiggled the locked doorknob, trying to enter the jailhouse. Private Maydew cracked the door open and peered outside, finding Corporal Rhoades. Maydew opened the door and saluted the corporal.

"Private Maydew, the general wishes to speak to you immediately."

"Yes, sir," answered Maydew, then he reached for his hat on the nearby chair and placed it on his head. He glanced over at Corporal Stevens, tilting his head and shrugging his shoulders.

Looking through the doorway, Stevens asked, "What's this about, Corporal?"

"Don't know, Stevens. The general just instructed me to retrieve Maydew and return to his quarters."

Maydew began to wonder if he was in trouble for the condition of the Mexican prisoner when they arrived. He glanced at Stevens again, who was staring at the floor in heavy thought, figuring he was fearing the same thing. Maydew quickly saluted Stevens and turned back to Corporal Rhoades.

"Ready, sir," he said.

"Good day, Stevens," said Rhoades as he saluted and turned away, heading to his horse as Maydew followed closely behind to his.

Maydew glanced back at the jailhouse just as the door shut.

The two soldiers made their way through town, heading toward the fort.

Shaking his head, Maydew thought, *Damn! This is all Stevens's fault. I told that asshole we should have just kept going that night instead of making camp.* He looked onward as his animosity grew higher than old glory flapping high above the fort.

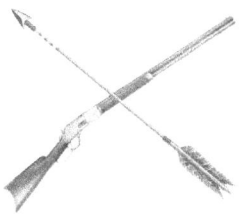

CHAPTER 23
A FAMILIAR FACE

Domingo awoke to Corporal Stevens and Deputy Collins banging and shouting.

"Wake up, scum suckers," said Stevens as he dragged a metal cup across the bars.

Domingo's vision was now almost normal, though around his eyes was still a bit swollen. He looked at the two men in front of the cell, then to his right, at the Apache who was also just waking.

"Dinner time," said Stevens as he went to the cell door. "Just beans. It's not all we got, but it's all you're getting." He snickered. "Oh, and good news, Domingo. Wells's brigade should be returning early tomorrow, so this might be your last meal." Pointing towards Red Sleeves in the corner, he spat, "Now back your ass away from the door and go sit next to your squaw."

Domingo slowly climbed from his cot, walked to the corner near Red Sleeves, and sat on the floor.

Stevens took out his key, opened the gate, and slid the plates inside. He then pulled his pistol out and pointed it at Domingo. "You move one inch, and I'll put a bullet right through your forehead." He turned toward Deputy Collins, who stood close by. "Grab that piss bucket."

A disgruntled Collins went inside and grabbed the bucket, left the cell, and sat the bucket on the floor outside the cell as Stevens locked the door.

Domingo reached down and grabbed both plates.

"Nah, amigo," said Collins. "You let the savage get his own."

Domingo sat one plate down on the floor and returned to his cot.

The Apache raised his head and stared at the men but made no attempt to get his plate.

"Come get it, boy," said Collins.

The Apache just looked back down at the floor.

Having gotten his first good look at the Indian since his vision had improved, Domingo realized that he was none other than the Indian he'd met while returning from the Gila River. The same man Domingo had blamed for the American troops destroying his home. At first surprised, he soon became angry. He'd thought the Apache were friends with the Americans, so why was he in an American jail? Wanting to be sure it was the same man, he set his plate on the floor and walked over to the Indian. He reached to lift the Apache's face, but as he closed in, Red Sleeves grabbed his hand and jumped to his feet.

The Indian was quite tall and towered over Domingo, staring down. Then he squinted and drew his brows closer as the realization of who Domingo was became evident on his face.

Domingo jerked his hand away from Red Sleeves while continuing to glare up at the Apache.

"Oh shit," said Collins. "These boys know each other!"

Domingo and Red Sleeves had a half-minute stare down until Domingo turned and sat back down on his bed. He more than wanted to beat the hell out of Red Sleeves but knew he needed to save his strength and not risk further injury.

"Damn," said Stevens with a chuckle. "I thought we were going to see something."

"Probably stole from each other," said Collins.

"Yeah, most likely. Mexicans and Indians ain't nothing but a bunch of thieves," added Stevens.

"Hey, señor, bring me that," said Collins, pointing to the untouched plate of food on the floor.

Domingo grabbed the plate and walked to the cell door.

Collins reached through the gate and grabbed the plate of beans, spilling them on the floor as he turned the plate sideways to slide it through the bars. "Since you all are friends, there's no reason you can't share," he said.

Collins and Stevens laughed as they walked away, then the deputy began telling Stevens of some run-ins he'd had with natives in the past.

Domingo sat on his cot glaring at Red Sleeves, and Red Sleeves stared right back. The two men were both injured, but their adrenaline was pumping, and neither felt anything. Domingo had not lost many fights in his life and was not afraid of any man. If the two had come face to face in any other situation, he would be trying to squeeze the life from the

Indian's throat. However, this situation was different, and they both knew it.

Domingo reached for his plate of beans and began to slowly eat while still staring at Red Sleeves. Realizing the Indian was in no rush to sit back down, he figured if the chief hadn't turned away by the time he finished his beans, there might be trouble yet. Just as he scraped the last couple beans from his plate into his mouth, Red Sleeves sat down on the floor where he had been. Domingo set his plate down, then lay back on his cot. He was surprised by how angry the Indian seemed to be at him, then laughed at the thought of how foolish he'd been to side with the Americans.

Red Sleeves glared up at Domingo.

"Americanos your friends, huh?" said Domingo. "I see where that friendship got ya." He put his hands behind his head and closed his eyes.

A few moments went by in silence.

"I remember when we met by the river," said Red Sleeves in broken Spanish.

Domingo opened his eyes and listened.

"I always regretted not killing you then."

Anger rising, Domingo sat up on his cot and glared down at Red Sleeves. "It would have been me doing the killing, Chief. Your friends may have gotten me, but long after you were dead."

Red Sleeves shook his head. "Ever since you arrived, it's been nothing but hardships for my people." Placing his fist in front of his heart, he added, "You have brought great pain to my heart, where used to be happiness."

The veins in his neck and face throbbing, Domingo stood

from his cot and shouted, "I have brought *you* pain? You brought the Americans to my home. They killed my son!"

Red Sleeves's face flushed red as he stood and returned Domingo's angry stare. "*You* brought the Mexican army to my home. I lost my brother and many of my warriors. We had to find shelter in the north. No time to hunt or rest. Little children had to keep up because we were too weak to carry them. So many died, starving and sick."

"How can you say it was me who did that? I did nothing!" said Domingo. "All I wanted was to live in peace and raise my family. The war you have with Mexico was your doing, not mine!"

"Mexico, your country, placed bounties on the Apache. They murdered our chief and left him for the buzzards!" said Red Sleeves.

"I can't believe I'm hearing this shit," said Domingo. "You fucking asshole, blaming me when *you* are the problem."

"You're a coyote whore," replied Red Sleeves. "I will be glad when you die tomorrow."

"You're gonna hang too, prairie nigger," said Domingo, sitting back down on his cot. "Oh yeah, looks like kissing the Americans' asses really worked well for you." He lay back down and looked up at the ceiling, breathing heavily.

Corporal Stevens walked over to the gate. "You two either fight or shut the fuck up!"

After a few minutes of silence, Red Sleeves sat back down in the corner. Never taking his eyes off the Mexican, he waited for another round of attacks, but none came. He looked at the floor and back at his cellmate several times as his anger slowly dissipated. Thinking about the things the brown man had said to him, especially the Americans killing his son, Red Sleeves came to realize Domingo wasn't the Apache's enemy. They were both just guilty by association.

He looked over at his cellmate still lying on the bed, eyes open, with his hands behind his head. "I made mistakes as war chief. Sending a party to remove you from our land was one of them, and it cost my people dearly." He slowly turned away and looked down at his hands. "When I became chief, trusting the hair faces was another mistake." He leaned back against the cell wall. "I have no more fight left in me for you, Domingo. My people are without their chief, without their land; without food and shelter. They are tired, scared, and sick, what's left of them. I must help them; lead them into an alliance with all Apache, to unite them. I must make peace with all who will help us and prepare for war with the hair faces."

Red Sleeves glared up at the ceiling for a few seconds with the back of his head against the cement, then drew several deep breaths and closed eyes. "I have said all I can say. I have nothing else."

Domingo shook his head. After several more moments passed, he glanced over at the Apache, who sat in the corner with his head against the wall. As he looked at Red Sleeves this time, he didn't have the anger inside him that he'd had moments before. Instead, he felt sorry for the Indian in the realization that they shared similar pain. His emotions had been pulled from one side to the other in a matter of minutes. He began thinking about his own family. They were also alone and scared, Arabella without her husband and the children without their father.

Still laying down on the cot, he rubbed his aching temples and thought of his father, his mother, and Marcello. All the struggling he'd endured over his entire life played through his mind. How Arabella stood right by him no matter how bad it got. How hard he'd worked to build a comfortable life for his family. How all that hard work and years of suffering had just begun to pay off. He thought of his country fighting so long for independence only to lose so much of it to the Americans. He thought of how the squabbles between Mexico and the Apache paled in comparison to the much greater threat they both now faced.

"The Americans," he whispered.

His anger toward the Americans became almost uncontainable.

Domingo's mind raced over the next hour until he thought of a way to escape. Not tomorrow—when the guards would lead them out to the gallows and the town would be swirling with people, lawmen, and soldiers—but now. Right now. He remembered how the guards had watched them about to fight earlier, and if they could fake a fight now, the guards might unlock the cell and come inside. He didn't even need them to come in—just get close enough so he could grab one of them through the bars. The idea of grabbing Stevens and choking his skinny neck until his eyes rolled back and he breathed his last bit of air made his heart pound with excitement. The lion inside him began to roar, more than ready to be free or die trying.

Domingo sat up in his cot and put his feet to the floor. "Chief," he said quietly.

Red Sleeves looked over at him.

Domingo checked that the guards weren't paying attention and then said softly, "I know the pain you feel because it's the same that I feel. My family is also scared and without their father and husband. Neither of us deserves to be in here, but we are. I want to help you get back to your tribe, and I want to get back to my family. Chief, I am not sure if you are my friend or enemy, but we can figure that out later." He checked outside the cell again to make sure no one was coming, then said, "I have an idea to get us out of here."

Red Sleeves grinned. "Well, if it works, I think friends."

Domingo chuckled, then explained to Red Sleeves about faking a fight to get at least one of the guards close enough to grab. How he didn't need the guards to open the gate, and they probably wouldn't, but if he pretended to be knocked out and posed no threat, they would lower their guard. "Just keep me close to the gate, and I'll grab one of them and get their pistol," he finished.

Red Sleeves squinted his eyes and shook his head. "No good."

Domingo's arms fell to his side, then he quickly raised them again. "Chief, let's just try. What do we got to lose? If the opportunity does not come, then I won't make a move, I promise. We will wait for another chance tomorrow." He stared at Red Sleeves, waiting for a response.

Red Sleeves looked at the gate for a moment, then back at Domingo. "Let's go home," he said with a confident nod.

Then he stood up and crept toward Domingo in a fighter's stance. "So does this mean I get to hit you?"

"Well, you might have to, so it looks more convincing," replied Domingo.

"That's not a problem," said Red Sleeves, grinning wide. "I been wanting to do that all day."

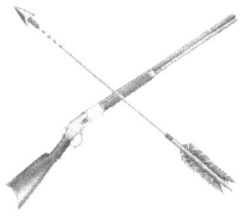

CHAPTER 24
EVERYTHING IS IN FRONT OF US

Domingo grabbed Stevens's arm through the cell gate and slammed his head into the bars. The corporal's mouth hit the hard metal, knocking a front tooth out and busting his lip. Domingo wrapped his arm around Stevens's neck and braced him against the bars while grabbing his sidearm with the other hand.

Deputy Collins reached for his pistol, but Domingo quickly put the stolen pistol to the corporal's head.

Red Sleeves rushed over and helped hold Stevens, partially concealing himself behind the corporal.

"Let him go! Let him go *now*!" yelled Collins, pointing his pistol at Red Sleeves.

"Listen, this can be really simple," said Domingo calmly. "Now put your gun down."

A shocked and nervous Collins shook his head. "Stevens! What do you want me to do?"

Domingo squeezed Stevens harder against the bars, preventing him from replying. "No, we're not talking to him," he said. "Now put the gun down and no one has to be hurt."

"Stevens!" said Collins.

Barely able to breathe, much less talk, Stevens muttered, "Do it."

Now even more confused, Collins asked, "Put it down?"

Stevens nodded his head as best he could.

Domingo watched Collins's movements closely as the deputy raised his left hand up slowly while still pointing the pistol with his right. "Put it down," he said. "Red Sleeves, keys."

Red Sleeves started feeling around in Stevens's pockets.

Collins shook nervously, making the barrel of his gun twitch about.

"Put it down," said Domingo again, jamming the pistol hard into Stevens's face.

"If I put it down, they could kill us both," explained the panicked Collins while taking a few steps back.

Scared for his life, Stevens muttered, "Don't leave. They will kill me."

Red Sleeves finally found the keys to the cell and showed them to Domingo.

"I've got him. Go ahead and open it," said Domingo.

"Throw your pistol!" said Stevens. He could breathe a little after Domingo loosened his grip a bit.

"They will kill us both! I'll go get help!" said Collins, taking another step back.

Stevens's face turned white. "No!"

"Put it down, amigo," said Domingo. "Or he's dead!"

Red Sleeves struggled with the keys, trying with no success to get the gate open.

His patience running out, Domingo looked for a clear shot at Collins. He figured he would have to kill Stevens and then take a quick shot at Collins, but what he really needed was Red Sleeves to get the door open. Realizing the Indian had probably never used keys before, he said, "Red Sleeves, come here and hold him."

Collins took a few slow, deliberate steps backward toward the door. Then Red Sleeves moved to take over for Domingo holding Stevens, and Collins spun on his heel and rushed for the door.

"No!" shouted Stevens.

With no time to think it out, Domingo fired, and Stevens dropped to the ground as blood splattered the walls and floor. Domingo quickly took aim at Collins and hit him in the leg, but Collins still managed to stumble outside.

Domingo handed the gun to Red Sleeves and grabbed the keys. "We've got to hurry," he said. "Dumb gringo," he muttered, pushing Stevens out of the way and opening the cell door.

Red Sleeves followed Domingo out of the cell and quickly searched the jailhouse for another pistol but could not find one. There was a rifle in a case, but it was locked. They tried breaking the door off, but to no avail.

"Out the back," said Domingo.

The two outlaws flew out the back door. It was just getting dark outside as they walked swiftly away from the jailhouse to look for a horse.

Red Sleeves tapped Domingo on the shoulder, saying, "Over there!" He pointed to a horse tied up in front of the barber shop.

They started toward it when they were spotted by a bystander who quickly ran away. When they reached the horse, Red Sleeves slipped alongside the building to avoid drawing attention to them as Domingo went to untie the animal.

"Stop!" yelled someone from inside the shop.

Two men rushed outside, one pulling his pistol.

Red Sleeves grabbed the armed man from behind and took the pistol from his hand, then head butted and threw him to the ground. The other man turned and ran back inside. Red Sleeves raced toward Domingo and the horse. A shot rang out, grazing the back of Red Sleeves's leg. Domingo and Red Sleeves turned toward the direction the shot came from and saw four more men coming. One of them was Ricks. They both fired at the approaching men, sending them flying for cover.

Domingo climbed up on the horse. "C'mon, Chief!" he shouted. Then he fired another shot in the direction of the men still ducking for cover.

Red Sleeves also fired a shot at the men and then jumped on the back of the horse, and they took off. About twenty yards down a side road heading out of town, a man hidden from view on the side of a building swung his rifle, missing Domingo but knocking Red Sleeves from the horse. Domingo was home free and could have kept going, but he looked back and saw Red Sleeves fighting three men. He turned the horse around, firing his pistol in the air, and rode right into one of the men.

Reaching for Red Sleeves, he yelled, "Chief!"

Red Sleeves struggled to break away from the other two men as Domingo and the horse danced around the fray, throwing dirt and dust in the air from the frantic horse's hooves, while trying to free the Apache.

One man reached for the rifle strapped to the saddle, and Domingo jumped from the horse, landing on the man before he could get the rifle. Another man rushed into the ruckus, making it four against two as Domingo pummeled the man he'd knocked to the ground.

Red Sleeves grabbed one man's knife right out of his hand by the blade. He flipped it in the air, grabbed the handle, and stuck the knife into the man's chest. After being hit from behind, he spun and stabbed another man in the neck, then climbed onto the horse as Domingo finished beating a man in the face until he stopped moving.

Domingo stood and looked up at Sheriff Ricks standing a short distance away with his gun aimed toward he and Red Sleeves. He turned to get on the horse, then noticed three more men approaching, and one of them was Collins limping along.

"Shoot 'im!" yelled Collins to Ricks.

Red Sleeves turned the horse toward Domingo, reaching out his hand.

Domingo glanced one more time at Ricks, then grabbed Red Sleeves's hand and swung up to get on the horse.

Bang!

The sheriff's bullet went through Domingo's back and out his chest.

Red Sleeves tried to pull Domingo up on the horse.

Blood trickling from his mouth, Domingo looked up at Red Sleeves and shook his head no. "Go," he said with a gurgling gasp.

Red Sleeves held on to him, leaning way over on the Indian side of the horse. He was about to lose his balance and fall off, but Domingo jerked his hand out of the chief's hand and hit the horse on the rump. The horse jumped forward, and Domingo fell—face up and motionless—to the ground.

Red Sleeves turned the horse toward Ricks and charged him.

Sheriff Ricks lost his balance while dodging the horse's charge and clumsily fell to the ground.

Civilians had begun to gather, and Red Sleeves was running out of time. He looked down at Domingo, seeing the extent of his injury and that he wasn't moving, then whipped the horse to charge through the gathering civilians.

With one eye cracked open, Domingo watched his new friend blast through the crowd. He gasped for air as he smiled at the sight of the frightened mob. The men talked about assembling a posse as Sheriff Ricks approached Domingo.

Ricks looked down at Domingo's dying face, clearly upset that he had killed a man.

Domingo's vision slowly drifted toward darkness. It was like walking farther and farther into a cave where it just kept getting darker and darker. His breaths came slower as blood filled his lungs. He saw Arabella and his daughters sitting at the table, eating dinner. They were talking and laughing, but there was another man there he could not recognize. Then his son appeared next to him, dressed in a fine suit and somehow already a full-grown man. He reached for Domingo's hand and helped him to his feet. Both excited and confused, Domingo looked at his son as the two walked down the street. Domingo began to turn for a look behind him, but Marcello stopped him.

"Don't look back, Papá. Everything is in front of us. Come on, you will see," said Marcello, reaching for his hand, and they continued down the street.

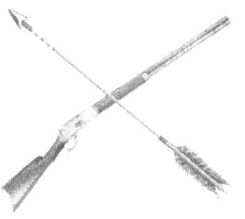

CHAPTER 25
OLD FRIENDS & NEW FRIENDS

IN THE TWO MONTHS SINCE Arabella returned to the ranch, Jose, Luis, and Pedro repaired much of the fences, rebuilt the barn, and even built a roomier bunkhouse complete with a stove and a window. They still had close to two hundred sheep, although they lost several to wolves while away. Without the constant demand from Sanchez and his men, there was no need for any more cattle than a milk cow.

There had been no word from Domingo, and Arabella's hopes of him returning were fading. She so badly wanted to know if he was alive.

Pedro had been very helpful, and she appreciated him greatly. She knew he loved her, but she could not bring herself to love him in that way. She deeply cared for Pedro but was careful to never show emotion toward him, lest she mislead him.

Pedro was working out back when Arabella came outside with a glass of tea for him. As she made her way over where he was pounding a new piece of fence post in the ground, she noticed a man riding through the valley below. He was wearing a sombrero. Heart pounding, Arabella dropped the glass of tea.

"Oh, my God," she said, staring intensely into the distance.

Vicente had recently mentioned in a letter about coming to the ranch, but it was way too soon for it to be him. Tears formed in Arabella's eyes as she got her feet moving toward the man.

Pedro came up from behind Arabella and followed her gaze into the distance.

"Is it him, Pedro?" she asked.

Pedro looked as hard as he could, then said, "We can only hope so."

The man riding toward them waved, and Arabella cried out in joy as she ran toward him. When she reached the edge of the fence and saw that it was not Domingo, she stopped and tried to gather her wits.

Now less than fifty feet away, the man waved at her again. "Hello, Arabella!" he said cheerfully.

Arabella remained unsure of who it was until he was close enough for her to see his familiar smile. General Sanchez was not in his army uniform and looked different with longer hair, a full mustache, and a lot of gray hair, or she would have recognized him much earlier.

She smiled big and wiped her eyes. "Oh, General," she said, laughing. "So good to see you."

Sanchez brought his horse to a stop about ten feet from Arabella. "My God, you are as beautiful as ever," he said with a grin.

"You sweet man. Get down from that horse and give me a hug," said Arabella.

Domingo

Sanchez climbed down from his horse on a wooden leg he seemed to be quite well acquainted with. He and Arabella held hands as they walked toward the house.

Pedro met them partway, then extended a hand toward Sanchez. "Hello, I'm Pedro."

Sanchez reached out and shook his hand.

Seeing the general's confusion, Arabella said, "We will talk when we get inside, General."

Sanchez smiled. "Okay, Arabella, but just call me Ramon. I'm out of the military now. Wasn't that good at it anyway," he said with a giggle.

Arabella stopped and looked up at him. "You know, I never knew that was your name," she said with a smile. "Ok, Ramon, come on in. We have a lot of catching up to do."

"Yes, ma'am."

When the three reached the porch steps, Arabella motioned for Pedro to wait outside.

Pedro nodded and went back to the fence he had been working on.

Sanchez and Arabella entered the house and sat down at the table as the girls came running from their room to see who was there. Camille remembered him well. Laila was too young, though she was still excited to see someone stop by.

"Go outside, girls. You will have plenty of time to see him later," said Arabella.

The girls waved to Sanchez and rushed out the door.

Quiet settled over the table for a moment as Arabella placed two glasses and a pitcher of tea upon it, then gathered the strength for what she was about to tell Sanchez. As she told him of the horrors of that fateful day, she cried.

A sympathetic Sanchez put his hand to his forehead, then

shook his head in utter disbelief and shock that the Americans had killed Marcello. When Arabella told him the American soldiers had asked about him specifically and the Mexican fort nearby, Sanchez lowered his head and rubbed the back of his neck.

"I wish I could have made it back here to warn you of the Americans," he exclaimed with his brows drawn close as he fought back tears. "They placed themselves directly between us, and I had to retreat south."

Arabella reached for Sanchez's hand to comfort him. "You great man," she said, wiping tears from her eyes. "You had already warned us months earlier." She poured a glass of tea for each of them.

"Marcello was some young man. Strong and smart, just like his father," said Sanchez, wiping a tear from his eye and nodding.

Arabella closed her eyes and took a deep breath. "Domingo went out after the soldiers who killed him over two months ago, and still no word."

Concern washed across the general's face as he lowered his head. He made a fist, clamping his hand so tightly, the knuckles turned white. A few moments later, he began nodding. "Domingo is a strong man, and I believe he could survive such an endeavor."

"I couldn't stop him. I begged and begged, but he left with the fire of the devil in his eyes," Arabella said, then she pressed her palms to her temples and leaned back in her chair. After a few moments of silence, she leaned forward and placed her hands on the table, letting her head hang down.

"I will do my best to find out where he is, Arabella," said Sanchez, reaching across the table for her hand. "He shouldn't be hard to find. There are not many like him," he added with a smile.

The two sat and talked for almost two hours. Sanchez informed Arabella how the American invasion had claimed much of Mexico's land, and Arabella shared what she'd seen of this transition while in Tucson.

"Will this become America too?" she asked.

He shook his head. "I'm really not sure. If they do come this far, they should honor the land grant Mexico gave you. But of course, you have to pay taxes in American dollars." Sanchez felt in his pockets, then quipped, "I don't have any of those."

Sanchez looked at Arabella with her hand on her chin, staring at the table. "Arabella," he said, dropping his smile and nodding. "You should head south. Load up your daughters and belongings and head back down to your family."

Arabella shook her head, then looked at Sanchez. "I'm going to stay. Domingo may return."

Sanchez took a drink of his tea, then nodded. "Yes, he will, and he will find you wherever you go, I promise you." He leaned back in his chair. "With the Americans so close, he wouldn't be able to stay here anyway."

Arabella nodded in agreement.

"If he killed an American soldier, they will most certainly be coming for him." Sanchez lit a cigar and continued, "Besides, the Apache are still around and coming farther south every day now that the Mexican army has been cleared out."

Arabella listened intently as her eyes darted back and forth, considering what he was telling her.

"They may want to get some payback for how I drove

them north, and they know of my presence here; how we were friends," said Sanchez.

Arabella took a few deep breaths.

"Come with me, Arabella. You, your girls, and your friend can stay with me and my family for a while."

Arabella smiled, then stood and refilled the general's glass. "You are such a sweet man," she said, placing her hand on his shoulder. "Tell me how to find you just in case I do, in fact, leave, but as for now, I must stay."

Sanchez smiled. "You are quite the woman, Arabella."

Arabella smiled back. "Please try your best to find out something about Domingo."

"I will, but I want you to think about what I told you and about getting out of here," said Sanchez. "I can't stand the thought of those Apache sons o' bitches hurting you and your girls."

"I will discuss it with Pedro and the ranchos, I promise," replied Arabella as Sanchez stood from the table. "You're not leaving, are you?"

Sanchez finished his tea and said with a smile, "Well, this is not the safest place for me to be. Those Apache bastards would come skin me alive if they knew I was here."

Arabella smiled as Sanchez put his hat on. "Never knew you to be so easily rattled by a few Apache," she teased.

"Those savages already took one leg. They ain't getting nothing else," he replied, grinning. "As long as I don't have to try and outrun them, I'll be good." He looked down at his wooden leg. "Now, let's go outside and walk along the fence; talk of more pleasant things."

Arabella grabbed his hand and said, "That sounds great."

The two walked out the door and were quickly greeted by

Domingo

Camille, Laila, and Pedro, horsing around on the porch. They took a short stroll around the yard slowly following alongside Sanchez as he kept a hand on the fence to keep his balance.

Two days after Sanchez left, Arabella was still thinking heavily on the things he'd said to her and had talked to Pedro several times about it. Fearing for herself and her children, and believing the Apache were moving farther south each passing day, she was finally convinced it was time to travel home to Guadalajara, and Pedro agreed.

After breakfast, Arabella, Pedro, Luis, and Jose talked about her plan to head south. Luis and Jose were not happy about her leaving, but they agreed it was probably the safest thing to do. They planned on discussing the business side of the ranch after dinner, giving time for Luis and Jose to check on the woolies. The ranch hands thanked Arabella for breakfast, then went outside to the horses and rode off in search of the herd. It was Arabella's hope that the brothers could buy her half of the sheep and pay a little something for the house so she would have something to get established with once they reached Guadalajara. She decided to leave a letter for Domingo, just in case he returned, and told Pedro about it while cleaning up the table.

Pedro replied, "That's a good idea. I will feed and water the horses, grease the wagon wheels, and gather up my tools from the barn, so we will be ready to leave in the morning."

Arabella nodded, and with a disheartened smile, said, "I will get things together from the house. No need to worry with any more chores, I suppose."

Pedro smiled, then gave Arabella a hug and went outside.

Arabella sat the girls at the table and gave them biscuits, beans, and canned milk. She began telling them they were moving south to a safer area, where she had lived as a child. The girls were already showing their displeasure when she saw something out of place through the window. She focused for a moment, realizing it was dust being kicked up from several horses' hooves trotting at a brisk pace toward the ranch.

"Stay here and finish your breakfast," Arabella told the girls before quickly heading outside.

Watching as she swiftly made her way down the porch steps and toward the barn to find Pedro, Arabella realized there were about twenty Indians coming up the road. Her heart pounded heavily as she ran toward the barn, screaming in a panic, "Pedro! Pedro! Indians!"

She looked back at the porch at the sound of the screen door slamming and saw her oldest daughter running down the porch steps.

"Mama, what is it?" asked a frightened Camille.

"Inside! Now!" shouted Arabella with a deep rage in her voice, her face completely red. "You go watch your sister!"

Camille quickly turned away and ran back inside, shutting the door behind her.

Pedro came darting out of the barn, already on alert from the fear in her voice. Looking at the rapidly approaching Indians, he ran past Arabella to get his rifle from inside the house, and she quickly followed. Once inside, she told the girls to hide in the keep, grabbed a pistol, and went back by the door to look out.

The Indians came to a stop right in front of the house.

Arabella's heart was full of fear, and her eyes swelled with tears. *Why didn't I leave with the general?* she thought. *Why didn't we leave this morning?*

She looked around for Pedro but didn't see him anywhere.

Domingo

Reaching the screen door, she stared out at the Indians as the one who appeared to be the chief climbed down from his horse, looked toward the far side of the house, and raised his hand in a friendly gesture. *What is he doing?* she thought, then realized Pedro must have been over there.

The chief turned toward Arabella, who looked through the door and raised his hand high, letting her know they came in peace.

She stood there for a second, then saw Pedro walking over to them with his rifle pointed toward the dirt. She opened the door and cautiously made her way to the porch, then joined Pedro while wiping away tears and regaining her composure.

The chief looked at them for several moments without saying a word, then spoke in broken Spanish. "My name is Mangas Coloradas. Father of the Chiricahua Apache. Chief Red Sleeves," he explained. "I have brought many from my tribe with me, including my wife and children. I have done this so they will hear the words I say and understand them." The chief nodded to Arabella and looked to his family a few yards behind him, then turned back toward Arabella. "I have fought many who entered the Apache land. I have fought many who are enemies of the Apache. This fight was all I knew as a young man. This fight will continue until I am an old man." He brought his fists to his chest. "This fight has led me to many places, to many victories, to many defeats, and to many others who also fight for their land, their way of life, and their families, like your husband, Domingo."

Arabella clasped her hands in front of her chest, her eyes filling with tears.

"Your husband took his fight to the white man, to avenge

your son's death. He was victorious, but then was captured and beaten."

Arabella took a breath, wanting to ask if Domingo was alive, but Red Sleeves continued before she could speak.

"We were locked up together for two days"—he crossed his wrists in front of him—"before we realized we'd met before. We at first blamed each other for what happened, and soon after, found these thoughts were wrong. We agreed that although once enemies, we would make peace." He drew his open hands toward his chest. "We escaped by working together. During our escape, I was knocked off the horse and surrounded. Domingo charged our horse into the men, and we fought side by side. Even though we are not of the same people, in that moment, we were brothers." He pushed his fists together, then looked down at the ground for a moment and back at Arabella. "Your husband was shot in his back, and I tried to lift him to the horse. I would not leave without him, and I continued to fight. Domingo smiled and struck the horse to get it moving and saved me."

Arabella covered her mouth as the tears came streaming down her face, her head tilted forward and her eyes closed.

Red Sleeves waited a few moments until she regained her composure and looked back toward him. "I know these words I speak do not bring peace to your heart." He placed his fist in front of his chest. "But know that our people will always remember his sacrifice." He walked over to his tribe and grabbed the reins of three horses. "Take these pintos as a gift from my people."

Pedro walked over and took the reins from the chief.

An Apache woman of similar age to that of Arabella got down from her horse and walked over to another Apache nearby, grabbing some blankets. Then she approached Arabella and Pedro, placing blankets of many colors and patterns into Arabella's arms.

The chief walked over to Arabella, towering over her, and placed a necklace with a small turquoise pendant around her neck. Then he placed a hand on her shoulder and said, "This was worn by my chief, then by me when I became chief, and now it is yours. May this give you strength and protect you." He turned and walked toward the woman who had given Arabella the blankets, helped lift her back onto her horse, and went to his own horse and climbed up. After a few moments, he added, "No matter how many lines the great fathers of nations draw on their maps to create invisible borders and divide the people, there can't be and never will be a line between friends and family, mothers and their children, lines between those living or those who are now with the spirits. Wherever the sun god, the great mother, and the great spirits lead us, let our friendship survive through all lines and last though all days." Then Red Sleeves held his hand out and above his head in an offer of friendship and peace.

Arabella smiled, tears flowing from her eyes as she happily raised her hand high to affirm their new friendship. "Thank you, Chief Red Sleeves! Thank you!" she exclaimed, keeping her hand high and making eye contact with the other Apaches as several began raising their hand to her as well.

Still holding the pintos and reeling from what just happened, Pedro's eyes filled with happiness and tears as he raised his hand and thanked the chief as well.

Chief Red Sleeves nodded to Pedro, then to Arabella, and leaned a little on his horse to look around Arabella, giving a little smile to Domingo's girls peering out the screen door.

He and his tribe turned their horses around and rode away, distancing themselves from the ranch.

Arabella stood watching as they slowly disappeared into the valley. She felt great relief at the burden of not knowing what happened to Domingo finally being lifted. Her beloved Domingo was gone, but he had managed to give her one last gift of love and safety.

Pedro stood frozen in disbelief as Camille and Laila made their way outside. The girls jumped with delight and raced toward the beautiful pintos at the end of leads still in Pedro's hand.

Her eyes filled with tears, Arabella turned toward Pedro and embraced him, then pulled away to look at the girls who were calling to her. Sharing a glance and a smile, Pedro and Arabella moved to lift the girls up on the horses.

Pedro looked at Arabella and said, "With these horses, it will make our trip much easier and a lot quicker."

Arabella rubbed the neck of one of the horses and smiled that lovely smile of hers. "I don't feel much like leaving today. Let's just enjoy this moment for as long as we can."

CONTINUARÁ

If you enjoyed reading this novel, please return to your favorite online retailer and leave a review. The author appreciates any and all feedback from readers.

ABOUT THE AUTHOR

Born in 1973, Bozwick Abel resides in Pinckney, Michigan near the chain of lakes. He spends a fair share of time boating, fishing, and eating ribs with the wolf pups. Abel is a firm believer that passion is the marrow of the soul and can take you anywhere you want to be.

Visit the author's website: https://bozwickabel.com/
Connect with the author on Facebook:
https://www.facebook.com/bozwick.abel

ACKNOWLEDGEMENTS

A song I heard several years ago put the wheels in motion for the Pariahs of War series. After writing most of the first book and then setting it aside for quite some time, the curiosity of friends and family helped me refocus to finally finish it. Even though the Pariahs of War series has just begun, it has been quite a journey already.

I'd like to say thanks to those friends and family, you know who you are.

I also want to thank Debra L Hartmann and her team at IAPS.rocks. Being my first book, I needed plenty of help and they were with me all the way through. I cannot say enough about their expertise and knowledge of not only editing, proofreading, and book design, but the entire self-publishing process.

I'd especially like to thank all those who read the book and the unspoken heroes from days of old.

Milton Keynes UK
Ingram Content Group UK Ltd.
UKHW040040270124
436770UK00001B/10